NOW'S THE TIME

NOW'S THE TIME
JOHN HARVEY

Slow Dancer Press

U.S. DISTRIBUTOR
DUFOUR EDITIONS
CHESTER SPRINGS
PA 19425-0007
(610) 458-5005

Published in Great Britain in 1999 by
Slow Dancer Press
91 Yerbury Road London N19 4RW

Stories, Introduction & Coda ©John Harvey 1999

British Library Cataloguing-in-Publication Data.
A catalogue record for this book is available from the British
Library.

ISBN   1 871033 53 5 – Paper
ISBN   1 871033 58 6 – Cloth

Slow Dancer Fiction titles are available in the U.K. through
Turnaround Publisher Services and in the U.S.A. through Dufour
Editions inc.

Cover design: Keenan

Printed in Great Britain by The Guernsey Press Co. Ltd.

This book is set in Sabon 10/13

Slow Dancer Press

THE COMPLETE RESNICK SHORT STORIES

ACKNOWLEDGMENTS

'Now's the Time' first appeared in *London Noir*, edited by Maxim Jakubowski, Serpent's Tail, London, 1994. Reprinted in *Das Grosse Lesebuch Des Englischen Krimis*, Goldmann, Germany 1994.

'Dexterity' first appeared in *No Alibi*, edited by Maxim Jakubowski, Ringpull Press, Manchester, 1995. Also available in a limited edition from Scorpion Press, Blakeney, Gloucestershire.

'She Rote' first appeared in *Fresh Blood*, edited by Maxim Jakubowski and Mike Ripley, The Do-Not Press, London, 1996. Reprinted in *The Year's 25 Finest Crime & Mystery Stories*, Carroll & Graf, 1996.

'Confirmation' first appeared in *The Orion Book of Murder*, edited by Peter Haining, Orion, London, 1996.

'Bird of Paradise' first appeared in 'Ellery Queen's Mystery Magazine', May 1997. Reprinted in *The Cutting Edge*, edited by Janet Hutchings, Carroll & Graf, 1998, in *The Year's 25 Finest Crime & Mystery Stories*, Carroll & Graf, 1998

'Cheryl' first appeared in *City of Crime*, edited by David Belbin, Five Leaves Publications, Nottingham, 1997.

'Stupendous' first appeared in *Eine Leiche Zum Geburtstag*, edited by Ronald Gutberlet, Rowohlt, Germany, 1997.

'My Little Suede Shoes' first appeared in *Mean Time*, edited by Jerry Sykes, The Do-Not Press, London, 1998.

'Cool Blues' first appeared in *Blue Lightning*, edited by John Harvey, Slow Dancer Press, 1998.

CONTENTS

INTRODuCTION

SOMEWHERE BACK in the late eighties, I was living in Nottingham, writing – mainly – for television and wondering if maybe I should have a crack at a crime novel again. I'd tried before, a little over ten years earlier, and the results had not been encouraging: a series of four paperback originals, their titles lifted from the Bob Dylan songbook, and featuring Scott Mitchell, a mawkish private eye with his office in London's Covent Garden and his character stranded awkwardly over the mid-Atlantic. The immediate models for this misbegotten project were obvious: the first four Spenser novels by Robert Parker and, to a lesser degree, the Hazell books written by Terry Venables and Gordon Williams under the pen name of P. B. Yuill. Behind these, of course, hovered the domineering influence of Raymond Chandler – classics of the form and first consumed by me in their green Penguin editions when I was still at school.

Cocky and naive as I was, my avowed intention was to soar where Venables and Williams had flown and others had stuttered and fallen back to earth – the Scott Mitchell books were going to be the first perfect distillation of Chandler's literate, wisecracking style into a true English setting. Of course, though I couldn't see this at the time, they failed miserably. Chandler's style, while easy to parody, is dangerously difficult – near impossible – for another writer to achieve. So the books were derivative, stereotypical, over-sentimental, devoid of originality, observation or wit. And worse, there they were in their appropriately garish covers, reproaching me for my presumption, my lack of judgement – for trying to run when I could scarcely walk.

But by 1987, two things had happened: I'd become involved in a television series called *Hard Cases* and I had – albeit belatedly – discovered Elmore Leonard.

Hard Cases, which ran for two seasons, was a drama series which revolved around the work and lives of a team of probation officers based in Nottingham's inner city and its genesis lay in the long-running American police series, *Hill Street Blues*. As a writer, I was fascinated by the construction of *Hill Street*, its pace and verve, the swerving shifts of tone, the number of running characters and story lines it juggled with apparent ease. So I sat down with my video tapes, my stop watch and my note book and plotted it all out, minute by minute, scene by scene; stripped episodes down to their constituent parts and examined the machinery before, first laboriously, later happily, reassembling something with a similar form – only instead of focussing on a stressed-out, over-worked and under-financed group of police officers, my story lines revolved around the probation service and its clients.

Luck played a hand. I was putting the finishing touches to my master plan when I read an interview with the near-legendary drama supremo, Ted Childs, asking why there were no British scripts with the qualities of *Hill Street Blues*. I phoned my agent, my agent phoned him… all right, it wasn't quite that simple, but eventually Central Television commissioned and ran six episodes of *Hard Cases*, which, if they didn't set the world alight, did contain some strong dramatic moments, some flights of fancy.

In possibly my favourite sequence, a young officer, faced with a psychotic transsexual actor threatening suicide, talks him down from his locked dressing room by doing Erich von Stroheim to the actor's Gloria Swanson, allowing us to pay an elaborate homage to *Sunset Boulevard*. But this was, after all, British television, and British television is, for historical reasons, steeped in the documentary tradition. So the far-fetched moments of the imagination were always going to be anchored by the left-leaning social concerns of such film makers as Ken Loach. And no bad thing.

Besides, there we were filming on the streets of Nottingham, the same streets and pubs that had been frequented by the young D. H. Lawrence and later by the Alan Sillitoe of *Saturday Night and Sunday Morning*. There were traditions to be upheld.

The tradition behind *Hill Street Blues*, of course, that of the multi-character, multi-storyline police drama, leads in other directions: the pioneering 87th Precinct novels of Ed McBain and the later, L.A. based books by policeman turned writer, Joseph Wambaugh.

Elmore Leonard, as I'd been discovering, comes from a different part of the crime tradition. Less concerned with cops and private eyes, as heroes at least, and shunning the prevalent fascination with serial killers and the profilers and pathologists that follow in their wake, Leonard's books revolve, in the main, around those who strut and stumble around the lower reaches of the criminal world. These are character studies, deftly assembled with humour and affection, and the characters are defined by private moralities and impossible ambitions; these are people who see the world askew and are thus incapable of seeing the impossibility – or the humour – of their situation. For these are also comic novels: comedy of character and situation spun along by dialogue which, in common with the best of its kind – Mamet, Higgins, Ross Thomas, Bill James – suggests truth and realism through artifice, by means of artfully constructed rhythms and repetitions.

Leonard's books lean, I think, more towards Hammett than Chandler – though there is some of Chandler's romanticism present – while his characters might find their roots in the worlds of James M. Cain and, especially, Horace McCoy. I wouldn't be surprised if Leonard read and enjoyed Donald Westlake and Ross Thomas and when I saw somewhere that his favourite crime novel was George V. Higgins' *The Friends of Eddie Coyle* that was no surprise at all.

La Brava is, I think, my favourite Leonard novel, though *Freaky Deaky* and parts of *Bandits* run it close. What is certain is that reading these and others made me want to get back into the water myself and write crime again. Only by now I hope I'd learned a lesson: I didn't want to try and write *like* Elmore Leonard, I wanted to write *as well*. And if I haven't managed it yet, hey! What's wrong with a little ambition?

What I wanted was to take Leonard's dialogue-led, character-led approach and bring it to the mix of multiple narratives and urban realism that had been at the heart of *Hard Cases*. A police series set in the streets of Nottingham.

And at this stage another piece of good luck presented itself. Not long before, teaching on an Arvon Foundation writing week, I had met the writer Dulan Barber and we had quickly become good friends. Dulan liked opera, Sarah Vaughan, Dusty Springfield and good wine – though, at a pinch, indifferent would do; he wrote crime novels under the name of David Fletcher and supernatural thrillers as Owen Brookes; he knew as much about putting a book together as anyone I have ever met and was generous and selfless with his time. We started to talk about the ideas I had for a projected novel – the one that would become *Lonely Hearts* – and for a central character, a conscientious but shabbily-dressed policeman, who would gradually emerge, prompted by Dulan's comments and questions, as Detective Inspector Charlie Resnick.

Rockford, as I would say, dressed by Columbo's tailor.

A sober, shadow version of the policeman played so expertly by Robert Foxworth in Harold Becker's film of Wambaugh's *The Black Marble*, a hard-drinking, soft-centred officer of Russian descent.

Little by little, as Dusty would sing, the pegs on which to hang Resnick's character came clear: the Polish background, the delicatessen sandwiches, the cats, the love of jazz. And then the squad that would work with him: Lynn Kellogg, able, fresh-faced, overweight; Graham Millington, dour and unimaginative, steadfast, eternally smitten by Petula Clark; Divine, in whom all the blinkered prejudices of the worst police officers reign incarnate.

Lonely Hearts was first published here by Viking in 1989; an American edition by Henry Holt in the same year. Nine other novels have followed, finishing in 1998 with *Last Rites*, which brought the sequence to an end after ten books. Ten books, five years, give or take, in the lives of Resnick and his team and of the city in which they are set. From the Thatcherite eighties to the New Labour nineties –

I suspect for many of those who people these novels, little has changed.

And Resnick? Older certainly, still capable of inspiring respect and affection from his team, though he'll never ascend to the middle-management excellence exhibited by Frank Furillo in Hill Street Blues. Readers have observed a certain mellowness of late, a coming-to-terms; though his temper's probably closer to the surface now than at any time since 1989. He still relaxes listening to Monk and Billie, Spike Robinson and Lester Young; despite similar eating habits, he seems to have learned to work his way through a triple-decker sandwich without spraying the contents over shirt and tie.

From my point of view, he's tired; needs a rest.

In the short stories, some of them, he gets just that. Often he's a peripheral figure, keeping his counsel and his distance while the hapless Snapes and Ray-os of his world go round in ever decreasing circles.

That there are stories at all is down to Maxim Jakubowski, who commissioned me to write the first and then several more; latterly to others like Ed Gorman and Jerry Sykes who liked what they'd read and wanted more.

Even though I'd tried my hand at most kinds of writing, the short story was something I'd steered clear of. Out of fear: fear of not being able to do it right, not being able to do it at all. I'd read them, of course: Hemingway, Fitzgerald, Updike, Malamud; Alice Adams, Jayne Anne Phillips, Elizabeth Tallent, Bobbie Anne Mason, Lorrie Moore, Raymond Carver, Richard Ford; Lawrence Block, Donald E. Westlake and John Lutz. The two or three attempts I'd made had finally found homes for themselves in the littlest of little magazines.

But Maxim was forceful; he didn't brook much argument. And besides, a tale in which Resnick comes down to London, maybe listens to a little jazz. What's the problem? Where's the harm?

I suspect 'Now's the Time' may be the weakest story here (so if you're reading them in sequence, show some forbearance!) but the important thing was it got me started. More importantly, I found that I enjoyed it. And so ten more followed, each named after a Charlie Parker composition, some light enough for the wind to blow through them, some carrying, in a concentrated fashion, the same burdens as the novels.

I found I was thinking more and more of the stories as footnotes to the longer work, as testing ground on which to walk characters who might graduate into the bigger leagues. So 'Now's the Time' concludes the story of Ed Silver, the jazz musician who appears in *Cutting Edge*, while Raymond Cooke – Ray-o – the adolescent abattoir worker from *Off Minor*, scabs and scavenges his way across four stories only to re-emerge in the final novel, *Last Rites*. Indeed, if you read 'She Rote', 'Confirmation', 'Work' and 'Stupendous' in that order, the story of Raymond and his extended family, his Uncle Terry and various crooked cohorts, and, not least, Terry's troubled girl friend, Eileen, they become a novel in their own right, albeit one with overlaps and gaps.

The Snape family – Norma, Shane, Sheena and Nicky – first appeared in 'Dexterity', before featuring centrally in *Easy Meat* and more tangentially in *Last Rites*. Grabianski, the compassionate burglar who first shinned up a drainpipe in *Rough Treatment*, holds the centre of 'Bird of Paradise', in which he evinces a passion both for the little-known canvases of the British Impressionists and for Sister

Teresa of the Sisters of Our Lady of Perpetual Help – both obsessions travelling with him into *Still Water*.

There are two stories in this collection which have not appeared before. 'Work' was written for a book of erotic crime fiction, edited by Ed Gorman and entitled *Careless Whispers*; sadly, some of the fiction – not I think, mine – was adjudged by the prospective publishers to be too erotic by half and its appearance has been put on hold. 'Slow Burn', the longest story here, is based upon a radio script I wrote for BBC Radio 4, for whom it was produced by David Hunter. Anyone who listened to that broadcast, and blessed with an especially good memory, will notice significant changes in plot and character – though nothing as severe as in my radio adaptation of *Cutting Edge*, in which I changed the identity of the murderer between printed page and spoken word. Author's privilege.

I hope you enjoy some of these stories as much as I enjoyed writing them, as much as I have enjoyed writing about them.

John Harvey, London, 1998.

NOW'S THE TIME

"THEY'RE ALL *dying, Charlie.*"

They had been in the kitchen, burnished tones of Clifford Brown's trumpet, soft like smoke from down the hall. Dark rye bread sliced and ready, coffee bubbling, Resnick had tilted the omelette pan and let the whisked eggs swirl around before forking the green beans and chopped red pepper into their midst. The smell of garlic and butter permeated the room.

Ed Silver stood watching, trying to ignore the cats that nudged, variously, around his feet. Through wisps of grey hair, a fresh scab showed clearly among the lattice-work of scars. The hand which held his glass was swollen at the knuckles and it shook.

"S'pose you think I owe you one, Charlie? That it?"

Earlier that evening, Resnick had talked Silver out of swinging a butcher's cleaver through his own bare foot. "What I thought, Charlie, start at the bottom and work your way up, eh?" Resnick had bundled him into a cab and brought him home, stuck a beer in his hand and set to making them both something to eat. He hadn't seen Ed Silver in ten years or more, a drinking club in Carlton whose owner liked his jazz; Silver had set out his stall early, two choruses of 'I've Got Rhythm' solo, breakneck tempo, bass and drums both dropping out and the pianist grinning, open-mouthed. The speed of thought: those fingers then.

Resnick divided the omelette onto two plates. "You want to bring that bread?" he said. "We'll eat in the other room."

The boldest of the cats, Dizzy, followed them hopefully through. The *Clifford Brown Memorial* album was still playing 'Theme of No Repeat'.

"They're all dying, Charlie."

"Who?"

"Every bugger!"

And now it was true.

SILVER Edward Victor. Suddenly at home, on February 16, 1993. Acclaimed jazz musician of the be-bop era. Funeral service and memorial meeting, Friday, February 19 at Golders Green Crematorium at 11.45 a.m. Inquiries to Mason Funeral and Monumental Services, High Lanes, Finchley.

Resnick was not a *Guardian* reader; not much of a reader at all, truth to tell. *Police Review,* the local paper, Home Office circulars and misspelt incident reports, *Jazz Journal* – that was about it. But Frank Delaney had called him Tuesday morning; Frank, who had continued booking Ed Silver into his pub long after most others had turned their backs, left Ed's calls unanswered on their answerphones. "Seen the *Guardian* today, Charlie?" Resnick had taken it for a joke.

Now he was on the train as it approached St Pancras,

that copy of the newspaper folded on the seat beside him, the debris of his journey – plastic cups, assorted wrappings from his egg mayonnaise sandwich, bacon and tomato roll, lemon iced gingerbread – pushed to one side of the table. There was the Regent's canal and as they passed the gas holders at King's Cross, Resnick got to his feet, lifted his coat down from the rack and shrugged his way inside it. He would have to walk the short distance from one terminal to another and catch the underground.

Even at that hour, King's Cross seemed jaded, sour, down at heel, broad corners and black cabs; bare-legged girls whose pallid skin was already beginning to sweat; men who leaned against walls and railings and glanced up at you as you passed, ready to sell you anything that wasn't theirs. Ageless and sexless, serious alcoholics sat or squatted, clutching brown bottles of cider, cans of Special Brew. High above the entrances, inside the wide concourse, security cameras turned slowly with remote-control eyes.

The automatic doors slid back at Resnick's approach and beyond the lights of the computerized arrivals board, the Leeds train spilled several hundred soccer fans across the shiny floor. Enlivened by the possibility of business, two girls who had been sharing a breakfast of chips outside Casey Jones, began to move towards the edges of the throng. One of them was tall, with badly hennaed hair that hung low over the fake fur collar of her coat; the other, younger, smudging a splash of red sauce like crazy lipstick across her cheek, called for her to wait. "Fuck's sake, Brenda!" Brenda bent low to pull up the strap of her shoe, lit a cigarette.

"We are the champions!" chanted a dozen or more youths, trailing blue and white scarves from their belts.

In your dreams, Resnick thought.

A couple of hapless West Ham fans, on their way to catch an away special north, found themselves shunted up against the glass front of W. H. Smith. Half a dozen British Rail staff busied themselves looking the other way.

"Come on, love," the tall girl said to one of the men, an ex-squaddie with regimental colours and a death's head tattooed along his arms, "me and my mate here. We've got a place."

"Fuck off!" the man said. "Just fucking fuck off!"

"Fuck you too!" Turning away from the tide of abuse, she saw Resnick watching. "And you. What the hell d'you think you're staring at, eh? Wanker!"

Loud jeers and Resnick moved away between the supporters but now that her attention had been drawn to him, Brenda had him in her sights. Middle-aged man, visitor, not local, not exactly smart but bound to be carrying a quid or two.

"Don't go."

"What?"

The hand that spread itself against him was a young girl's hand. "Don't go."

"How old are you?" Resnick said. The eyes that looked back at him from between badly applied make-up had not so long since been a child's eyes.

"Whatever age you want," Brenda said.

A harassed woman with one kiddie in a pushchair and another clinging to one hand, banged her suitcase inadvertently against the back of Brenda's legs and, even as she swore at her, Brenda took the opportunity to lose her balance and stumble forwards. "Oops, sorry," she giggled, pressing herself against Resnick's chest.

"That's all right," Resnick said, taking hold of her arms

and moving her, not roughly, away. Beneath the thin wool there was precious little flesh on her bones.

"Don't want the goods," her friend said tartly, "don't mess them about."

"Lorraine," Brenda said, "mind your own fucking business, right?"

Lorraine pouted a B-movie pout and turned away.

"Well?" Brenda asked, head cocked.

Resnick shook his head. "I'm a police officer," he said.

"Right," said Brenda, "and I'm fucking Julia Roberts!" And she wandered off to join her friend.

The undertaker led Resnick into a side room and unlocked a drawer; from the drawer he took a medium size manila envelope and from this he slid onto the plain table Ed Silver's possessions. A watch with a cracked face that had stopped at seven minutes past eleven; an address book with more than half the names crossed through; a passport four years out of date, dog-eared at the edges; a packet of saxophone reeds; one pound, thirteen pence in change. In a second envelope there were two photographs. One, in colour, shows Silver in front of a poster for the North Sea Jazz Festival, his name, partly obscured, behind him in small print. He is wearing dark glasses but, even so, it is clear from the shape of his face he is squinting up his eyes against the sun. His grey hair is cut in a once-fashionable crew cut and the sports coat he is wearing is bright dog-tooth check and over large. His alto sax is cradled across his arms. If that picture were ten, fifteen years old, the other is far older – black and white faded almost to sepia. Ed Silver on the deck of the *Queen Mary,* the New York skyline rising behind him. Docking or departing, Resnick couldn't tell. Like many a would-be bopper, he had been part of Geraldo's navy, happy to play foxtrots and waltzes in exchange for a fervid forty-eight hours in the clubs on 52nd Street, listening to Monk and Bird. Silver had bumped into Charlie Parker once, almost literally, on a midtown street and been too dumbstruck to speak.

Resnick slid the photographs back from sight. "Is that all?" he asked.

Almost as an afterthought, the undertaker asked him to wait while he fetched the saxophone case, with its scuffed leather coating and tarnished clasps; stuck to the lid was a slogan: *Keep Music Live!* Of course, the case was empty, sax long gone to buy more scotch when Ed Silver had needed it most. Resnick hoped it had tasted good.

In the small chapel there were dried flowers and the wreath that Frank Delaney had sent. The coffin sat, cheap, before grey curtains and Resnick stood in the second row, glancing round through the vicar's perfunctory sermon to see if anyone else was going to come in. Nobody did. "He was a man, who in his life, brought pleasure to many," the vicar said. Amen, thought Resnick, to that. Then the curtains slowly parted and the coffin slid forward, rocking just a little, just enough, towards the flames.

Ashes to ashes, dust to dust,
If the women don't get you, the whisky must.

While the taped organ music wobbled through 'Abide With Me', inside his head Resnick was hearing Ed Silver in that small club off Carlton Hill, stilling the drinking and the chatter with an elegiac 'Parker's Mood'.

"No family, then?" the vicar said outside, anxious to find time for a cigarette and a pee before the next service.

"Not as far as I know."

The vicar nodded sagely. "If you've nothing else in mind

for them, we'll see to it the ashes are scattered here, on the rose garden. Blooms are a picture, let me tell you, later in the year. We have one or two visitors, find time to lend a hand keeping it in order, but of course there's no funding as such. We're dependent upon donations."

Resnick reached into his pocket for his wallet and realised it was gone.

The 'meat rack' stretched back either side of the station, roads lined by lock-up garages and hole-in-the-wall businesses offering third-hand office furniture and auto parts. Resnick walked the gauntlet, hands in pockets, head down, the best part of three blocks and neither girl in sight. Finally, he stopped by a woman in a red coat, sitting on an upturned dustbin and using a discarded plastic fork to scrape dog shit from the sole of her shoe. There were bruises on her neck, yellow and violet, fading under the soiled white blouse which was all she was wearing above the waist.

"Ought to be locked up," the woman said, scarcely glancing up, "letting their animals do their business anywhere. Fall arse over tit and get your hand in this, God knows what kind of disease you could pick up." And then, flicking the contents of the fork out towards the street, "Twenty-five, short time."

"No," Resnick said, "I don't…"

She shook her head and swore as the fork snapped in two. "Fifteen, then, standing up."

"I'm looking for someone," Resnick said.

"Oh, are you? Right, well," she stood straight and barely came level with his elbows, "as long as it's not Jesus."

He assured her it was not.

"You'd be amazed, the number we get round here, looking to find Jesus. Mind you, they're not above copping a good feel while they're about it. Took me, one of them, dog collar an' all, round that bit of waste ground there. Mary, he says, get down on your knees and pray. Father, I says, I doubt you'll find the Lord up there, one hand on his rosary beads, the other way up my skirt. Mind you, it's my mother I blame, causing me to be christened Mary. On account of that Mary Magdalene, you know, in the Bible. Right horny twat, and no mistake." Resnick had the impression that even if he walked away she would carry on talking just the same. "This person you're looking for," she said, "does she have a name or what?"

The hotel was in a row of similar hotels, cream paint flaking from its walls and a sign that advertised all modern conveniences in every room. And then a few, Resnick thought. The manager was in Cyprus and the youth behind the desk was an archaeology student from King's, working his way, none too laboriously, through college. "Brenda?" he said, slipping an unwrapped condom into the pages of his book to keep his place. "Is that the one from Glasgow or the one from Kirkby-in-Ashfield?"

"Where?"

"Kirkby. It's near…"

"I know where it's near."

"Yes? Don't sound as though you're from round there."

"Neither do you."

"Langwith," the student said. "It's the posh side of Mansfield."

Resnick had heard it called some things in his time, but never that. "That Brenda," he said. "Is she here?"

"Look, you're not her father, are you?"

Resnick shook his head.

"Just old enough to be." When Resnick failed to crack a smile, he apologized. "She's busy." He took a quick look at his watch. "Not for so very much longer."

Resnick sighed and stepped away. The lobby was airless and smelt of... he didn't like to think what it smelt of. Whoever had Blu-Tacked the print of Van Gogh's sunflowers to the wall had managed to get it upside down. Perhaps it was the student, Resnick thought, perhaps it was a statement. A – what was it called? – a metaphor.

If Brenda was as young as she looked and from Kirkby, chances were she'd done a runner from home. As soon as this was over, he'd place a call, have her checked out. He was still thinking that when he heard the door slam and then the scream.

Resnick's shoulder spun the door wide, shredding wood from around its hinges. At first the man's back was all he could see, arm raised high and set to come thrashing down, a woman's heeled shoe reversed in his hand. Hidden behind him, Brenda shrieked in anticipation. Resnick seized the man's arm as he turned and stepped inside his swing. The shoe flew high and landed on top of the plywood wardrobe in the corner of the room. Resnick released his grip and the man hit the door jamb with a smack and fell to his knees. His round face flushed around startled eyes and a swathe of hair hung sideways from his head. His pale blue shirt was hanging out over dark striped trousers and at one side his braces were undone. Resnick didn't need to see the briefcase in the corner to know it was there.

From just beyond the doorway the student stood thinking, there, I was right, he is her father.

"She was asking..." the man began.

"Shut it!" said Resnick. "I don't want to hear."

Brenda was crying, short sobs that shook her body. Blood was meandering from a cut below one eye. "Bastard wanted to do it without a rubber. Bastard! I wouldn't let him. Not unless he give me another twenty pound."

Resnick leaned over and lifted her carefully to her feet, held her there. "I don't suppose," he said over his shoulder, "you've got anything like first aid?"

The man snatched up his briefcase and ran, careening between the banister and the wall. "I think there's plasters or something," the student said.

Resnick had gone to the hospital with her and waited while they put seven stitches in her cheek. His wallet had been in her bag, warrant card, return ticket and, astonishingly, the credit card he almost never used were still there; the cash, of course, was gone. He used the card to withdraw money from the change kiosk in the station. Now they were sitting in the Burger King opposite St Pancras and Resnick was tucking into a double cheeseburger with bacon, while Brenda picked at chicken pieces and chain-smoked Rothmans King Size.

Without her make-up, she looked absurdly young.

"I'm eighteen," she'd said, when Resnick had informed her he was contacting her family. "I can go wherever I like."

She was eleven weeks past her fifteenth birthday; she hadn't been to school since September, had been in London a little over a month. She had palled up with Lorraine the second or third night she was down. Half her takings went to Lorraine's pimp boyfriend, who spent it on crack; almost half the rest went on renting out the room.

"You can't make me go back," she said.

Resnick asked if she wanted tea or coffee and she opted for a milk shake instead. The female police officer waiting patiently outside would escort her home on the last train.

"You know you're wasting your fucking time, don't you?" she called at Resnick across the pavement. "I'll only run off again. I'll be back down here inside a fucking week!"

The officer raised an eyebrow towards Resnick, who nodded, and the last he saw was the two of them crossing against the traffic, Brenda keeping one clear step ahead.

The *maître d'* at Ronnie Scott's had trouble seating Resnick because he was stubbornly on his own; finally he slipped him into one of the raised tables at the side, next to a woman who was drinking copious amounts of mineral water and doing her knitting. Spike Robinson was on the stand, stooped and somewhat fragile-looking, Ed Silver's contemporary, more or less. A little bit of Stan Getz, a lot of Lester Young, Robinson had been one of Resnick's favourite tenor players for quite a while. There was an album of Gershwin tunes that found its way onto his record player an awful lot.

Now Resnick ate spaghetti and measured out his beer and listened as Robinson took the tune of 'I Should Care' between his teeth and worried at it like a terrier with a favourite ball. At the end of the number, he stepped back to the microphone. "I'd like to dedicate this final tune of the set to the memory of Ed Silver, a very fine jazz musician who this week passed away. Charlie Parker s 'Now's the Time'."

And when it was over and the musicians had departed backstage and Ronnie Scott himself was standing there encouraging the applause – "Spike Robinson, ladies and gentlemen, Spike Robinson." – Resnick blew his nose and raised his glass and continued to sit there with the tears drying on his face. Seven minutes past eleven, near as made no difference.

DEXTERITY

IF RESNICK had bumped into Nicky Snape early that Saturday morning, he could have become the proud owner of a bargain price, next-to-new CD-player, fully programmable, random play facility, digital filter, the whole 16-bit. And all for thirty quid. Twenty-five, should that have been all the cash Resnick could lay his hands on at the time.

True, there were one or two things missing, bits and pieces really, incidentals. No manual, but then anyone with a bit of intelligence could work out which switch did what for himself. And the box: no, there was no box. Who needs a box, when the whole unit tucked so neatly under the front of a loose-fitting leather jacket, or, for ease of carrying, under one arm? The remote control transmitter, though, Nicky had to admit that was more of a problem; nobody wanted to be jumping up out of the armchair every few seconds to fiddle through the tracks by hand. But he'd dropped it, hadn't he? Sliding his skinny arse back out through the bathroom window, the remote had squeezed out of his hand like a bar of soap and landed in the open toilet bowl with a splash.

Shit!

Legs waving in the wind, CD clutched to his chest, Nicky had not reckoned the risk of going back for it. Especially considering where it had fallen. Given on a quiet night he could hear the Turveys farting from four doors away, Nicky didn't fancy diving his hands into their khazi without a pair of rubber gloves.

No matter, he'd boost one from the electrical shop on the corner, one of those universal jobs that lets you programme everything from the telly to the microwave. Legs up on the settee with a can of Tennents, few flicks of that and you could tape *EastEnders,* listen to a tasty bit of Jungle, and make yourself a toasted ham sandwich all at the same time. Meet us here tomorrow and it's yours for a tenner, right? Five, then. Five, OK? Five. Do without, you tight cunt!

But Resnick had neglected to make his way into the city via Radford Road and so missed sampling the sales patter and burgeoning entrepreneurial skills of the fourteen-year-old Nicky Snape. What Resnick did was leave his car in the Central Police Station car park, nip into the market for an espresso, then wander down Market Street to SuperFi and purchase a brand-new Rotel RCD965BX at fifteen per cent off, last year's model. Box, manual and remote control included.

Now at last he had something on which to play the Billie Holiday boxed set he had bought himself the Christmas before last.

One thing Nicky was good with, his hands. Arms, too. Slide them down inside the smallest window crack, delve

into the deepest letterbox, ease back the tightest bolt, slip
the toughest lock. Like most things, it came with practice.

When Nicky got back home that Saturday afternoon he
was feeling cool. Black denim shirt loose over baggy black
jeans. Reversed on his head, the Chicago Bulls baseball cap
he'd swapped with some kid from school. Music zapping
through his Walkman at nearly 200 beats per minute and
bright new Reeboks on his feet. Nicky felt like... Nicky felt
like a fucking star!

Then smack! Three paces into the room and his mother
caught him such a round-arm slap that he went stumbling
sideways, legs jellying under him, cap flying and one ear-
piece of his headphones all but piercing his inner ear.

"What? What the fuck was that for? What?"

Norma hit him again: once for asking stupid questions
and once for using language like that inside her house.
"Don't you come in here swearing at me, you loundering
trail-tripes, don't you bloody dare! This is your mother
you're talking to and don't you bloody forget it!"

Nicky pulled off his headphones and, scooping up his
cap from the floor, jammed it back on his head. "What?"
he shouted in his mother's face. "What?"

At five-foot-eight, Norma Snape was a couple of inches
taller than her youngest son and outweighed him by some
forty pounds. It should have slowed her down more than it
did. The next blow Nicky ducked, but not the one after.
Norma's open hand struck him on the same side of the face,
right around the ear, and Nicky's skin burned red.

"What the fuck've I done now?"

"Didn't I just tell you... ?"

"Don't!" When Nicky scrambled back around the
settee, he was close to tears.

"For fuck's sake!" shouted Nicky's seventeen-year-old

half-brother, Shane. "Why don't the pair of you cut it out and let me watch this in peace?"

Neither paid him the slightest heed. The four o'clock at Kempton was under starter's orders and Shane had a twenty each way riding on the second favourite.

"Look," Norma said, pointing at her youngest son's feet. "You think I'm blind or stupid or what?"

"What?"

"Jesus and Mary, can't you ever say anything but that?"

"If I knew what you were talking about," Nicky said, "I might."

Norma narrowed her eyes as if she were in pain; someone knocked at the front door and she yelled at them to go away. "Those shoes," she said. "Those trainers you've got on your feet. They're new, aren't they? Brand sodding new."

"So?"

"So you picked 'em off the trees alongside the Park and Ride, did you? You thieving little bowdykite, you've been up the Viccy Centre, thieving again, that's what."

Nicky's face contorted into a smirk. "Yeah, well, that's just where you're wrong, 'cause I never nicked them at all."

"And I've told you before, I'll not have you lying to me."

Nicky tried vaulting his brother's legs in a dash for the kitchen door, but Shane's kick caught him high on the back of the thigh and brought him low. "Get out the bloody way!" The leaders were only at the second furlong mark and Shane's horse was back amongst the stragglers already.

"Right. Now, you listen." Norma had Nicky jammed up against the open door, holding him by his hair. "You're going to get those off your feet and take them back right now."

"No way."

She pulled his head back before slamming it against the door. "You'll do what you're sodding told."

Nicky wriggled the fingers of his right hand down into the back pocket of his jeans and came up with a crumpled receipt. "Don't believe me, look at that." There were tears in his eyes now and no mistake.

"What?"

"Now who can't say nothin' else?"

Norma slapped him for being smart and took the receipt. "One pair Reebok training shoes, forty-nine pound, ninety-five."

"Yeah, and today's date, see there, today's date, date and time, where and when I bought 'em, today."

"Forty-nine, ninety-five."

"Yes."

"Almost fifty quid."

"Yes."

"For those?"

"Yes."

Norma punched him so hard in the chest that Nicky nearly stopped breathing. "Where in the name of buggery did you get fifty pound to spend on your scuttering feet?"

It had been snowing when Resnick arrived back at his car; just lightly, a thin skein of flakes filtering down from an almost blue sky. Careful, he had locked the CD-player inside the boot, knowing better than to tempt providence, even in the police car park.

Phoning through to his own CID room at the Canning Circus sub-station, he half smiled at Kevin Naylor's diffident voice, asking him to please hold. Blurred down the line, he heard the fall and rise of voices, the scrape of chairs, the computer printer's broken rhythm, the sound of whistling that could only come from Graham Millington, a shrilly confident version of 'The Way We Were'.

When Naylor returned to the phone it was to report the normal mix of break-ins and minor assaults, drunk and disorderlies, and vehicles taken without consent. Like CID teams up and down the country, those of Resnick's officers who were not hard-pressed by long-term investigations were busy sweeping up the leftovers of another urban Friday night. And there was still Saturday to come: the traditional weekend of two halves.

"Not at the match, sir?" Naylor asked.

Resnick hung up. These past weeks of the season, frustrated by a series of games in which, if their visitors could not find a way of doing it for themselves, his team's defence had all but kicked the ball into their own net – and sometimes done exactly that – Resnick had voted with his feet and stopped attending. Since when, predictably, although County were still in prime relegation position, they had achieved some memorable results. Had actually won matches.

With a small degree of guilt, Resnick thought that, had he stopped going sooner, the team might have had a chance of staying put.

To cheer himself up he set out for the Old Market Square, spurred on to brave the youth of the city, clustered with numbed insouciance around the listening posts in the Virgin Megastore, and brush his way into the jazz section at the rear in order to supplement his meagre collection of CDs.

There were times when Norma Snape thought that if she'd not come south from Huddersfield, things would have been all right. No one had told her that, aside from being the self-confessed "poetry capital of the country", Huddersfield had recently been voted the town in which folk were most likely to be burgled. West Yorkshire police statistics, official. Put her Nicky in with a chance of knocking off another sonnet or knocking over the corner shop, it didn't take fourteen lines of iambic pentameter to tell which was the most likely.

At least tonight she knew where he was, playing pool with his Uncle Vic and under pain of death to be back in the house before eleven. Shane was... well, the Good Lord alone knew where Shane was... and Sheena – Sheena was sitting here alongside Norma, sipping a rum and Coke to make it last, knowing after that she'd be on halves of lager like everyone else.

"Where you off to now?" Norma asked, as Sheena shuffled from her seat, smoothing her skirt down in the far direction of her knees.

"Loo."

"Be sharp, then. Karaoke's set to start any minute."

Sheena made a face and wiggled away, more than half the eyes in the pub turning to watch her go. Norma had put her on the pill to celebrate her fifteenth birthday, but knew that was never enough. Times had changed since she was a lass herself, and there were things far worse you could catch now than a baby.

"Been gone long enough to piss for me too," Norma said, as Sheena finally returned. Up at the mike a Barton bus driver, still wearing his uniform trousers, was making a passable meal of 'The Green, Green Grass of Home'.

"Party upstairs," Sheena said, sitting down. "Cheryl Rogers's eighteenth."

"Not a mate of yours, is she?"

"Can't stand her, stuck-up cow. And her vol-au-vents taste like cardboard stuck round sick." Sheena leaned back and used a chipped fingernail to pick some shredded chicken from between her teeth.

For Resnick, it was a pretty basic sandwich. Ham, a few slices of strong Lancashire, some shallots, what remained of a green pepper and a smear of mustard pickle. The bread – his favourite caraway and rye – he had toasted on one side. Lately, he had been drinking Worthington White Shield.

The Billie Holiday tracks with Ben Webster and Barney Kessell were coming to an end, and he was looking at his purchases from Virgin, wondering how on earth you were supposed to read the notes on CDs without a magnifying glass. He turned the cases over in his hand. Spike Robinson: *The Gershwin Collection.* Spike, who had dedicated a number to Resnick's late friend Ed Silver from the stage at Ronnie Scott's. Monk, of course. The set of piano solos which included 'Memories of You'. Duke Ellington's *New Orleans Suite,* with Johnny Hodges playing one of his last solos on 'Blues for New Orleans'. And Charlie Parker – *Bird:* the *Dial Masters.* Resnick set the disc to play.

Broadway at 38th Street in New York, 28th of October, forty-seven. A Tuesday. Duke Jordan at the piano, Max Roach on drums. Miles Davis was just twenty-one. The rolling, rubato opening to 'Dexterity', before muted trumpet and alto play the theme, a little riff repeated clean and simple before the band drops out and leaves Parker wheeling through space alone, fingers, breath and soul manoeuvring together with agile blue grace.

Smiling, Resnick touches the remote and plays the track again.

Norma and Sheena had arrived home a shade after ten-thirty to find that Nicky was already there, head bent over some new computer game or other, can of Coke close to hand. He barely shrugged when his mother and sister came in.

"Where's our Shane?" Norma asked.

"In his room."

"What doing?"

"Sara Johnson."

Norma's coat dropped to the floor. "He better not geck-ing be! He…"

She was at the foot of the stairs before Nicky's laughter stopped her in her tracks, Nicky all but doubled over, Sheena joining in with it, pleased to see their mum caught out.

"You little bugger!" But Norma was laughing too, pleased she could still see the funny side.

"What's all the racket?" Shane asked, appearing in the doorway, magazine at his side.

"Never mind," Norma said happily, picking up her coat. "Sheena, just set kettle on, there's a love."

"God," said Sheena, "why's it always me?" But it wasn't a real protest, only routine. "Maybe we could all watch a video?" she called from the sink.

"What? Like together?" Shane laughed. "What d'you think this is all of a sudden, happy families?"

"Why not?" Norma said.

The tea hadn't had time to mash before Pete Turvey and his cousins were hammering at the front door.

The Turveys, all three of them, along with their respective wives, had spent the early part of the evening in their local before moving on to Radford Boulevard and Cheryl Rogers' birthday party. Cheryl's mum and Pete Turvey's wife worked the early shift at Player's, grateful to be hang-ing on to their jobs longer than most.

"Come back to the house after," Bev Rogers had said. "Trevor's got some drink in, haven't you, Trev?"

Cheryl's dad had nodded with less than enthusiasm. What the chuffin' hell did she want to be asking that pack back for? Piss up your leg as soon as look at you, most of the time. But all Pete Turvey had done was drop a shoulder in Trevor's direction and nod his head. "Nice one, Trev. We'll be there, no problem at all."

"Look here," Bev said, once they had all arrived and were standing, the three Turvey men close to six foot apiece, planted in the centre of the Rogers' living room with glasses in their hands. "This lot of presents our Cheryl got. Too much really. Way over't top. But then, like I was saying, you're only eighteen once."

"Aye," Pete Turvey had said, lifting his glass and winking in the girl's direction. "Sweet eighteen and scarce been kissed."

Cheryl's face and neck showed several shades of red and Turvey, who knew a few things about her that her mum did not, grinned and winked again.

"See what her dad give her, here, look," Bev said from across the room. "Stereo, all of her own."

Turvey could see it right enough, units stacked on one another, not quite matching: twin-deck Technics cassette-player, JVC amp, Kenwood tuner and, perched on top of them all, a Panasonic CD-player, almost new.

"Nice," said Turvey, moving in for a closer look.

"Course," Bev said, "Trevor had to match them up himself, piece by piece, didn't you, Trev?"

"Very nice," Turvey said over Trevor's grunt. "CD, specially."

"That was what I really wanted most of all, wasn't it, Dad?" Cheryl said, colour almost back to normal.

"Shame," Pete Turvey had said, turning back into the room, "the one he got you had to be fucking mine!"

"Let me get my hands on the bastard!" Pete Turvey said now, pushing his way across the Snape's front room; but he had Norma to get by first and then there was Shane. "Thievin' shit-arse!"

"Let him be."

Eyes wide, Nicky was crouching down beside the TV.

"Sort him out of there," Turvey said to his cousins, pointing, but when one of them moved there was Shane to block him and the other one stood his ground. "Go on!"

But nobody did.

"Happen," Norma said, "you should tell us what this is all about."

"I'll tell you what it's all about," Turvey shouted.

"Right. Then why don't we all sit down first?"

"I don't want to fucking sit down!"

"Suit yourself."

From the kitchen doorway, Sheena glanced over at Nicky and saw that Nicky was fit to piss himself with laughter. "I don't suppose anyone'd like a cup of tea?" she asked.

Nicky clapped a hand across his mouth and headed for the door.

"You stay bloody there!" Pete Turvey called.

"Nicky, stay there," Norma said.

Still fighting the urge to laugh, Nicky leaned against the wall. "Tell 'em what happened," one of Turvey's cousins said. "What happened," said Pete Turvey, "is that sniggering little toe-rag over there broke into my place Friday, stole the CD and sold it to Trevor Rogers for thirty quid so's Rogers could give it to his kid for her soddin' birthday."

Now it was Shane's turn to laugh.

"Shut it!" Norma said. And then, "Nicky, is that true?"

"Course it isn't."

"Don't you lie to me now."

"I'm not."

"He fucking is!" Turvey made to get at him, but this time the settee was in the way. The settee and Shane.

"You bring him round here, this bloke then," Shane said. "Rogers, that his name? Get him round here tomorrow, first thing. Say it all to Nicky's face. And mine. If he does and Nicky's lying, we'll sort it out."

"How?"

"We'll sort it out."

Turvey stared hard into Shane's face, but Shane didn't waver. Turvey knew he was heavier, older, taller; he had to ask himself if he fancied it, and the truth was he did not. Not there and then.

"Right," Turvey said, backing off. "Tomorrow, right?" He nodded at his cousins and with a hunch of their shoulders they turned and went, slamming the door at their backs.

Norma moved fast and she had hold of Nicky before he could dodge from the room.

"Mum!"

She slapped him both ways with her open hand, both cheeks, forward and back. Then slapped him again, tears hot against the laughter that still clung to the corners of his eyes.

"Tea's cold," called Sheena from the kitchen.

"Then mash some more."

Shane Snape was known. One conviction for aggravated burglary and with the next one he would do time. Serious though, Shane, about some things – money in his pockets, Special Brew, screwing Sara Johnson, supporting Mansfield

Town, politics of a sort. Responsibilities, he was serious about those too. Norma didn't ask him where he was going, didn't want to know, although, of course, she knew.

Shane hammered on the Rogers' front door until Bev came down.

"Trevor, I want to see him."

"It's past one in the morning."

"I don't care if it's past Monday. Get him down here now."

The two men stood, uneasy, in the cold back room; Bev, too nervous to go back to bed, sat on the stairs behind the closed door. Trevor old enough to be the other's dad.

"Pete Turvey," Shane said, "he was round ours earlier tonight."

"Yes."

"'Bout something you said."

"Yes."

"Me, I think he must've heard you wrong."

Trevor Rogers looked into Shane's eyes and remembered what he'd been told. How Shane had put this bloke in hospital for letting his dog piss on Shane's foot while he was waiting in the betting shop. Two weeks in intensive care. Definitely touch and go. It didn't matter that it wasn't true. What mattered, he believed it, Trevor, staring into Shane's unsmiling face, his unfaltering grey eyes.

"Yes," Trevor said, "he must've got, you know, wrong end of the stick."

At the door, Shane turned: "I was you, Trevor, I'd see Turvey got his CD-player back."

So Cheryl said goodbye to the most prized part of her stereo without ever having heard it; Trevor bunged Pete Turvey an extra twenty and mumbled something about one bloody kid looking much like another, must've made a mistake. "Right," said Turvey, copping the player and the twenty and gobbing full in Trevor's face, "that's what you did all right."

"You," Shane said, wrenching Nicky's arm up high behind his back. "Next time you shit on your own shoes, you can wipe it off yourself."

"I hope you realize," his mum said, "just how lucky you are."

Nicky did: and he thought it was never going to change. He lay low for a couple of weeks, swapping comics, playing the same old computer games, bunking off school and nicking stuff from shops, nothing out of the way. Then he broke into the Turvey house again and stole their CD-player for the second time.

Pete Turvey did something he thought he'd never see himself do – he went to the police.

"What you goin' to do about it, that's what I want to know. What you goin' to fuckin' do?"

From the door to his office, Resnick looked across the CID room to where Kevin Naylor, seated at his desk, was trying to calm an irate Pete Turvey into being rational. About thirty years, thought Resnick, and three bites at the education system too late.

"Kevin," Resnick said from near Turvey's shoulder, "anything I can do?"

"This gentleman…' Naylor began.

"What you can do," Turvey said, "is get that little arsehole Snape up in court and this time, instead of feedin' him with lollipops and promises and pats on the head, stick him inside so the rest of us can step out the house without comin' back and findin' anything not bolted down's been nicked."

"This isn't Shane?" Resnick said. "This is Nicky?"

"Christ!" exclaimed Turvey. "I must've come to the wrong place. Someone who knows what he's on about."

"Why don't you," Resnick said, "let DC Naylor have an accurate list of dates, what's been taken, anything else that's useful? I'll go along and have a word with the Snapes myself. OK?"

"Yeh," said Turvey. "Right. Yeh, right." And, wind from his sails, he took a seat at Naylor's desk.

❐

Resnick had known the family for a long time, through a whole catalogue of case conferences and supervision orders, periods for all three of the kids in local authority care. He knew Norma and liked her well enough, though he would never have been as foolish to think that she liked him. Why would she? From where Norma was standing, trouble came in shiny suits and waving warrant cards.

Like him or not, she made him a cup of tea. Pointed at the best chair for him to sit down in.

"How's Sheena?" Resnick asked, balancing the cup on one raised knee. At one side of the room, the television was switched on, an Open University broadcast on engineering. Resnick doubted anyone was following.

"Is it her you've come about, then?" Norma asked. Resnick shook his head.

"It's those Turveys, isn't it?"

"Is it?"

"Putting in their spoke where it's not wanted. Stirring trouble."

"They're making it up, then? About Nicky?"

Norma's expression changed, sour, as if she had found

something floating on the surface of her tea. She sighed. "What's the caufhead done now?"

Resnick voiced the complaint: the constant break-ins, the CD-player stolen twice.

Norma shook her head. "Even our Nicky wouldn't be that daft." Resnick let it ride. He knew there was no evidence, only Turvey's suspicions, though for himself, he thought they were probably correct. But if the machine had been taken it would have been off loaded within hours; the one risk Nicky would have kept to a minimum was being caught with it on his person.

As Resnick sipped the strong tea, he could feel it forming a lining inside his stomach. Silent, Norma lit one cigarette from the butt of another.

"You can see where it's heading, Norma. Clear as I can myself."

She shook her head and tilted it back, eyes closed. "You think I haven't told him till I'm blue in the face? Eh? Pleaded with him, belted him, tried shutting him in his room? Doesn't do a ha'p'orth of good."

Resnick doubted Norma was old enough ever to have seen a halfpenny. "Do you want me to talk to him? D'you think that might help?"

Norma let herself slump forward. "If you can find him, why not? One thing's sure, it can't make nothing worse."

Nicky was in town, standing with a crowd of youths in the amusement arcade on the north side of the square.

"Let's go outside, Nicky," Resnick said. "Sit in the car."

"Fancy me, then, do you?" Nicky grinned, adding a slight lisp to his voice. "How much is it worth?"

Ignoring the laughter, Resnick took hold of his arm. "I'll not ask twice."

Leaving the arcade, the boy turned back to his friends and laughed, miming masturbation with his hand.

He listened to Resnick for ten minutes, biting his already too-short nails and fidgeting with the ring in his left ear. All of the time his attention seemed to be outside the car, watching whoever was passing by; Resnick doubted if he'd heard one word in ten and was certain he didn't care.

"Nicky, have you heard what I've been saying?"

"Course," Nicky smiled. "Not stupid, you know. I can listen."

Yes, Resnick thought, but not to me. "OK," he said, "you can go."

Through the mirror, Resnick saw the boy stick two fingers high in the air before going back into the arcade.

"You've talked to him?" Turvey said, incredulously. "What sort of soddin' good's that supposed to do?"

His complaint would still be looked into, Resnick explained, the details of the missing property would be logged and if it turned up, of course, Turvey would be informed.

"And Snape?"

"We'll keep an eye on him."

"What you mean," Turvey said, "you're not goin' to do a bare-arsed thing."

Resnick shook his head. "We'll do what we can."

"Well, then," said Turvey, puffing out his chest. "I know someone who'll do a whole lot more."

"I have to warn you," Resnick said, "about taking the law into your own hands."

"Yeh?" Turvey said. "Yeh? The law? What's that then, round here? The law? What's that? You, that what it is?" He laughed. "Look around you. What d'you think?"

Resnick couldn't remember who it was had told him the best place to keep vodka was in the freezer, Russian vodka, at least. Whoever it had been, he was grateful. It was close to midnight, but somehow he didn't want to go to bed. In the living room, he turned off the central light and sat with one of the cats curled in his lap, another stretched out, long and slim, along one of the arms. The vodka glass was cold against his hand. He thought about Norma Snape, struggling to bring up three kids against all the odds. Then he tried not to think about it. There was a ballad track on the *Dial* set and he played it now, only the occasional flutter of notes embellishing the melody, the sharp edge of Parker's tone cutting all but the smallest residue of sentimentality away. When it came to an end, Resnick cued it again. 'Don't Blame Me'.

Nicky knew he was late and his mum would give him a thorough bollocking and he didn't care. The rhythm that tore through his headphones was fast and ragged and it seared his mind clear of everything else but the warmth of the cigarette he lifted to his mouth as he walked towards his home. He didn't hear the car approaching, didn't hear Pete Turvey's angry shout, the whoosh of the bottle as it sped, flaming, through the air, nor the crash of glass as it shattered at his feet.

What Nicky saw was the burst of flame as the petrol bomb exploded, and all he knew beneath his screams was the pain which claimed his hands and face and which clung to his legs like blistering skin.

SHE ROTE

SHE WROTE *Ray-O on her arm, scratching the letters with the blunted point of a compass she'd borrowed from one of the girls in Maths class. Scratched them and then went over the outline in blue biro, painstakingly slow.*

She wrote SARAH 4 RAY-O one hundred and twenty seven times in felt-tip on the inside of the toilet door. Only the persistence of two of the older girls, anxious to get in and light up, stopped her writing it one hundred and twenty eight, one hundred and twenty nine, one hundred and thirty.

She wrote a letter to the problem page of Just Seventeen: *"my boy frend wont use a condom he says theres no need cos I'm only 13. Please will you tell me if this is true. I need to no."*

But by then it was too late; by the end of the month she was bleeding but not enough, not the right kind.

Ray-o was nineteen, rising twenty. His real name was Raymond, Raymond Cooke, but everyone called him Ray-

o. The longest job he'd held down before going with his Uncle Terry had been in the wholesale butchers, down by the abattoir on Cattle Market Road. Hefting carcasses from the hooks of the conveyor belt, emptying tubs of tripes and offal into the incinerator bins; blood under his fingernails, gristle in his hair; the smell of it insidious on his skin.

Terry had saved him from all that. "How 'bout it, Ray-o? How d'you fancy working for me?" His uncle had taken a lease on a shop in Bobber's Mill, just to the north of the bridge. Second-hand stuff, that's what they'd be selling. Refrigerators, cookers, stereos, the odd bit of furniture – there was always a call.

"There's a couple of rooms over the top, an' all. Could live there if you want. Shan't charge you no more'n you're paying now. What d'you say? You and me, workin' together, eh?"

Raymond hadn't needed asking twice. A chance to get away from that poxy little room he had in Lenton, turn his back on all the shit and guts he'd been up to his elbows in. And besides, Terry, he was like a father to him really, more than his own father, that was sure; a father and a mate, both at the same time. Terry would take him out drinking, buy more than his fair share of pints, have a laugh about women, you know, doing it, having it away. "Now then, Ray-o, how d'you fancy sinking your teeth into that lot? Need a pair of flippers and a bleedin' snorkel!"

And Terry knew what he was talking about – ever since that cow of a wife of his had left him, he had new girl friends all the time. Raymond didn't know how he did it: forty if he was a day. And that one he was going with now, Eileen, she couldn't have been much older than Raymond himself. Great looking, too. Really gorgeous. If ever she came round to the shop, Raymond couldn't look at her without blushing.

Off duty, Mark Divine and Kevin Naylor were propping up the bar in the Mason's Arms, a little removed from their normal stalking grounds, but Divine had half a mind he might set eyes on one of his snouts who'd been avoiding him. Three pints and a couple of shorts down the road, so far he had had no luck.

"Another?" Naylor asked, hoisting a crisp new twenty in the barman's direction.

"Go on," Divine said. "Why not?"

Naylor's wife, Debbie, was off to her mum's, hatching plans for her sister's wedding; underskirts enough to bandage a battalion and more sequins than *Come Dancing*. Divine's on-again, off-again relationship with a staff nurse from the Queen's was decidedly off-again, and all he had to go home to was a video of *Baddiel and Skinner's Fantasy Football League* and the remains of last night's king prawn biriyani, adhering to its aluminium container in the fridge.

"This," Divine said, at the end of a copious swallow, "tastes like piss."

"Yes," Naylor said, licking the residue of froth from where he was considering growing a moustache. "Agreed."

Over to the far side of the room, in what would, before these democratic days, have been partitioned off as the public bar, a group of a dozen or so lads were in increasingly party mood. A good score of jokes, sexist, of course, ribald laughter, angry words, a bit of informal karaoke, spilt beer, a few choruses of 'Happy Birthday', a slight accident in the passageway outside when one of them didn't make it all the way to the bogs.

"Nice to see," Divine said.

"How's that?"

"People enjoying themselves."

Naylor nodded. He had personally felt the collars of at least two of them in the past eighteen months, one a suspected burglary, the other for being in possession of a controlled substance. Neither case had gone to court.

"Hey up!" Divine said, nudging Naylor in the ribs. "Catch a look at that."

The young woman who had come into the bar had long red hair, shading towards chestnut, and it hung loose past the collar of the oversize beige raincoat she was wearing. Aside from the hair, and the brightness of her lipsticked mouth, what marked her out most clearly was the policewoman's cap she wore at a jaunty angle on her head. A moment to take in the room and then she strode purposefully to where the lads were sitting.

"You don't think there's been a complaint?" Naylor said.

"Not yet."

First the table, then the whole pub fell quiet.

"Which one of you is Darren Matthews?" the young woman asked, not a tremor in her voice.

A few shouts and jeers, pointed fingers and sniggering behind hands and the aforementioned made a passable attempt at getting to his feet, pale face and tie askew, speech slurred. "Who wants to know?"

Before you could say Robert Peel, the woman had her raincoat unfastened and whisked away; she had obviously done this before. She was wearing police uniform skirt and tunic, black tights and three inch heels. "Darren Matthews," she said. "You're nicked."

In the resulting uproar, Divine caught the barman's

attention and got in another couple of whiskies, doubles. Someone had switched on the pub stereo and Janet Jackson was breathing encouragement to the woman, as, on the table now, she danced and swayed in front of the birthday boy's face, removing her uniform piece by piece as she moved. With a semblance of unison, the others around the table clapped encouragement.

"Debbie do that for you this year, Kev?" he asked.

"Did she, heck as like. Set of socket wrenches and a pair of Paul Smith socks."

The redhead stepped out of her skirt and revealed a pair of handcuffs tucked into the elastic of high-sided silk briefs with *Go to Jail* in tasteful red lettering over the crotch.

The object of her attentions did his best to make a bolt for it, but his mates grabbed him and pushed him back down.

"Only kind of arrest that poor sod's about to have," Divine said, "is of the cardiac variety."

With a professionalism that many of Divine's and Naylor's colleagues would have envied, the woman cuffed Matthews' wrists to the arms of the chair. So many were on their feet then, crowding round, it was difficult to see exactly what happened next, but what flew in the air above their heads was clearly Matthews' trousers.

"Jesus!" Divine exclaimed, shifting along the bar for a better view. "She's only going to do the business."

"She's never."

"Want to bet?"

Naylor grabbed Divine by the arm. "Then we're leaving."

"You're bloody joking!" He could no longer see the swaying head of red hair and he guessed she must be down on her knees.

"You want to get in there and put a stop to it?" Naylor demanded.

"No, I bloody don't."

Naylor pulled at the front of Divine's shirt. "Then we're out of here. Now, Mark, now."

Divine drove with almost exaggerated care; he didn't want to get pulled over and be ordered to blow into a plastic bag.

"What d'you reckon she gets for that?" he asked. "Side from a nasty taste in the mouth."

Naylor shrugged. Ever since leaving the pub, he'd been hoping against hope Debbie would be back from her mum's by the time he got in. "Fifty, hundred."

Divine whistled appreciatively. "Only need to do that a few times, pull in more than you or me."

"You fancy it then?"

"What? Spot of the old Chippendales? Why not? Might as well make some use of that old uniform, eh?" He laughed. "You read about that bloke, did this act dressed as a copper, strip-o-gram, like. Poor bastard only got three years, didn't he? On account these women he stripped for complained how he'd – what was it? – humiliated and degraded them."

"Maybe he had."

"Yeh? Shame they hung around long enough for him to get his tackle out of his Y-fronts, then, might not've been so fucking degraded if they hadn't."

Nodding, not really listening, Naylor glanced at his watch. He'd get Divine to drop him off at the Paki shop on the corner, pick up a bottle of that Chardonnay Debbie liked, glass or two to put her in the mood.

Terry was not quite asleep when he heard the key in the

lock, a smile on his face as soon as he recognised Eileen's footsteps on the stairs.

"Hello, love. How'd it go?" Reaching up for her as she leaned across him, brushing the top of his head with a kiss.

"Fine. Yeh, it was fine."

"Good tip?"

"Sixty. Not bad."

Terry pulled her down towards him. "Maybe we should celebrate."

"Not now. I want to take a shower first, clean my teeth."

"Okay, sweetheart. Whatever you say."

But by the time she had come back again, Terry had begun to doze off, so that when she slipped under the covers beside him, what he did was slide himself against her gently, one arm covering hers, the pair of them slotted together like spoons. It was what he liked most: what he missed those nights she stayed away.

From her room along the landing, Sarah had heard Eileen come in too; had lain there listening to the litany of doors – bedroom, bedroom, bathroom, bathroom, finally the bedroom once more. Sometimes, if she tip-toed across the floor, opened her own door just a crack and listened long enough she would hear her dad cry out and know that they'd been doing it. The same sound that Ray-o made, she knew what it meant.

Ray-o. Sarah lifted the covers over her head and said the name out loud. Ray-o. Ray-o. Ray-o. Abruptly, she stopped, realising that she had been shouting and even muffled like that she might be heard, if not by her dad or Eileen, then by her grandmother in the room adjoining hers. Ray-o. If only they knew... She remembered the first time she'd gone with him, ages she'd been, deciding which skirt to wear, which top, using this article she'd torn from a magazine to get her make-up just right.

Ray-o had met her in the rec and they'd sat on a bench near the kids' swings, drinking cider and smoking Raymond's Silk Cut. After a bit, he'd said how it was getting cold and taken her up to his room. All his mates, the blokes he shared with, had been out. She remembered a smell of sour milk and something else which seemed to come from Raymond himself. When he kissed her he pushed his tongue so far into her mouth she almost choked.

"Wash that stuff off," he said. "Here." Offering her a cloth.

"What stuff?"

"That muck you've got all over your face."

When she'd finished, he took the cloth back from her and wet one corner of it with spittle, the way her mum had used to do when she was little; carefully, he wiped away the eye shadow that had smeared her cheek.

"Ray-o," she said quietly.

"What?"

"Nothing." She'd read somewhere it was a mistake to tell a boy you loved him too soon.

"That's all right then." He started to take off his clothes and she thought that she should do the same.

When she was stretched back on the bed, one arm across her face to shield her eyes, she felt him touching her, her breasts and down between her legs. He hurt a little but not much.

"Here," he said. "Here."

He was kneeling over her, his thing sticking out, hard and thin. His balls were tight in wrinkled skin. "Here." He took her hands and placed them on him, sliding them back and forth. After a while he closed his eyes, pushed her hands away and did it for himself. She didn't know what was more surprising, the way his stuff sprayed across her or the shout that was more of a scream. Concerned, she asked him if it hurt. He lifted the cloth coloured by her make-up from the floor and wiped himself then gave it to her to wipe the stickiness away.

"Ray-o," she said.

"What?"

"I love you. Honest." She couldn't help herself. After all, he hadn't done it to her the first time; that proved he respected her, right?

Without really wanting to, Sarah ran her hands gingerly over her stomach, the swell of her belly. She was larger each day now, she'd swear it, though when she was standing straight it wasn't as if she even showed. Her clothes she wore loose and shapeless, just in case. Careful to lock the bathroom door. Ray-o. She couldn't understand why her dad had flown off the handle when he'd seen Ray's name written on her arm. Crack! The back of his hand across her face so fast she'd scarcely seen it coming and the next thing she knew she'd been picking herself up from the floor. "You stupid little cow! What d'you want to do a thing like that for?" And when she'd said it didn't mean anything, only that she liked him, he'd hauled her off the floor and shaken her until her eyes seemed to rattle in her head. "Flesh and blood, you horny little cow! He's your own flesh and fucking blood!"

Well, he wasn't. He was only her cousin. In the bible, cousins did it all the time. She'd read it at primary school.

Through the wall Sarah could hear her gran's low, reverberating snore.

❒

More months passed. The first frost caught Resnick by surprise. Opening the front door to retrieve the bottles (yes, still bottles) the milkman had left on the step, his feet nearly went from under him. Then he saw that the leaves that had collected in the lee of the wall were rimmed with white along their brittle edges; Dizzy's coat, when he ran his fingers along it, bristled cold and dampish to the touch.

Back in the kitchen, coffee ground and ready, he warmed the milk for all four cats before pouring it into their bowls. While the rye bread was toasting, he sliced Jarlsberg cheese and pulled the rind away from several rounds of Polish salami. The local weather forecaster was predicting a further drop in the temperature of five to ten degrees, but clear and sunny skies. One of the pullovers he had neglected to take to the cleaners had a bronze stain all down one side; the other was coming unravelled beneath the left arm. In the back of the drawer he found a sleeveless cardigan and he put this on over his pale blue shirt and beneath the brown tweed jacket he'd bought seven or eight years before, at a shop which now sold charity Christmas Cards and next year's calendars with twelve different picture of Madonna or Ryan Giggs.

The previous night he'd been listening to some Gerry Mulligan – the California Concerts from the early fifties – and he fancied hearing a handful of the tracks again, but there wasn't time. He had arranged for Graham Millington to give him a lift into the station, and, sure enough, there was the sergeant now, punctual as ever, sounding his horn.

"Cold enough to frighten brass monkeys," Millington

said, as Resnick climbed into the car.

"Happen we'll be busy, Graham. Take our mind off the weather."

Millington stubbed his Lambert and Butler out in the ashtray between the seats and set the car in gear.

Busy wasn't the word for it. Aside from the ongoing investigations in which all the officers in Resnick's team were involved, the cold night had fostered a flurry of activity through the early hours. Amongst the items stolen from the good burghers of the city were seven fur coats, including two minks and one sable, two cases of five-star brandy, three electric blankets and a state-of-the-art gas fire with full three-dimensional coal effect, neatly removed from its marble fireplace home. And this was without the usual plethora of jewellery, CD collections and VCRs, most of which would, even now, be exchanging hands as part of the system on which the invisible economy depended. How else were people supposed to get pissed, book holidays in Spain, buy something decent for the kids, score weed, pay the tally man, eke out child support, place a bet or put a little aside for a rainy day? If they didn't win the lottery, that is.

"Then there's this, boss," Divine said. They were sitting round the CID room, tea getting stewed, blue cigarette smoke frescoing the ceiling. "British Telecom van broken into, two gross of new DF50 fax machines gone missing."

"Soon be a lot of those around on discount, then," mused Millington. "Shouldn't mind one myself."

"All right," Resnick said, getting to his feet. "Let's keep our eyes peeled. Known fences, second hand dealers, car boot sales, any of these fly-by-night merchants sailing along by the seats of their pants. Graham, we've got a list, let's parcel it out. And while Lynn's off on that course, you'd best put a few my way as well."

For some reason, Raymond had caught himself thinking about Sara: not his cousin Sarah, Sarah with an h, but the Sara he used to go out with a couple of years before. The one who had been with him when... well, some of what had happened back then Raymond didn't like to remember. That little girl who'd gone missing and then all that business with the Paki copper as got knifed... but Sara, he didn't mind thinking about her. Nice, she was. Pretty and posh, sort of posh. Clever, too. Never able to understand what she'd seen in him, Raymond, and after a month or two, neither had Sara herself. She'd written him this letter, full of words he didn't properly understand – except he knew what they meant. She was dumping him, that was what. Raymond had tried to talk her out of it, get her to change her mind, but it hadn't been any good. "I'm sorry, Ray, but I'm afraid my mind's quite made up." And she'd walked off to where one of her customers was waiting to pay for a large bag of mixed soft-centres, head stuck in the air in that toffee-nosed way she had.

He hadn't been good enough for her, that's what it was. Of course, she hadn't come straight out and said it, Sara, not in so many words. She wasn't like that, better brought up. Whereas his cousin Sarah, she was pathetically grateful if you as much as looked at her, never mind anything else. Always hanging round though, that was the trouble. Wouldn't leave him alone. Not even indoors; in her house, his Uncle Terry's house. There they'd been, one day, Raymond feeling her up on the settee, thinking Terry was clear and instead he'd come breezing in, nearly caught them at it. "I shouldn't like to think, Ray-o," Terry said after Sarah had scarpered upstairs, "that you were taking advantage of me."

After that, of course, Raymond had backed off and told Sarah to do the same. Stop mooning after him, finding excuses to come to the shop, looking at him all the time like he was God's fucking gift – though from Sarah's point of view, most probably he was. Raymond couldn't see anyone else fancying it, scrawny little tart with a bony arse and tits like doorbells. Mind you, having said that, he thought she might have been putting on a bit of weight lately. All that ice cream and chocolate she was stuffing herself with, Raymond thought, making up for the fact that he wasn't giving her any. He was near the back of the shop, chuckling about that, when the street door opened and Detective Inspector Resnick walked in.

Raymond recognised him right off and the blood flew to his face. Half-turning a clumsy step away, he sent a clock radio crashing to the floor. The plastic top splintered clear across and the radio started playing Jarvis Cocker's 'Underwear'.

"Raymond, isn't it?" Resnick said, letting the door swing to behind him. "Raymond Cooke."

Down on one knee, mis-hitting the control buttons and switching on the alarm instead, Raymond mumbled yes.

"So, what you up to these days?" Resnick asked, flicking idly through a shoebox of second-hand CDs. "Keeping out of trouble?"

"Yes."

"And you've got a job?"

"Yes, here. I work here. My uncle, he…"

"Uncle Terry?" Resnick asked. "Terry Cooke?"

"Yeh."

"His place, then?"

"Yes."

"And you, you're what? Helping him out?"

"No, no, like I said, I'm here all the time. Live here, too. Upstairs." Raymond pointed towards the ceiling, past a couple of slightly battered kiddies' mobiles and a string of plastic onions that could have done with a dust.

"Nice," Resnick said. "Handy."

"Yeh."

"Of course…" Resnick had taken one of the CDs from the box now and was studying the writing on the back. "…not so handy for the park, the rec, watching little girls on the swings."

"I don't…" Breath caught high in Raymond's throat and for a moment he thought he wouldn't be able to breathe.

"Don't what, Raymond?"

"I'm not…"

"Yes?"

Raymond steadied himself against a tumble drier, cleared his throat, found a screwed-up tissue in his pocket and blew his nose. "I've got a girl friend," he said. "Going steady."

"That's nice, Raymond," Resnick said pleasantly. "Anyone I know?"

"No, no. Shouldn't think so, no."

"You're not…" Resnick looked upwards, "…living together?"

Raymond shook his head. "Thinking about it, you know."

Resnick reached out suddenly with his free hand and, as Raymond flinched, flicked something from the shoulder of the youth's leather jacket. "Treat her well, I hope, Raymond?"

"Yeh, yes, of course."

Raymond gulped air and Resnick stepped back and glanced at the CD in his hand. "How much?"

"Fiver."

"Good condition is it? I mean I'm not going to get it home and find it doesn't play?"

Raymond shrugged. "Far as I know it's okay."

"You've not heard it then?"

"Jazz, isn't it?" He shook his head. "Look, you can have it for four. Three-fifty."

"You're sure? Only I wouldn't want to get you into trouble with Uncle Terry."

"He doesn't mind. What I do in the shop here, it's up to me."

"Responsibility."

"Yeh."

Smiling, Resnick gave him a five pound note and waited for his change. "You wouldn't have anything in the way of fax machines, I suppose? You know, the kind with the telephone. Integral."

Raymond's face brightened. "Terry did say something, yes. I reckon we'll be getting some in, the next couple of days. You could always call back. You know, if you were passing."

Resnick hesitated for a moment at the door. "All right, Raymond, I might. Maybe you could even put one aside."

Sarah had shut herself in the bathroom, the cabinet where her dad kept his aftershave and deodorant, his spare razor blades and his condoms pulled over against the door. There were days – most days – when she could forget what was happening to her, happening to her inside, but this wasn't one of them. Sometimes the pain was so sudden and sharp, she had to bite her bottom lip to stop the screams; sometimes she almost went as far as thinking she would call her gran, ask her to help, but she knew she wouldn't do that. Not really. What she wanted – if she couldn't have Raymond – were friends to turn to, girl friends to ask for advice, but none of the girls at school would give her as much as the time of day.

After a while, she didn't know how long, she heard her gran going down the stairs, on her way to the early evening bingo. Her dad was already out, had been most of the day, she didn't know where. Squatting in the bath, Sarah bore down on the toothbrush she had placed across her mouth and bit it clean in half.

Millington was laughing as Mark Divine set down fresh pints between Resnick and himself. "And that's what he said? Come back in a couple of days and I'll have one here ready?"

"More or less."

"Daft twat!"

Resnick nodded. The more he thought about the way Raymond had reacted when he'd walked into the shop, the more he thought the lad might have something to hide, something he might like to ease off his chest. He doubted if it were anything as straightforward as a few BT fax machines.

"Turn him over, shall we?" Millington asked. "What d'you think?"

Resnick set down his glass. "Why not? Take Mark here and Kevin; pay them a call. Out of shop hours. But, Graham..."

"Yes?"

"This Cooke youth, Raymond, let's not drop him in it, not with the uncle. Let him stay clear."

"Plans for him, have you?"

"Maybe." He shrugged heavy shoulders. "Stay on his good side for a while, that's all."

Millington tapped the last Lambert and Butler from the packet; no sense in buying any more now till the morning, not with the wife how she was about him smoking. "Just as you like."

They went in with a warrant two days later; still not light. They had the door down before Raymond, deep asleep, could stumble down the stairs to let them in.

"Your uncle here?" Millington asked sharply.

Standing there in boxer shorts and an Oasis T-shirt, one hand cupped across his balls, Raymond just shook his head.

"Call him. Then get yourself back up there out of the way."

The DF50s were in the store room on the first floor, below where Raymond slept. Two dozen, neatly boxed. All in all, they hauled away a van load of stuff, mostly electrical; nice job that would be for someone, checking them against the stolen goods inventory.

"Course," Millington winked, "you've got the paperwork on all this lot."

Beside him on the pavement, hands deep in pockets, no time to grab a topcoat, freezing bloody cold, Terry Cooke didn't say a thing.

Sarah sat there in her room, curtains closed tight. She didn't know if it were day or night. Her eyes were open and then her eyes were closed. The pain came and then it went. Slowly, she reached from the side of the bed down into the drawer and lifted the baby with both hands. So small and light. So cold. Carefully, she unbuttoned her blouse and pressed him to her chest, the spongy top of his head soft against the nub of her breast.

Seeing it on the table where it had been left, poking out from the pages of last night's *Post*, Resnick realised he had never got around to playing his bargain price CD. *Charlie Parker: from Dizzy to Miles*. Pouring himself a glass of the bison grass vodka he had won in a raffle at the Polish Club he took the CD from its case, set it on the machine and pressed play.

It began with two of the tracks Parker had recorded with Max Roach and Miles Davis in 1951, but through some quirk of programming, the third tune didn't appear till some way into the disc. One of those unison statements so beloved of boppers to begin and then Parker takes off in surprisingly light, long fluid phrases before giving way to the choppy sound of Miles' muted trumpet; a chorus of so-so piano which Parker can't wait to end before he's muscling back in, stronger now, more aggressive, grabbing the piece by the scruff of its neck and hurtling it into four bar exchanges with the drums. Three minutes and six seconds later, abruptly, it's over. *She Rote*.

Settled back in his chair, Resnick smiled: well worth three-pounds-fifty of anybody's money.

The grandmother found the baby the next morning, searching through Sarah's drawers for an old jumper to unpick for wool. He had been wrapped in several layers of clothing and set snug against the drawer's edge, buttons across his eyes.

Her dad found the note in the kitchen, propped up between the stacks of plates near the back door.

Dear Dad,

I am riting to let you no you dont have to worry about me. I shall be OK. I'm sorry but I took the money from where you keep it in your room beside the bed and also from Grans bag. Im telling you this cos I didnt want you to blame Eileen or Ray-o.

Im sorry for what Iv done – and about the baby.

Love,

Sarah

xxxxx

CONFIRMATION

TERRY COOKE went to the pool every morning because it was good for his health. His doctor had told him so. Or, rather, his doctor had said, squinting above a pair of glasses held together with orange Elastoplast, "Terry, you're going to have to change your lifestyle, that is if you're going to have any life at all. Future tense."

A quarter past eleven on a sunny January morning, Terry was finally in Dr Max Bone's surgery after forty minutes shared with old copies of the *Guardian* magazine and the usual selection of bad backs, hacking coughs, and unmarried mums-to-be about to drop their firstborn on the worn carpet. The *Guardian,* for Christ's sake, where did Bone think this was, West Bridgford? And there was the doc ignoring his request for a referral to a chiropodist so Terry could get rid of his troublesome bunion on the NHS, and engaging him instead on issues of mortality. Life or death. His. Terry's.

"I'll stop smoking," Terry said, prepared to be alarmed.

"You should."

"Cut back on the drink."

"Yes."

"For pity's sake, I'm not even fifty."

"You want to be?"

Terry got up from the chair and walked to the window. In the street outside, two kids in bomber jackets, neither of them above ten years old, and both wearing nearly-new Nike trainers that had come down the chimney with Santa, were dismantling a black and silver mountain bike whose owner had optimistically left it chained to a parking meter.

"Exercise," the doctor said.

Terry couldn't see himself in one of those poncey jogging suits, sidestepping the dog shit round the edges of Victoria Park.

"Specifically, swimming; that's the thing."

The only time in the last fifteen years Terry had been swimming, Carrington Lido had still been an open-air pool and not a bunch of cramped chi-chi houses with satellite dishes the size of dinner plates and shiny gold numbers on the doors.

"It's not just the aerobic activity," Bone said, "though you need that without question. It's the effect of the water. Calming." He removed his glasses and pinched the bridge of his nose. "It's the stress, Terry, it's making too great demands upon the heart."

His back to the window, Terry could feel it, angry and irregular against his ribs. Cautiously, he returned to the chair and sat down. "Swimming," he said, uncertainly. "That'd really make a difference?"

Bone nodded. "If not, I know a wonderful masseuse. Shiatsu. Unfortunately not on the National Health."

Terry thought he would try the swimming first. He

shook Bone's hand and, out on the street, clipped the ear of an eight-year-old demanding a pound to look after his car, make sure no one tried to nick the radio, see it didn't get scratched.

"Listen, you, I find one mark on that motor you're for it. This is Terry Cooke you're talking to, right?"

"Yeah, and my Dad's Frank Bruno."

Terry shrugged; anything was possible. He walked as far as the corner of Carlton Road and sat in the side bar of an empty pub with a half of bitter and a large Bells. Stress, the doc was right. Terry had it in spades.

There was his daughter, Sarah, for instance. Several months back she had followed her mother's inexact path and taken the overnight National Express north to Edinburgh. No note, no reason, though Sarah's gran, Terry's own mum, that is, had acted strangely about the whole thing and Terry was sure she knew more about it than she was letting on. One of these fine days, when she'd suckled enough gin, it'd all come pouring out. Till then, it was the occasional reversed-charge call from Sarah and a postcard of Greyfriar's Bobby with a scrawled message to say that she and her mum were fine. Terry could imagine the pair of them shacked up in some scabby flat, more likely than not a squat. As long as her mother wasn't into sharing needles, it might not work out so bad.

At least it made it easier with Eileen, Terry's live-in girl-friend. Eileen was a stripper of considerable abilities who, since moving in with Terry, had taken herself upmarket and now specialised in delivering personalised birthday mes-sages dressed in her own version of a WPC's uniform.

Terry tried to tell himself he didn't mind Eileen going out and cuffing some spotty car salesman to a chair while she gave him a tongue lashing, but the truth was that he

did. After all, the first time he'd ever laid eyes on her himself, it had been the speed with which she'd got down to her
spangled g-string that had taken his eye. Slowly, very
slowly. Now whenever Eileen went out on a job, part of
him was terrified she'd encounter some muscled hard boy
who worked out six days a weeks and made love like a
power machine on the seventh. Twenty-three, Eileen, and
young enough, just about, to be Terry's daughter herself.

Sarah... then Eileen... and the star over the sodding
stable hadn't long faded before Inspector bloody Charlie
Resnick had been sniffing round the secondhand shop
Terry rented out by Bobbers Mill. Resnick like some scruffy
Santa with a ho-ho-ho and turkey gravy on his tie, offering
to do a special New Year inventory of suspect goods. It was
only good luck that Terry had been there himself that day,
and not his gormless nephew Raymond, otherwise it might
not have been so easy to steer Resnick away from the several gross of Sega and Nintendo that had escaped the
Christmas market. To say nothing of the camcorders.

Stress? Of course he was suffering from stress. A life like
this, how could it be anyway else? But fifty was something
he did want to see. It wasn't altogether off the cards that he
and Eileen might want to start a family.

Terry lowered himself into the water gradually, none of
those bravura dives off the pool edge for him, and began
the first of thirty slow, laborious lengths. Not so very long
from now he'd be back out and across the road, sitting in
the market café with a strong tea and a sausage cob.

Resnick got into the station that morning late and less than
happy. His own car was in for what might prove to be its
last ever service and the Vauxhall he'd borrowed had
recently been used for a spot of undercover observation

and smelled of hastily bottled urine and too many Benson Kingsize. Halfway along Lower Parliament Street a corporation bus driver had ploughed into the back of a Burger King delivery truck and the consequent brouhaha had blocked the traffic both ways from the Theatre Royal to the Albert Hall and Institute.

"Bit of a lie-in?" Millington asked when Resnick finally pushed his way through the door to the CID room, the smile edging its way, ferret-like, from beneath the sergeant's moustache. "Deserved."

"Last night's files on my desk?" Resnick asked, barely breaking stride en route to the partitioned-off section that was his office.

"Likely need a bit of an update by now."

"Tea, Graham," Resnick said. "I don't suppose there's any chance of a cup of tea?" Coffee was his preference, but experience had long since taught him that within the confines of the station the cup that cheers was the safer choice.

"Kev," Millington called, head inclined towards the far corner of the room.

"Boss?" Telephone in hand, Kevin Naylor peered round from his desk.

"When you've a minute, get kettle on, mash some more tea."

Naylor sighed, spoke into the receiver, made a mark alongside the list of names and addresses on his desk and got to his feet. He glanced across at Lynn Kellogg as he passed, Lynn sitting impervious at her computer, strolling through the county database detailing offenders with a penchant for carrying firearms with malicious intent. That'll be the day, he thought, when anyone dares ask her to make the bloody tea in this team.

Leaning over the shuffle of folders and papers that covered his desk, Resnick scanned through the outline of the previous night's events. Three men had been arrested and held in the cells overnight: two on charges of drunk and disorderly; the third, apparently sober, had driven his fibreglass-bodied invalid tricycle into a Kentucky Fried Chicken franchise and attempted to run over his ex-lover, who was one of the customers.

There had been eleven burglaries reported from the Victorian splendours of the Park estate and seven more, all of them in the same short street, from the less salubrious east side of the Alfreton Road. Carl Vincent was out there now, checking some of these door to door, while Naylor was talking to other aggrieved homeowners on the phone.

All routine: it was the last entry in the night's incident file which claimed most of Resnick's attention. At eleven minutes past three a message had been received giving information of a burglary taking place at a television and electrical goods suppliers in Radford. The officers who had responded, PCs Mark McFarlane and Mary Duffy, had initially reported seeing no obvious signs of forced entry, but in the narrow alley at the rear had run into a gang of four men armed with a sawn-off shotgun, iron bars and a long-handled sledgehammer. A mercy, Resnick thought, that the shotgun had not been brought into play, though he was by no means certain the officers would have agreed. Mark McFarlane was in Queen's with a suspected fractured skull and Mary Duffy was in an intensive care bed in the same hospital, a splintered rib having pierced her lung. Such descriptions as they had been able to give of their assailants were necessarily brief and incomplete – balaclavas and coveralls, boots and gloves – it had been dark in the alley and McFarlane's torch had been smashed early in the struggle.

Resnick snapped open the door from his office. "Graham…"

"On its way. Kev, what you doing with that tea?"

"This pair in hospital," Resnick said, "when did we last get a report?"

"Not above half-hour back. No change."

Resnick nodded. "Any list yet of what was taken?"

"I've called the owner twice," Millington said, handing Resnick his favourite Notts County mug. "Promised it within the hour."

"Get on to them again, Graham. Sitting on it this long, likely all they're busying themselves with is massaging the totals for the insurance. If they keep stalling, maybe you should get down there yourself."

Millington nodded, right.

"Sir," Lynn said, swivelling at her desk. "I've got a print-out of likely candidates for carrying the shotgun. Local, anyhow."

"Good. Cross-check with the information officer at Central, might be a body or two worth pulling to get things started. Let me know how it's going when I get back." Resnick took a couple of swallows at his tea and set it down. "I'm off out to the hospital, take a look at the wounded, see if anything's jogged their memory." He hoped the traffic had died down and that Duffy and McFarlane would be up to talking to him when he arrived.

He was hoping in vain. McFarlane had lost consciousness again by the time Resnick got to his side and all that Mary Duffy could tell him through bruised lips was that one of their attackers had seemed taller than the rest, two or three inches over six foot, and another might have been stockier and shorter than the other two.

"Voices?" Resnick asked. "Accents?"

Quietly, Duffy began to cry. "I'm sorry, sir. I'm sorry."

Resnick patted her hand and hoped she wouldn't notice when he glanced at his watch.

Terry Cooke collected his tea and roll from the counter and went to his normal seat by the window. Across Gedling Street, the stalls of the open market were attracting a slow scuffle of elderly shoppers, collars turned up against the keenness of the wind. He watched as a lean, slope-shouldered figure, white haired, turned away from where he had been buying what looked like a couple of pounds of potatoes, a few carrots and onions, and crossed towards the café.

Like Terry, Ronnie Rather was a creature of routine. Monday, Wednesday, Friday, he would push his olive-green shopping trolley sedately from stall to stall, before treating himself to tea and toast and a small cigar that burned like anthracite and had a similar flinty smell. On alternate Fridays, he splashed out on beans as well.

Since Ronnie had been adhering to this particular routine longer than Terry himself, and had made a habit, when it was vacant, of sitting at the window table, Terry could hardly object when as today the old man parked up his trolley against the table edge and joined him.

"Ron."

"Terry."

There would be no more said until Ronnie had cut his slices of toast into thin strips – soldiers, Terry's mum would have called them, when she had been readying them for the young Terry to dip into his boiled egg – which Ronnie would then sprinkle with salt before chewing methodically. Two or three pieces despatched into the gurgles and groans of Ronnie's antique digestive system and Terry's breakfast companion would lean forward across the table, resting on one elbow, and engage him in conversation.

Which usually meant, as was the way with those old jossers well above the pensionable age, talking about the dim and distant past when a pint of beer was a pint of beer and the sound of a horse-drawn cart approaching along the road outside was enough to send every self-respecting householder running for his dustpan and broom. Or, in Ronnie Rather's case, when there was a dance hall on every corner, each of them keeping a dozen or more musicians in full-time employment, and when names like Joe Loss and Jack Hylton were enough to quicken the pulse and set up a tremble at the back of the knees.

Trombone, Ronnie had played; first or second chair with every dance band ever to grace Mayfair and the West End or tour the provinces, where, according to Ronnie, so many women would throng round the stage door it often needed the police to clear them away. If he had really done all the things he claimed, played with all those people in all those places, Terry figured Ronnie Rather had to be the wrong side of eighty if he was a day. Which was just about right.

"Here, Terry..." Ronnie began, and Terry waited for the night the Prince of Wales came into the Savoy and insisted that everyone else was sent packing so that he and Mrs Simpson could dance alone. Or the time at the Queensbury Club just before the end of the war, when Glen Miller recognised him in the audience and insisted that he step up and sit in with the band.

But no, it was "Terry, you hear about them two poor bloody coppers, got their heads smashed in?"

Terry nodded; he had heard it on the news driving to the pool. A gang of four masked men, heavily armed, disturbed while carrying out a burglary – well, he reckoned he could fit names to at least two of those hidden faces, possibly three, and it wouldn't surprise him if by the time he got out to the shop there hadn't been a call enquiring, in the most roundabout of terms, if he might be interested in enlarging his stock to the tune of a couple of dozen state-of-the-art wide-screen, digital sound TVs.

"One of 'em a woman, an' all, that's what sticks in my craw. The bloke, copper, I mean, whatever's comin' to him, fair deal. But not the woman – only a kid, too." Ronnie Rather shook his head in disgust and a piece of undigested toast reappeared at one corner of his mouth. "Call me old-fashioned, if you like. Don't hold with hitting women, never have."

"No, no," Terry said. "I agree with you there. Ninety-nine per cent." And he did. "Listen, Ronnie," he said, checking what remained of his tea was too cold to drink, "like to stick around and chat, but you know how it is, got to run. Business. See you soon, yes?"

Ronnie nodded and watched as Terry scooted out through the door and hurried off to where his car was parked on a meter outside the leisure centre doors. Ulcer, Ronnie thought watching him, that's what he's going to get if he doesn't watch out. An ulcer at least.

Millington and his merry team had stuck the proverbial pin in Lynn Kellogg's list of likely candidates and, backed up by a crew of eager uniforms, each and every one of them anxious to avenge their fellow officers, had gone knocking on doors and feeling collars on the Bestwood and Broxtowe estates and in those all-day pubs and twenty-four-hour snooker halls where villains of like minds were wont to congregate. Great sport, but to little long-term avail.

"Anything, Graham?" Resnick asked.

It was late enough in the afternoon for any pretence at daylight to have given up the ghost, and the sergeant's moustache was drooping raggedly towards his upper lip. "Bugger all!"

It would have taken Petula Clark herself to have walked into the CID room and given out with 'The Other Man's Grass (Is Always Greener)' – a perennial favourite of Millington's – to bring the smile back to his eyes.

"I thought Ced Petchey…"

"Ced Petchey coughed to a break-in out at the University Science Park which netted a couple of outmoded Toshibas and three cartons of double-sided three-and-a-half-inch floppy disks."

"Ah. I thought we'd already charged the Haselmere youth with that one?"

"Precisely."

It was that time of the day when Resnick's energy was at its lowest and his need for a quick caffeine injection at its most pronounced. "Look at it this way, Graham. What we've done today, clear out the dead wood. Tomorrow, we'll strike lucky."

"We bloody better."

Resnick thought there was no harm in giving luck a helping hand. He left his car on the lower floor below the Victoria Centre and took the lift up to the covered market. Doris Duke was winding sprigs of greenery into a bouquet in which pink and white carnations featured prominently.

"Three of these for your mates out at the hospital this morning, Mr Resnick. By the sound of it, fortunate they wasn't wreaths."

Resnick slid a ten-pound note along the surface where she worked. "If you've a customer for that already, Doris, you could make me up another."

"Fifteen, Mr Resnick. Got to be worth that, at least."

"Prices going up, Doris? I didn't see a sign."

Doris pushed the bouquet away and sat straighter on her stool, hooking the heels of her shoes over the lower rungs. "Special orders, special price; you know how it goes." She lifted a pack of ten Embassy from the breast pocket of her pink overall, leaned sideways and slid a lighter from the side pocket of her jeans.

Resnick set five pound coins, each neatly balanced on top of the other, down on the centre of the ten-pound note.

"Word is it's Coughlan. He was the one carrying." Doris's voice could only just be heard.

"Whoever that was," Resnick said, "didn't do the beating."

"I'm sorry, Mr Resnick," Doris said, "this time of the year they're scarce, good blooms. That's the best I can do for now."

Resnick nodded. "Look after yourself, Doris."

"You too."

Somehow, when he walked away in the direction of the Italian coffee stall, Resnick forgot to take his bouquet.

"Coughlan," Millington said sceptically. "Bit of a change of pace for him, isn't it?"

"Self-improvement, Graham. Most likely comes from listening to his probation officer."

Resnick and Millington were in the left-side bar of the Partridge, what would have been called the Public in more openly divided times. Their fellow drinkers – and it was not crowded – were either single men staring morosely into pints of mixed, or students wearing slimming black and sporting silver rings.

"You think it's true?" Millington asked. He was trying not to stare at a skinny seventeen-year-old, the largest of whose three noserings was decorated with three emerald stones and from whose left eyebrow a tiny crucifix hung from a loop of chain.

"About Coughlan?" Resnick said.

"They get themselves pierced all over? All over their bodies?"

"I don't know, Graham. No idea." He knew the superintendent's daughter had come back from her first term at university with a gold stud in the side of her ear and a plaited ring through her navel.

"Blokes, too." Millington shook his head, eyes close to watering at the prospect of a pierced foreskin.

"Coughlan, Graham."

"It's good information?"

"More often than not."

"Go wading in, all we're like to do is warn him off. Come up empty handed."

Resnick nodded. Coughlan had been involved in maybe a dozen break-ins in the past two years, but each foray to turn over the council house he lived in off Bracknell Crescent had found the neat three-bedroom semi as clean, in Millington's words, as a pair of Julie Andrews' knickers. A shotgun, though; for Coughlan that was a step in a dubious direction. Why go armed to do an empty shop in the wee small hours? Maybe he was trying to get the feel of it, readying himself for bigger things.

"No word who he was working with?"

"'Fraid not."

"What's that cousin of his called? Barker? Breaker?"

"Breakshaw. Norbert Breakshaw."

"Didn't he go down for five last time?"

"Carrying a weapon with criminal intent."

"Maybe the shotgun was his."

"Then what was Coughlan doing carrying it?"

"Norbert likely give it him to hold, leave his hands free for belting McCrory and the girl. He's a nasty bastard. Certificates to prove it."

"One thing, Graham, isn't he still inside? Lincoln?"

"I'll check first thing. If he's out and we can put the pair of them together, Breakshaw and Coughlan…"

"Confirmation, Graham, that's what we need. Confirmation."

"Right," said Millington. "Sup up and we'll have another before I get home to the missus. Chicken chasseur tonight, unless I'm much mistaken. Say what you like about Marks, you know, can't fault 'em for reliability."

Resnick's quip about Karl or Groucho remained frozen on his lips.

Terry Cooke had fallen asleep with the *Mail* open on his lap and orchestral versions of Burt Bacharach's hits lilting out of the stereo. When he opened his eyes with a start, Eileen was framed in the living-room mirror and the violins were just cascading into the theme of 'This Guy's In Love With You'. There were times, Terry thought, life could be pretty nearly perfect.

"I was just going," Eileen said. She was wearing a red dress, tight at the hips, high black heels, and her red hair was pinned high above her head. A camel coat was slung over one arm.

"Without saying goodbye?" Terry smiled.

"You looked so peaceful."

"So?"

Smiling, she crossed the room and he turned to greet her, Eileen bending to plant a red-lipped kiss on the oval of thinning hair where the scalp showed through.

"What time'll you be back?"

"Late."

"Why don't you let me meet you?"

She took a step away. "Terry, let's not start all that again, eh?"

When they had first started living together he had insisted upon picking her up outside whichever hotel or club she had been working, but Eileen had insisted it was bad for business and finally convinced him it was true. No birthday boy for whom she'd just table-danced in a g-string and policewoman's hat would enjoy the sight of her being whisked away by her live-in lover, likely back home to a bowlful of hot cereal and his and hers mugs of Ovaltine. "It won't do, Terry, it's bad for the image. You've got to see that?"

Terry knew she was right; knew, too, what she wasn't quite saying: picked up by some bloke old enough to be my father. Most nights now, unless he had to go out on a bit of business himself, Terry stayed home, television turned low so he'd hear the cab pulling up outside, the clatter of Eileen's heels up to the door.

"What is it tonight?" he asked.

"A stag night and two twenty-firsts."

"OK, see you later. Have fun."

Eileen hated lying to him, but sometimes he didn't leave her any choice. If Terry knew she'd gone back to working the pubs – not often, and then only when the landlord had organised a lock-in, which meant bigger tips and less chance of the punters getting out of control – he would not be happy. But that was what Eileen missed, working an audience, feeling all their eyes on you and knowing if you played it right you could keep them there, glued. That feeling of control.

For tonight, she'd been brushing up one of her old routines with a banana and half a dozen ping-pong balls; if that didn't put at least a couple of hundred quid in the pot, she didn't know what would.

No chicken chasseur for Resnick to go home to; no wife. A predatory black cat to greet him, hungry, at the front door and three others, more docile, waiting inside. After seeing to them, he fixed himself a sandwich from gorgonzola and smoked ham, forked two pickled cucumbers from a jar and snapped open a bottle of Pilsner Urquel. In the front room, he fished out an old vinyl album, *Eddie Condon's Treasury of Jazz*, bought a hundred years ago, and set it to play. When Billy Butterfield was taking the introduction to 'I've Got a Crush on You', trumpet and piano with the verse to themselves, Resnick recalled seeing Butterfield in person: the 'seventies it would have been, down the M1 at a club in Leicester, a portly old boy wearing stay-pressed flannels and a blue wool blazer. The number was coming to an end, Ralph Sutton filigreeing under the final chords, when the telephone rang. Resnick recognised Ronnie Rather's voice right away.

Ronnie was in the downstairs bar of the Old Vic. "Get your skates on, Charlie, and you'll just catch the last set."

The band were into something modal, bluesy; sax and rhythm set up on a low stage deep to the rear of the low-ceilinged room. Maybe half the tables were taken, couples mostly, caught up in quiet conversation. Ronnie Rather was sitting midway between the door and the stand, his white hair resting back against the wall, eyes closed, listening.

Resnick went over to the bar, and when the girl had solved seven across she got to her feet and served him a bottle of Worthington White Shield, which she left him to pour for himself, and a large brandy with a touch of lemonade. Dropping his change back into his suit pocket, he stayed there listening: all of the musicians he recognised, was on nodding terms with; he had seen them playing in everything from pubs like this to the pit band at the theatre: they were of an age. Second Nature was what they were calling themselves now; the last time he had seen them it had been something else. The pianist, Resnick thought, had likely been with Billy Butterfield when he had seen him in Leicester.

As the number came to an end, a tenor cadenza over bowed bass, Resnick walked back across the room and placed the brandy down alongside Rather's empty glass.

"Cheers, Charlie."

"Pleasure."

Ronnie nodded in the direction of the band. "Heard Mel Thorpe do his Roland Kirk, have you?"

"Not recently."

Ronnie tasted his brandy and lemonade and smiled. "Considering he's not black or blind, he does a pretty fair job."

On flute now, the soloist sang, hummed and grunted as he blew, spurring himself along with intermittent shouts and hollers which raised the temperature of the playing to the point that one or two of the audience began drumming on their tabletops and the barmaid set aside her crossword puzzle in favour of polishing glasses. The applause was sustained and earned.

"I saw him, you know, Charlie. Roland Kirk. St Pancras Town Hall. Nineteen sixty-four."

Resnick nodded. He had seen Kirk once himself, but later, not more than a year before the end of his life –

Birmingham, he thought it had been, but for once he wasn't
sure. The musician had already suffered one stroke and
played with one side of his body partially paralysed; it had
been like watching a tornado trapped in a basket, a lion
shorn and bereft in a cage.

"This business with the copper, Charlie. The girl..."

"Mary Duffy."

"If you say so. I don't like it, treating women like that."

Resnick allowed himself a smile. "One of nature's gentlemen, that what you're saying, Ronnie?"

"Oh, I've known a few in my time, Charlie. Young
women, I mean."

"I'll bet you have."

"And never raised a finger, not to any of them. Not
one."

Resnick nodded again, drank some beer. The band were
playing a ballad, medium tempo, 'The Talk of the Town'.

"Bumped into Terry Cooke," Ronnie said, "café by the
market, Victoria Park. Soon as I mentioned it, the break-in
and that, he turned all pale and couldn't wait to be on his
way."

"You don't think he was involved?"

"Terry? Not directly, no. Have a heart attack minute
anyone said boo to him in the dark."

"What then?"

"Mates with Coughlan, isn't he?"

"And this was Coughlan's job?"

"Word is, on the street."

"I didn't know," Resnick said, "Cooke and Coughlan
were close."

"Who Cookie was close to," Ronnie explained, "was
Coughlan's wife."

"Second or third?"

"Third. Marjorie. Cookie was having it away with her the best part of a year. That was before he cottoned on to this young bit of skirt he's got now. Anyway, while all this was going on, he got himself into a card school with Coughlan. Poker. Dropped a lot of money there on occasion, so I heard. His way of paying for it, I suppose."

"Coughlan didn't know?"

"Some blokes," Ronnie said, leaning a shade closer to Resnick as if letting him into a greater confidence, "get off on the idea their bird's fresh from shagging someone else. Whether Coughlan's one of those, it's difficult to tell. But him and Cookie, still speaking. Doing business."

"You think Coughlan's going to be looking to his old pal Terry, then, to help him offload from the other night?"

Ronnie paused to applaud a particularly nice piece of piano. "Wouldn't you, Charlie? What friends are for."

Resnick bought another large brandy, nothing for himself. "Any word Breakshaw might have been involved?"

"Norbert? Not so's I've heard. But it'd make sense. Evil bastard. When he kicked inside his old lady's womb, he'd have been wearing steel-capped Doc Martin's."

The hand Resnick slipped down into Rather's jacket pocket held three twenty-pound notes. "Look after yourself, Ronnie."

Ronnie nodded and leaned back, closing his eyes.

When Terry Cooke arrived, waved through the lock-in on Coughlan's say-so, Eileen was down on all fours on the bar, waving an unzipped banana above her head and asking, should she put it in, if there was anyone there man enough to eat it out.

When Coughlan had phoned, the last thing Terry had wanted to do was be seen drinking with him so soon after the break-in and what had followed, but Coughlan had assured him it was a private party. Mates. No prying eyes. He hadn't said anything about Eileen. Maybe he hadn't known. Maybe he had.

Now Coughlan gripped Terry firmly by the upper arm and led him into a corner, some distance from the core of the chanting crowd.

"You'll not be bothered," Coughlan said, "not seeing the show. Nothing you won't have seen before."

Terry looked into Coughlan's face but, heavy and angular, it gave nothing away. In a wedge of mirror to his right, Terry could see the shimmer of Eileen's nearly nude body as she lowered herself into a squatting position, facing out. The banana was nowhere to be seen.

"What's up, Terry? Nothing the matter?"

Terry shook his head and tried to look away.

"Come over all of a muck sweat."

"Bit of a cold. Flu, could be."

"Scotch, that's what you need. Double."

The crowd, grinning, egging one another on, clapped louder and louder as Eileen arched backwards, taking her weight on the palms of her hands, the first brave volunteer being pushed towards her by his mates.

"Not hungry yourself, Terry?" Coughlan enquired, coming back with two glasses of Bells. "Had yours earlier, I daresay."

"What's going on?" Terry asked, feeling his own perspiration along his back and between his legs, smelling it through the cigarette smoke and beer. "What's all this about?"

"Marjorie sends her love," Coughlan said. "Told her I'd be seeing you tonight."

"For fuck's sake, Coughlan!"

"Exactly." Coughlan's hand was back on his shoulder, like a vice, and Terry, the glass to his lips, almost let it slip from his hand. "Bygones be bygones, eh, Terry? So much shafting under the bridge. Besides, things change, move on…" There was a loud roar from the jubilant crowd and then cheers. "…Musical beds, you might say. Keeps things fresh. Revives the appetite." Coughlan looked pointedly towards the mirror, turning Terry so that he was forced to do the same. "Lovely young girl like that, Terry, shouldn't take much persuading to get her round my place of an evening. Once in a while." His face twisted into a smile. "Genuine redhead, natural. I like that."

Terry held his glass in both hands and downed the scotch.

"I could have let Norbert loose on you, Terry. He'd have loved that. But no, this way's best. Pals. Pals, yes, Terry?"

Terry said nothing.

"And then there's the stuff from the other night. "Course I don't expect you to take it all. Dozen sets, say? Sony? VCRs? Stereo? Matt black, neat, you'll like those. I'll have them round your place tomorrow night. One, one-thirty. Norbert, I expect he'd like to make delivery himself."

Terry Cooke looked at the floor.

"I shouldn't wait around, Terry, to take her home. Someone'll see she gets a lift, you don't have to fret."

Back on her feet and shimmying along the bar to 'Dancing Queen', Eileen caught sight of Terry for the first time as he pushed through the door, spotted him and almost lost her step.

There was a light burning on the landing, another in the back room, and Eileen stood for a full minute on the step, key poised, running over her excuses in her head. She'd half expected to get back and find her bags on the pavement, clothes flung all over the privet hedge. Thought, when she got inside, that he might be waiting with a knotted towel in his hand, wet, she'd known men do that; at least his fist. But he was sitting, Terry, in the old round-backed chair that was usually his mother's, cup of tea cold in his hand.

"Terry, I…"

"You get on," Terry said. "Time you've had your shower and that, I'll be up." He didn't look her in the face.

Twenty minutes later, when he slid into bed beside her, the backs of her legs were still damp from the shower and he shivered lightly as he pressed against her.

"Terry?"

"Yes?"

"Put out the light."

Resnick and Millington were in the shop when Terry Cooke arrived, not yet ten-thirty and Millington poised to buy a nearly-new book club edition of *Sense and Sensibility* for his wife, while Resnick was thumbing through the shoe-box of CDs, looking for something to equal the set of Charlie Parker *Dial* sessions he'd bought there once before.

Terry's nephew, Raymond, stood in the middle of the room like a rabbit caught in headlights.

"Ray-o," Terry said, "get off and see a film."

"They don't open till gone twelve."

"Then wait."

"You know why we're here?" Resnick asked once Raymond had gone.

"Maybe."

"We've heard one or two whispers," Millington said, making himself comfortable on a Zanussi washing machine. "Concerning a certain nasty incident the other night."

"Not down to me," Terry said hastily.

"Of course not," Resnick assured him. "We'd never believe that it was. But others, maybe known to you…"

"You see, we've heard names," Millington said. "Confirmation, that's all we need."

"Though if you give us more…"

"Confirmation and more…"

Terry felt the muscles tightening along his back; he ought never to have missed his morning swim. "These names…"

"We thought," Resnick said, "you might tell us."

"Remove," Millington said, "any suggestion that we put words into your mouth."

Terry felt the pressure of Coughlan's hand hard on his shoulder, remembered the sick leer on his huge face when he had talked about sharing Eileen. "Coughlan," he said. "Him for certain."

"And?"

"Breakshaw. Norbert Breakshaw."

"Thank you, Terry," Resnick said, letting a Four Seasons anthology fall back into the box; just so many times, he thought, you could enjoy 'Big Girls Don't Cry'.

"Here," Millington said. "How much for this?"

"There's something else," Terry said, "something else you'll want to know."

When Norbert Breakshaw parked the van close to the back entrance to Terry Cooke's business premises, he wasn't alone; Francis Farmer and Francis's brother-in-law, Tommy DiReggio, were with him. Norbert had brought them along, partly for the company, partly to help him shift the gear; they had been with Norbert and Coughlan at the original break-in. Francis had hung back once Norbert had started swinging the sledgehammer and things got a little out of hand, but Tommy had enjoyed the chance to let fly with an iron bar, get the boot in hard.

"There's a light on," Norbert said. "He's waiting for us."

Not quite right. What was waiting for them was a team of some twenty officers, two of them, Millington included, having drawn arms just in case.

Burdened down by boxes of expensive electricals, Francis and Tommy had no chance to run; Norbert's retreat back to the van was cut off by a phalanx of men and women eager to try out their newly issued long-handled truncheons.

"Just like the military in the Gulf," Millington explained in the canteen later. "Not so often you get a chance to give the hardware a try, battle conditions and all."

Resnick had taken Vincent and Naylor for back-up, but left them downstairs, watching over Coughlan's wife as she offered them a choice of Ceylon or Darjeeling. Resnick read Coughlan his rights as the big man dressed, hesitating for longer than was strictly necessary over the striped tie or the plain blue. Either way, the custody sergeant would never let him take it with him into the cells.

"Some bastard fingered me, I suppose," Coughlan said, walking ahead of Resnick out of the room.

"Your mistake," Resnick said, "doing a job with Breakshaw, letting him wade into those officers the way he did."

"It wasn't Cookie, was it?" Coughlan stood facing Resnick at the foot of the stairs.

"Terry? No," Resnick said. "Besides, I thought the two

of you were close. Family, almost. Last thing I should have thought he'd want to do, drop you in it. Unless you've given him reason, of course."

"Whatever time is it?" Eileen asked. The faintest glow from the streetlamp, orange, filtered through the curtain of the room.

Terry picked up the clock and brought it closer to his face. "Half three."

"What you doing still awake?"

"Can't sleep."

She turned towards him, careful not to let the cold air into the bed. "You're not worried, are you?"

"What about?"

"I don't know. I thought maybe the other night…"

"Shush." Leaning forward, he kissed her lightly on the mouth. "It's happened. Done."

"I won't do it again."

"You said."

"I pr—"

Again he stopped her, this time with his hand. "Don't. Don't promise. There isn't any need."

She moved her mouth so that first one, then two of his fingers were between her lips. Terry reached down and hooked his thumb inside the top of his boxer shorts, easing them lower till he could kick them away to the end of the bed.

"I don't deserve you, you know," Eileen said, reaching for him, his tongue for that moment where his fingers had been.

"Yes," he said, when he could speak again. "Yes, sweetheart, you do." This had to be a better way, Terry thought, of relieving stress. No matter what the doctor said.

BIRD OF PARADISE

IT WAS still surprisingly cold for the time of year, already well past Lent, and Sister Teresa kept her topcoat belted but unbuttoned, so that the lower part of it flared open as she strode through the stalled traffic at the corner of Radford Road and Gregory Boulevard, revealing a knee-length grey wool skirt and pale grey tights which Grabianski, watching from the window of the Asian confectioner's, thought were more than pleasingly filled.

He popped something pink and sugary into his mouth and smiled appreciatively. One of life's natural observers, he never failed to enjoy those incidental pleasures that chance and patience brought his way: a brown flycatcher spied on the edge of Yorkshire moorland, the narrow white ring around its eye blinking clear from its nest; a chink of light just discernible through the blinds of a bedroom window, four storeys up, suggesting the upper window may have been left recklessly unfastened; the stride of a mature woman, purposeful and strong, as she makes her way through the city on an otherwise unremarkable April day.

Casually, Grabianski stepped out onto the street. He was a well-built man, broad-shouldered and tall, no more than five or six pounds overweight for his age, somewhere in the mid-forties. His face was round rather than lean and freshly shaved; the dark hair on his head had yet to thin. His eyes were narrowed and alert as he angled his head and saw, away to his right, the woman he had noticed earlier, passing now between two youths on roller blades, before rounding the corner and disappearing from sight.

Dressed in civilian clothes as Sister Teresa was, Grabianski would have been surprised to have learned that she was a nun.

The Sisters of Our Lady of Perpetual Help were dedicated to the deliverance of succour and salvation to the needy, those who were, for whatever reason, less fortunate than their neighbours. Or, as Sister Teresa's fellow worker, Sister Bonaventura expressed it, the more economically challenged members of the urban underclass. Sister Bonaventura was a *Guardian* reader through and through.

Originally, the Sisters had continued to wear their traditional vestments while working in the community, and could often be seen setting up their late-night soup stall in the Market Square or ascending the steps towards the old General Hospital, for all the world like sumptuous magpies denied the power of flight. But with the decline of the city into an awkwardly romanticised version of its former self, fake minstrels and archers on every street corner and working models of everything from flour mills to four-loom weaving, no one gave credence to the belief that nuns perambulating in their proper habit were real nuns at all.

Resting actors employed by the city council to entertain the tourists, drama students supplementing their grants in ecclesiastical drag, that was what people assumed. So now Sister Teresa and the others wore their simple white shifts and coarse grey wool only when they knelt to prayer each morning at six in the small community house where they lived, changing into civilian clothing before stepping out into the jostling world.

Most of what they wore came to them as a result of charitable donations or after-hours visits to the nearest Oxfam shop, though rumour, of necessity unsubstantiated, had it that Sister Marguerite's underwear was silk and had been ordered on approval from one of the boxed advertisements at the back of the *Sunday Times*.

The three of them, Sister Teresa, Sister Bonaventura and Sister Marguerite, had been working together now for almost two years and in the summer they were due to return to their convent outside Felixstowe for six months of silent contemplation and spiritual healing. As Sister Bonaventura put it, an enforced visit to the health farm without any of the benefits of whirlpools or colonic irrigation.

The house they lived in was attached to the community centre in Hyson Green, itself a former church which had fallen on agnostic times. Deconsecrated, it was home to a variety of worthy enterprises, from a twice-weekly mother-and-toddler club, through yoga and enabling sessions for recovering alcoholics to the evening youth club and disco. Fridays, Saturdays and alternate Thursdays, Sister Marguerite, whose room was closest to the dividing wall, was lulled to sleep by the insistently sampled bass lines of Jazzmatazz and the near-ecclesiastical pleading of black rappers whose every third injunction included the words "bitch" or "motherfucker" or both.

These and other highly colourful expressions had been tagged on the walls and stairwells of the low block of flats Sister Teresa was now entering, no longer even bothering to try the lift, but walking instead up to the third floor balcony, where cat shit and used works shared space with several tubs of late daffodils and bright purple pansies and washing hung from lines diagonally stretched from wall to railing, railing to wall.

Teresa rang the bell of number thirty seven and waited while Shana Palmer turned down the television, hushed the baby, pushed aside the three-year old and paused to light another Embassy Filter on her way to the door.

"Sister…"

"Shana, how are we today? The little one, she got over her cough, did she?" Teresa said nothing about the bruise that was thickening around the young woman's left eye. Eighteen, nineteen? For certain she had not reached twenty-one.

"Cup of tea, sister?"

"That'd be lovely, thanks."

Teresa followed her through the narrow hallway, jammed with pushchair and tricycle, free newspapers, unopened junk mail and broken toys, into the kitchen where the three-year-old pulled at the legs of her mother's jeans and whined for whatever she couldn't have. Waiting for the kettle to boil, Teresa looked out through the postage stamp window at the block of flats opposite, almost identical save that more of them were boarded up.

"Biscuit, sister?"

"No, thanks."

They went into the living room and sat at either end of the sofa that served as the three-year old's bed, the baby cosseted in blankets and sucking on its dummy in half-sleep. In the corner, on TV, a modishly efficient woman in a floral print dress and that morning's makeover, explained how to choose the best cuts of lamb from your local organic butcher.

Teresa waited until she had finished her first mug of tea and declined a second before leaning towards Shana and touching her lightly on the forearm. "Don't you think it's time, Shana, we had another talk about finding you and the children a place in a refuge?"

Grabianski had waited several minutes more before heading east along the Boulevard, his meeting with Vernon Thackray timed for the quarter hour and Thackray, like himself, was a stickler for punctuality. And sure enough there was the car, a dark blue Volvo estate, pulled in at the upper corner of the space on the Forest Recreation Ground allotted to drivers wishing to Park & Ride.

Grabianski skirted the parking area, so as to approach the vehicle from the driver's side. Thackray was behind the wheel, head resting back against the padded extension to the seat, eyes closed, the music seeping out through the inch of lowered window something Grabianski recognised as baroque and nothing more. Albinoni, Pergolesi, one of those. Vivaldi, he was certain, Thackray would have considered too common by half.

He was three strides away from the car when Thackray opened his eyes and smiled. "Jerzy. Good to see you again. Come on, get in why don't you? We'll take a drive."

The interior smelt of leather polish and astringent, doubtlessly expensive cologne. Anyone else who knew Grabianski well enough to greet him by his first name would have used the Anglicised Jerry.

As they pulled out onto the main road, Thackray made

a vague circling gesture with his head. "Find things much changed?"

Grabianski's response was noncommittal, vague.

"Three years, is it?"

"Four."

"I'm surprised you haven't been back before."

Beneath his coat, Grabianski was aware of his shoulders tensing. "I'm surprised I'm here now."

Thackray laughed and swerved inside a Jessop's van that was signalling right ahead of the Clarendon round-about. "Clumber Park. I thought we'd take a quick trip out to feed the ducks."

When he had last been in the city, those four years before, Grabianski had been partnered up with a skinny second-storey artist named Grice, an individual of notably limited imagination, save where gaining illegal access was con-cerned – there he was almost second to none.

Jewellery, that was their speciality, that and the few antiques Grabianski recognised as not only genuine but likely to fetch a good return; the baubles they sent Red Star to a silversmith with premises on Sauchiehall Street, Glas-gow, the eventual proceeds making their discreet way into a pair of pseudonymously held accounts a safe interval later.

All had been going well until they had the misfortune to come across a sizable quantity of almost pure cocaine in someone's bedroom safe and Grabianski had allowed Grice to convince him it was a good plan to sell it back to the owner, a television director of decidedly moderate stature. Unfortunately, he turned out to be only holding the coke for one of the local suppliers, after which things not only got complicated but nasty. And that was without Grabianski falling in lust with the director's wife.

In the end the only way Grabianski could avoid a lengthy prison term was to help the police with their enquiries, set up the aforementioned dealer and turn Queen's evidence on his partner. The result, a suspended sentence and an invitation from the local constabulary to get out of town. And now he was back.

No wonder his neck muscles were uncomfortably tight.

There was the usual selection of Mallards and Pintails, along with a small flock of Shovellers, consisting entirely of flatheaded, blue winged drakes. Lower down, at the far, northern, end of the main lake, a clamour of Canada Geese stalked the two men incessantly, greedy for anything they might have in their pockets and be prepared to throw away. The water looked grey and cold, its surface turning in the wind.

"I've had it checked four weeks out of the last five," Thackray was saying. "Leaves the house between seven and seven-twenty and never back before eleven-fifteen."

"Theatre? Cinema?"

"Bridge club. Up on Mansfield Road. Duplicate. Quite good, seemingly. Plays a modified Acol."

"Hmm." Grabianski nodded, unimpressed. He was a straightforward never-mess-with-a-minor-suit, four-no-trumps-is-strong-and-asking-for-aces kind of player himself.

"Here." Thackray took a sheet of graph paper from his inside pocket and the nearest dozen geese started honking in earnest.

The plan of the house interior had been neatly drawn in violet ink, the position of the alarm in red, the paintings marked clearly in green, one angled above the other on the drawing room wall, their exact dimensions noted at the

cop. 1

bottom right corner of the sheet. Neither so large that they could not be fitted into a large holdall.

"And the alarm, it's not connected directly through to the police?"

Thackray shook his head and they walked on, turning into a stiffening breeze. "Not any more."

"Any idea how she got hold of them?" Grabianski asked. "Dalzeils. Hardly ten a penny."

"Handed down, apparently. In the family for a couple of generations. Gambling debt originally."

"Sentimental value, then. Seems a shame."

Thackray fingered a three-inch cigar from his breast pocket and let the cellophane wrapping waft out across the lake. "Look at it this way, Jerzy, what we're doing, it's a public service. Liberating art for the nation."

"At least there'll be the insurance."

"Not so, apparently. Let the policy lapse, last day in March. Cost of the premiums, I suppose. Works of art like that in a private hands, can't be cheap."

"So if she loses them she's left with nothing."

"Social work now, is it? Distressed gentlefolk?"

Grabianski growled and continued walking.

"At least," Thackray went on blithely, "they're going to a good home, so that's one thing you don't have to fret about. Japanese banker, anniversary present for his second wife." Thackray's face broke into a rare smile. "Just the kind of sentimental gesture, Jerzy, I should have thought you would have appreciated more than most."

❐

Resnick had been woken that morning soon after four, without being sure the reason why. The smallest of the cats nestling near the edge of his pillows, he had lain there aware of a vague sense of foreboding, listening to the birds outside the window and watching the steadily brightening light.

At half-five, certain now he would not fall back to sleep, he had risen and padded to the bathroom and the shower. By the time he had pulled on some clothes and reached the kitchen, the other cats had joined him, all save Dizzy content to wait patiently by their bowls while Resnick opened a fresh can of food and found milk in the fridge. The six o'clock news summary told of slaughtered cattle and bankrupt British beef farmers, bombs in the Lebanon, first reports of a police officer being shot dead in Liverpool, more details promised as they became known. The magnolia tree that leaned across the low wall from his neighbour's garden had started, at last, to unfold into bloom. When he stood for a moment at the back door, staring out, he felt the first fall of rain against his face, faint and indefinite as if it too would not last.

He arrived at the police station early, earlier than usual; Kevin Naylor, the young DC who had drawn first shift, was still sorting through the duty officer's report of the night's activities, breaking it down into categories before setting the file on Resnick's desk. Burglaries Naylor would initially deal with himself, the rest would be for Resnick, as Detective Inspector, to prioritise and hand on to the other members of the squad.

"Quiet night?" Resnick asked, glancing at a fax that had come in from Manchester CID during the night, asking for information about a runaway girl of fourteen.

"Passable, sir. Usual bit of activity in the Park. Three houses broken into on Tennis Drive; last one the owner got up for a pee round about two, looked out the window and there were these blokes lifting his twenty-three inch Sony into a van."

"Blokes?"

"Two of them; another in the driver's seat he thinks. Not sure."

"And the van?"

"Green, apparently. Dark green. If you can trust colours under those antique gas lamps they're so proud of. Old post office van, sounds like, sprayed over."

"He wrote down the number?"

"Two letters missing. Like I say, the lighting…"

"Yes. I know. You'll get round there sharpish."

"First call."

The Park was not a park at all: a private estate principally made up of large Victorian houses sporting stained glass and ornate decoration and originally designed to show off the wealth and taste of the mine owners and lace merchants who had lorded it in the latter half of the last century. Now it was home to barristers and account executives and Porsche owners who never seemed to work at all. Smack in the centre of the city as it was, the place attracted burglars the way a mangy dog had fleas.

"Remember that couple who worked the Park a few years back," Naylor said, making conversation as he poured the tea. "One of them built a bit like you, big, the other a scrawny little bugger. Turning over this place when the bloke as lived there come back unexpected, took one look at 'em and had a heart attack. Big bloke called emergency services, hung around to give him mouth-to-mouth."

"Saved his life."

"What was his name now? Something foreign. Polish, wasn't it?"

"Grabianski," Resnick said, of Polish ancestry himself. "Jerzy Grabianski."

"Wonder what became of him then?"

Resnick shrugged broad shoulders. "Retrained, maybe. Paramedic, something of the sort." It was a nice idea and one he didn't believe for a minute.

Three hours later, when Resnick was in conference with his superintendent and Naylor was still out and about knocking on doors, Grabianski was watching with considerable pleasure as Sister Teresa crossed Gregory Boulevard. And a little more than an hour after that, Resnick selecting cheese and turkey breast for his sandwich at the nearby deli while Naylor checked through vehicle licences and registrations in the CID office, Grabianski was enjoying the fresh air and the ducks and contemplating the detailed drawing of the house in the Park which was home, just for the present, to a pair of watercolours by the British Impressionist, Herbert Dalzcil.

Sister Teresa had made three more home visits after calling on Shana Palmer, that particular issue no more resolved than it had been when she had arrived. At lunchtime, she had stopped off at the Help Line centre run in conjunction with the local BBC radio station, and busied herself with everything from sorting through the previous week's backlog of mail to counselling a fifteen year old boy who feared he might be gay, feared what his father would do if he found out, feared he might already have contracted AIDS.

She then went into the studio for her regular weekly spot on the afternoon show, answering questions from callers about spiritual and other problems that were bothering them, mostly, she found, the latter. As usual, she ended by asking for donations or volunteers for the Help

Line, thanked both presenter and producer and exited through the rear car park, having promised Sister Marguerite she would pop into Tesco's and buy a Sara Lee Pecan Pie for her birthday.

A dozen paces into the car park a hand grabbed at her hair, an arm was thrown tight about her neck and she was wrenched backwards and thrown heavily against the rear wall.

"Help?" Paul Palmer said, brandishing a fist in Sister Teresa's face. "I'll give you fucking help. All the help you fucking need."

And he began to punch her in the face and breasts, kick viciously against her legs and drive his knee into her groin.

Thackray dropped Grabianski at the York Street entrance to the Shopping Centre and carried on his way towards the London Road roundabout and the river; within the hour he would be safely ensconced behind closed doors in Stamford, hotting up his modem with discreet faxes to the Far East and cryptic messages on the Internet.

Grabianski had one of the swing doors half open, mind set on a bottle of vodka and some designer potato chips, when he heard cries coming from somewhere behind him: cries of pain and shouts of anger from the other side of the narrow street, from somewhere amongst the vehicles that were tightly clustered beyond the low brick wall. Others, passing, heard them and hurried on. Grabianski vaulted the wall and saw the couple towards the rear door, the man lashing out wildly and the woman half spreadeagled on the ground.

"Come near my wife again, you interfering bitch, and—"

Palmer broke off, hearing the sound of someone at his

back; half-turned, another warning on his lips, and met the heel of Grabianski's outthrust hand full force upon his nose. The snap of cartilage was dredged through snot and blood.

"Bastard!" Palmer tried to shout, but something blurred and muffled was all that emerged. Grabianski picked him off his feet and half-threw, half-pushed him across the front of a Ford Orion, Palmer screaming as he fell.

"Don't..." began the woman, easing herself up onto all fours. "Please, don't..." as she levered herself back against the wall, head sinking gingerly forward till it came to rest against her knees.

"Don't what?" asked Grabianski gently, bending down before her.

"Don't hurt him."

He recognised the dull sparkle of the ring upon her hand. Why was it they always defended them, no matter what? One of her eyes was already beginning to close.

"A beating," Grabianski said. "No more than he deserves."

"No, no. Please. She fumbled for then found his wrist and clutched it tight. "I pray you."

Something about the way she said it made Grabianski think twice; he recognised her then, the woman who had been striding out in shades of grey, and felt a quickening of his pulse. Somehow instead of her holding his wrist, he was holding her hand. Behind them, he heard her attacker scurry, slew-footed, away.

The muscles in the backs of Grabianski's legs were aching and he changed position, sitting round against the wall. Sister Teresa, blood dribbling from a cut alongside her mouth, was alongside him now, shoulders touching, and he was still holding her hand.

She found it strangely, almost uniquely, reassuring.

She said, "Thank you."

He said it was fine.

She asked him his name and he her's.

"Teresa," she said.

"Teresa what?"

And she had to think. "Teresa Whimbrel," she said and he smiled.

"What's amusing?" she asked, though a pain jolted through her side each time she spoke.

"Whimbrel," Grabianski said, "it's a bird. A sort of curlew." He was smiling. "Notably long legs."

He looked, she thought, decidedly handsome when he smiled, and something else besides. She wondered if that something might be dangerous.

"But I expect you know that already," he said.

She was looking at the fingers of his hand, broad-knuckled and lightly freckled with hair and curved about her own, smaller hand. And showing no intention of letting go. She nodded to signify, yes, she knew. There was a bird book back at the community house and Sister Bonaventura had pointed out the illustration. "A black and white cap on its head," she had said. "Just the way we would have looked once upon a time. Those unenlightened times."

"I think you should let go," she said.

"Um?"

"Of my hand."

"Oh." He asked another question instead. "Was that your husband? The man."

"Not mine."

He could feel the ring, though he could no longer see it. "But you are married?"

"In a way."

Grabianski raised an eyebrow, continuing to smile. "Which way is that?"

"A way you might find difficult to understand."

She lay on a narrow bed in Accident and Emergency, bandaged, strapped and salved. They had examined her carefully, wheeled her down to X-ray and back on two separate occasions, confirmed that two of her ribs were broken, but that, aside from internal bruising, there were no further injuries invisible to the naked eye.

"Lucky your saviour, he happened along when he did," the nurse said.

"Hmm," Sister Bonaventura commented, eying Grabianski appraisingly, "so that's who he is. He looks a little different in the pictures I've seen."

She and Sister Marguerite had rushed to the hospital as soon as they had heard, filling the small cubicle with anger, advice and concern. When the young police officer had arrived to take a statement, Grabianski had discreetly removed himself, returning an hour later with flowers, an artfully wrapped box of dark soft-centred chocolates from Thorntons and a copy of the Collins' *Field Guide to the Birds of Britain and Europe*, with the section on curlews clearly marked.

"Are you sure you're going to be all right?" Sister Marguerite asked, declining a second chocolate.

"Perfectly," Teresa replied. "The doctor's assured me there's no need for me to stay in overnight. And they'll provide an ambulance to take me home."

"That wasn't what I meant," Sister Marguerite said.

"I know what you meant."

Grabianski's presence filled the cubicle to the point of overflowing.

Leaving, the sister pressed an extra crucifix into Teresa's hand for good measure. The curtain she left ostentatiously open and after a few moments Grabianski reached across and pulled it closed. The bustle of Accident and Emergency went on around them, muffled but nonetheless real.

"There's one question…" Grabianski began.

Teresa laughed. "There always is. Prostitutes and nuns, it's always the same one: how did a nice girl like you…?"

But Grabianski was shaking his head; that wasn't the question.

Naylor knocked on Resnick's door and waited. Behind him, the CID room was the usual monkey house of movement and overlapping conversations; telephones rang and were curtly answered or left to flounder in their own impatience; officers scrolled down VDUs, pecked two-fingered reports from keyboards, doodled loved ones' names on the backs of envelopes, listened on leaking headphones to taped interviews. At his desk near the head of the room, Naylor's sergeant, Graham Millington, was sporting a new haircut and freshly trimmed moustache and an almost-new check sports jacket, in the inside pocket of which nestled reservations for seats on the London train and two tickets for that evening's performance of *Sunset Boulevard*. Andrew Lloyd Webber and Petula Clark in the one evening; it was almost more than ordinary flesh and blood could stand.

Naylor heard Resnick's call of "Come in" just above the sergeant's shrilly whistled version of 'As If We Never Said Goodbye'.

"Kevin?" Amongst the papers littered over Resnick's desk were the remains of a toasted tallegio and ham sandwich and several empty take-out cups still smelling of strong espresso.

"Licence plate on the van, sir. Likely belongs to a '94 Fiesta, reported stolen out in Bulwell three weeks back."

"Dead end, then."

"Not exactly. Youth as reported it missing, Tommy Farrell, been walking the thin and narrow since he left school."

"Charges?"

"Fraudulently claiming benefit, passing stolen cheques, possession of illegal substances, handling stolen goods. Probation on one, the others all dismissed."

"Insurance scam, then, the car? Nicked by his mates, switch the plates, sit back and wait for General Life or whoever to pay over the cheque."

"It's possible."

"So if one of Farrell's friends happened to own an old Post Office van..."

"Exactly."

Resnick leaned forward in his chair. "That piece of paper in your hand, Kevin; wouldn't be a list of Farrell's known associates would it?"

Grinning self-consciously, Naylor placed the sheet upon the desk.

"Mickey Redthorpe," Resnick read, "Michael Chester, Sean McGuane – he's in Lincoln doing three to five. Victor Canning, Barry Fielding, Billy Murdoch, Paul Palmer..."

Resnick looked up, fingers drumming across the name. "Aggravated burglary, Palmer, eighteen months inside?"

"Yes, sir. Released March 1st. Good behaviour."

"I wonder," Resnick said, smiling a little, "what the chances might be of finding friend Palmer the owner of a resprayed van?"

"A warrant or...?"

"Too early. Take Mark with you, have a little nose

around. Palmer's got a wife and kids, hasn't he? Probably not going anywhere in a hurry."

Naylor nodded. "Unless it's back inside."

Grabianski was not as cautious. And although he preferred making his way into other people's property under the cover of darkness, on this occasion, he was happy enough with the sound of the *EastEnders* theme tune and the sight of the living room door to the Palmer's flat closing behind Shana as she carried through the three-year-old.

Paul himself had made his way from the betting shop to the pub.

Grabianski checked both ways along the balcony, inserted the strip of plastic between front door and frame and slipped the lock.

As soon as he was standing inside the adrenalin grabbed him, jolting his veins. Being inside: forbidden. It was like sex, only better, purer; more controlled. He stood for several minutes, listening to sounds, breathing the air. Then made his way silently from room to room.

There was a rusted bayonet at the back of the cupboard alongside the double bed and a shoe box containing half a dozen stolen credit cards underneath it; burglary tools were secure in a duffel bag behind the waste pipe of the kitchen sink. The baby was sleeping in the back bedroom in a cot surrounded by several thousand pounds worth of electrical equipment, including a top-of-the-range wide screen Sony TV.

Just as Grabianski stepped out into the hallway, the living room door opened and Shana stood facing him, the almost empty mug of tea slipping from her hand.

"It's all right." Grabianski said softly. "There's no need to be afraid."

Which was when Paul Palmer entered through the front door, a six-pack of Special Brew at his side.

"You!"

Grabianski had the advantage of surprise and some forty extra pounds in weight; he grabbed Palmer by the front of his leather jacket and jerked him forward, kicking the door closed.

"You...?"

"You already said that."

Palmer's voice was distorted by the width of plaster taped across his nose. Grabianski spun him round and, firmly holding his shoulders, smacked him, face first, against the wall.

Shana screamed and Paul fainted, unused to having his nose broken twice in the same day. When he came to and saw Grabianski was leaning over him he flinched.

"Listen," Grabianski said, "if you ever go near that person again, I will break every other bone in your body. You know who I mean?"

Palmer blinked and grunted yes.

"And you believe me?"

He did.

"Good," Grabianski said, leaning away. "A little belief, it's a wonderful thing." He turned back at the door. "It might be an idea if you stopped thumping your wife, too. I imagine there's a self-help group you could go to, men and violence, something like that. You should look into it." And he walked off along the balcony, taking his time, though time was something he had precious little of – the owner of two rare Impressionist paintings would soon be sitting down to her first hand of the evening, busily counting points.

Since Resnick had stopped using the Polish Club with any regularity, when he did appear committee and staff fussed round him like swans with their wayward young; which only served to curtail his visits all the more. But halfway through a bottle of Polish lager with only the cats and CDs for company, he made a sudden decision to call a cab and go, even though it meant exchanging *Miles Davis Live at the Plugged Nickel* for an accordionist with a ruffled shirt and his heart on his sleeve.

He hadn't been in the club more than twenty minutes when, reflected in the mirror above the bar, he saw, approaching, someone he had thought he was unlikely ever to see again. He waited until Grabianski had taken the stool alongside his before holding out his hand. "Jerzy."

"Inspector."

"Charlie would do. Not as if I'm on duty."

"Ah." Grabianski smiled and ordered a bison grass vodka, Resnick declining with a shake of the head. "Maybe not."

"No coincidence, then? You being here like this?"

"I phoned ahead."

"Something that couldn't wait till morning."

Grabianski shrugged.

"You're here on business?" Resnick asked.

"An old friend to meet ." A smile spread across his face. "Two, if we include you."

It was Resnick's turn to smile. "That's what we are? Friends?"

They sat there a while longer, not speaking, two men who might easily have been mistaken for brothers; big men with broad, heavy features whose families had fled their mother country in the first months of the war. Sitting in that room, with so many framed photographs of generals and fighter pilots on the walls, it was unnecessary to ask which war.

"Paul Palmer," Grabianski said, paying for his second vodka. The slight shift of expression on Resnick's face told him the name was not unknown.

"What about him?"

"If he was caught with a quantity of stolen goods on his premises, a few choice artifacts of the burglar's trade, what are the chances he might see serious time?"

"Depends. Sometimes, as well you know, there are extenuating circumstances."

"Not for the likes of Palmer."

Resnick thought he would chance another lager after all; if they were going to pull Paul Palmer it would be before the milk and Graham Millington could take charge. Just the thing to get an overdose of Andrew Lloyd Webber out of his system.

"This isn't professional rivalry, I take it?" Resnick asked. "I mean, he's hardly in your class."

"Let's just say there are reasons for shutting him away where his temper won't do more harm."

Resnick frowned. "There's some history of domestic violence, I know. Is that what this is about? The wife? Shana, isn't it?"

"Not only her."

Resnick laughed. "I should have known with you there'd be a woman involved."

"It's not like that, Charlie."

"No?"

"Not this time."

Resnick remembered the alacrity with which the television director's wife had taken Grabianski to bed, bosom and bath. "Whatever happened to Maria Roy?" he asked.

Grabianski shook his head, grinning despite himself. "You don't want to know."

"And this time?"

"I told you..."But Resnick was staring at him from close range and for a confirmed criminal Grabianski could be a hopeless liar. "This is different."

"Yes," Resnick said, not meaning it.

"Platonic."

"Of course."

"Charlie, she's a nun for Christ's sake!"

Resnick's laughter was abrupt enough to turn heads way back across the room.

"No laughing matter, Charlie."

"So I've heard."

"This kid Palmer, he went for her. Could have been serious. Angry because she's been talking to his wife, advising her, you know, getting into a refuge, taking the kids."

Resnick nodded. "How come you're so certain about these stolen goods? They wouldn't be planted, by any chance, to lend us a helping hand?"

Grabianski shook his head. "Not my way."

"Okay. This is the second time I've got you to thank. Always assuming it pans out."

"Oh, it will." Draining his glass, Grabianski swung round on the stool and rose to his feet.

"You'll likely not be around to see it go down?"

"Likely not."

"Well," Resnick stood and again the two men shook hands, "it was good to see you again."

Grabianski nodded and began to turn away.

"I suppose I'd be wasting my breath telling you to keep your hands to what's rightfully yours?"

Grabianski kept on walking, through the door, along

the broad corridor and out onto the forecourt where he climbed into the taxi he had instructed to wait. Before it had pulled away, Resnick was speaking to Lynn Kellogg on the telephone, informing her of the cab company and registration. "Get onto their controller, find out their position; if you can get the destination without arousing suspicion so much the better. Then call in Mark and Kevin, sort out the surveillance between you, let me know how it's going. Send a driver to pick up my car and collect me here."

Grabianski stood in the first floor drawing room, heavy velvet curtains drawn against the night. He was wearing the same dark blue suit as earlier, smartly polished shoes, new white cotton gloves. He was holding a torch in one hand, a Polaroid camera in the other. The canvas holdall was on the floor near his feet.

He positioned himself carefully before taking the pictures, capturing the paintings separately and together. They were, he thought, a wonderful pair. The first, earlier by some fifteen years, showed a farm boy close by the half open gate to a field, some half dozen sheep in the middle distance, an avenue of poplars making a diagonal right to left behind. It was a perfectly respectable, cleanly executed rural painting of its time; the kind the Royal Academy in the 1880s would have cherished. Possibly still did.

But it was the second that Grabianski cherished, an earlier study for what most critics considered Dalzeil's masterpiece, *Departing Day*. It showed a stubbly, tilled landscape through the blur of fading light, the sun a yellow disc, faint through mottled sky. Patched along the low horizon were sparse purplish shadows, whether outbuildings or carts, or even cattle, it was neither possible nor desirable to know.

What had happened to Dalzeil between the two paintings, Grabianski was uncertain. Had he been smitten by the influence of Seurat, sudden as Saul on the road to Damascus, or had he fallen under the spell of Monet, who had exhibited in London only a few years before this work would have begun? More prosaically, had Dalziel's failing health and badly deteriorating sight meant that this hazy vision of the world was the only one he had left?

It didn't matter. For Grabianski, most of what gave him pleasure in painting was here: the interplay of light and colour, the shifting texture of the paint, the mystery.

It was exquisite.

He felt a thread of envy for the woman who had lived with the joy of this painting for so long and considered what he was about to do. He checked his watch and unzipped the canvas bag.

Divine turned his back in the direction of Resnick's car before uncapping his flask and tipping an inch or more of whisky into Kevin Naylor's coffee and then his own. Lynn Kellogg and Carl Vincent were somewhere off in the shrubbery, keeping guard over the rear of the house, while Divine and Naylor had positioned themselves to watch both the main entrance and the fire escape angling rustily down the side of the building. Resnick's driver had parked in shadow fifty yards along the street.

"Tell me why we're hanging about here like this, Kev?" Divine asked, "when there are nice warm pubs in spitting distance."

"Overtime?"

"Oh, yeh. Knew there was a reason."

"Hush up!" Naylor hissed. "Here he comes now."

They watched as Grabianski, somewhat larger than life, nonchalantly let himself out of the front door and headed for the low wrought iron gate, swinging the holdall a little as he walked. Beneath the even crunch of his feet on the gravel came the firm click of a car door and then the sound of Resnick's feet approaching.

Fifteen yards along, Grabianski stopped. "Coincidence, Charlie?"

"Hardly that."

Grabianski scarcely turned as Divine and Naylor moved up on him from behind.

"You wouldn't care to show us, Jerzy, what you've got in the bag?"

Grabianski hesitated but not for long. "Why not?"

Naylor shone his torch as the zip was eased back; save some gloves, a torch and a camera, the bag was empty.

"Not much of a haul," Divine observed.

"I've a receipt for the camera," Grabianski said, "if you think that's really necessary."

Resnick looked at him thoughtfully. "Why don't you come and sit in the car? Mark, Kevin, give the place the once over just in case. Tell the others to call it a night."

Resnick told his driver to take a walk. He pushed a cassette into the car stereo and kept the volume low: Monk playing 'April in Paris', 'I Surrender, Dear'. "Why the change of mind?" he asked. "Or was it a change of heart?"

"How about a conversion?" Grabianski's smile was as angular as the music.

"How about you realised the risk you took in coming to me was too great? You must have known there was a chance I'd have you followed."

Grabianski leaned back against the inside of the door. "The truth?"

"What passes for it, maybe."

"You do know about the paintings? You know they're rare."

Resnick nodded. "A little. The owner was in touch a while back about security."

"Always been a special favourite of mine, Dalzeil. Soon as I heard they were here I had to see them. And what chance would I have otherwise?"

"Written and asked permission? Knocked on the door?"

"Not my way, Charlie. Besides, half an hour with one of the unsung masters, worth any amount of risk. Like standing up to your armpits in cold water for hours just to catch a glimpse of an Ivory Gull that's got lost on its way from the Arctic."

"Any amount of risk?" Resnick said.

"Come on, Charlie," Grabianski laughed. "You'll not bother charging me with this, scarce worth the paperwork. Besides, your lads, they'll not find as much as a speck of dust disturbed. And then there's always that small favour to repay."

Resnick reached over and clicked open the door. "London nowadays, isn't it? Notting Hill? Camden? Work enough down there, I should have thought. Art galleries, too."

Grabianski held out his hand but this time Resnick didn't take it; instead he watched in his rear view mirror as the tall figure merged into the dull glow of street lamps until he was no more than a purple shadow without shape or contour.

A week later a package arrived at the community house addressed to Sister Teresa. It contained two Polaroid pictures of a landscape painting, which Sister Bonaventura assured her was firmly in the Impressionist tradition, and a single feather, mottled brown and white, close to five inches long. Sister Marguerite thought it might have come from a curlew, but Teresa assured her it was a whimbrel and produced her book as evidence. There was neither letter nor note.

Only later, looking at the photographs alone, did she see, faintly to the side of one of them, the reflection of a man seemingly holding a camera. Her saviour. At least, that's what she believed.

CHERYL

CHERYL HAD a scarlet embroidered leisure suit with padded shoulders and a matching belt, which she liked to wear when she delivered meals on wheels to the elderly, the housebound and the infirm. Cheryl thought it her mission to bring a little colour into their lives; she thought it cheered the old farts up. And it was true, although she hadn't been doing the job long, four months this coming week, she would have needed more than the fingers of both hands to count the number of faces that smiled, positively beamed, when they heard the beep-ba-ba-beep of her horn, the rhythmic jabber of her finger on the bell. Not that she was letting it go to her head; she wasn't the Angel of Old Lenton. At least, not yet.

The truth was, though it paid less, she liked it as well, if not better, than any job she'd ever had. Bar work, waitressing, a discouraging six months serving up double sausage, double egg, bacon and chips in the police canteen, five years – Cheryl still couldn't believe it – on the night shift at Pork

Farms. That had been when her Vicki was little and sleeping over at her gran's in the Meadows. Once Vicki had started at the juniors, Cheryl had gone to work there, playground attendant first and then dinner lady. That, she supposed was what had put the idea into her head, meals on wheels.

When it had been time to go to the comp, Vicki had begged her mum not to follow there, too. Reminders about writing to her dad and tidying up her room while doling out the mashed potatoes. So Cheryl, whose first real boy friend, a pipe fitter from Bulwell, had taught her how to drive, if little else, and who'd had a driving licence since her eighteenth birthday, if rarely a car, took a test to show the supervisor she could tootle along at thirty without shaking up several dozen foil wrapped dinners, filled in a form with the fountain pen she more usually saved for notes about late payment of the rent, and gratefully accepted a uniform overall which she almost never wore.

Drab, too drab: not the way Cheryl saw herself at all.

As she drove, Cheryl played tapes in the van. Not that it was fitted out with a stereo, of course, but there was this natty little cassette player from Dixons she hung from the handbrake: Jackie Wilson, Sugar Pie DeSanto, Aretha belting out 'Respect' and 'Think'; sometimes, when she was feeling soft and hopeful, 'I Say a Little Prayer For You'. Once she had clapped her Walkman on old Tommy Vickers' head and boogied him round the room to 'Let's Get It On', Cheryl keeping time to the slivers of treble and bass that slid through the headphones, singing along at the top of her voice, "Don't want to *push*!" Tommy had had to lie down afterwards for quite a long time.

This particular morning it was raining, that fine rain like mist which dulls the sky and seeps, almost unseen, under the skin and Cheryl needed her scarlet suit and her music more than ever. She was playing Dusty, *Dusty in Memphis*; proof, if proof were needed, that white girls can have soul, the voice, yearning and strong. 'Breakfast in Bed'. Cheryl braked sharply so as not to nudge a cyclist turning left off Lenton Boulevard and taking too wide a line. Her Vicki would still jump in with her now and then of a Sunday, those days she forgot she was near thirteen and it was no longer cool, jump right in amongst the pages of the *News of the World* and settle down to tea and toast and if they were feeling specially wicked, the pair of them, bacon cobs slavered all over with brown sauce. The kind of breakfast Dusty was singing about though, the kind you shared with a bloke, well, it wasn't to say she didn't have offers, but with a kid Vicki's age it was difficult, specially since Vicki's gran had passed on. No more easy all night sleepovers. For either of them. More often now it was quick kebab, a glance at the watch and oops, sorry, got to be getting back.

Cheryl's patch spread all around the Radford Flats where they lived, down past the Raleigh cycle works and through Dunkirk towards the railway. Her first call this morning, though, was Lenton. Sherwin Road. Mary Cole, who'd been living there alone since her husband died not so long back and Mary herself had a stroke. She was over it now, well, she could move at least, with the aid of a stick, five minutes to get from the back room to the door in a sort of grudging shuffle, one side of her still set, paralysed really, Cheryl supposed. Once in a while, Cheryl had seen her blink back a few tears if something was said that reminded her of Ted, but normally she'd find a smile and even a joke sometimes about the cod.

This morning, the trip to the door was slower than usual and at the sight of Cheryl, bright red on her doorstep, Mary broke down into tears, great gulping sobs that shook the half of her body that could still respond.

Cheryl helped her back inside, put on the kettle and sat her down. "You're not a social worker, Cheryl." her supervisor would say. "You're not a home help. There are others paid to do that. Trained. You have meals to deliver. Quick, in and out." Easy to say, Cheryl thought, when you're in an office most of the day rustling papers; not so easy sitting here watching the tears try to find a way down this poor old dear's twisted mess of a face.

Gradually, over a cup of strong sweet tea, the story emerged. Ted Cole had borrowed money the winter before last, sixty pounds that was all, at least all Ted had wanted was sixty, but the man who'd called round about the loan had talked him into borrowing seventy five, which meant Ted having to repay the neat round sum of a hundred at a fiver a week. Which was fine from his pension and hers and whatever they got from social security. Only then Mary fancied a few days away at Mablethorpe, just a week by the sea, maybe that caravan site back down the coast, the place they'd stayed before, and Ted hadn't felt he could begrudge her that. Nor a few presents for the nieces and nephews when they made the trip across from Glossop. Before you knew where you were it was winter again. Ted now owed a total of three hundred and seventeen pounds, which he had been struggling to pay off at seven pounds fifty a week, when he'd gone out in the frost one morning to fetch the Mirror, ten Embassy and a pint of milk and keeled over with his heart.

The first Mary had known about the loans, any of it, was when the collector knocked on the door and expressed his condolences. "He were a lovely chap, Ted. Lovely. Tell you what I'll do, this last two weeks, the repayments, I'll say nothing. Stick it in out me own pocket, sign of respect. So if you'll just get your purse, love, it's seven fifty, and we'll start as we mean to go on. Your Ted, he used to meet me in the pub, like, but easier for you, I dare say, if I come here."

This man standing there, face like steamed pudding and rings on the hand he stuck out towards her, rings that were heavy and dull.

"You should have told him," Cheryl said, "now there was just you on your own, you couldn't easily manage."

"Well, I did. Because it was difficult. It was hard."

"And what did he say?"

"Oh, he was nice about it. Understanding, you know. Firm, but fair. I'll say that for him, he was always fair. He offered to make a new arrangement, just for me."

"Nice of him."

"He said there was this new scheme for people like me, finding it not so easy, you know. Said how he would wipe out all the old debt, all the money Ted'd owed, and make out this new loan I could pay back little by little, just however much I could afford. He showed me this paper, I remember, well, of course, I never really understood it. But five pounds a week, he said, we'll try that for a start. And well... well..." Mary plucking at the table cloth now and not quite able to stop the tears. "At first it was fine, but then I started to fall behind, and today... today he came right in here, into my home and he... I've swept it up now... but he took a china pot from that shelf there, mine and Ted's anniversary ware it was, and dropped it, right there on the floor. Sorry, he says, clumsy. These clumsy old hands of mine. Do more damage sometimes than they've a mind. Next week, Mary, he says, ten pound. You'll not let me down. And then he left."

Mary heaved a sigh and groped for Cheryl's hand. "I was frightened."

"Of course you were," Cheryl patting her, nodding, all the while thinking, you bastard, you cowardly bastard. Asking her, before she left, "This paper you say he gave you, you haven't still got it, I suppose? That or something with his address, a card?"

She pulled out the card, cheaply printed, from behind the cups and saucers at the side. "I'll just borrow this, Mary, for a while, okay?"

Mary looked alarmed. "I wouldn't want to cause any trouble."

"Don't you worry," Cheryl said. "It'll all be fine."

The offices of the Sheriff Finance and Loan Company were on the Alfreton Road above a burned-out tandoori take-away and adjacent to a lock-up shop trading in second hand electrical goods and vinyl albums on which the names Neil Sedaka and Roger Whitaker were writ large. There was neither carpet nor lino on the stairs.

Sonia White was just scrolling another invoice into the Olivetti when Cheryl knocked and barged right in. Sonia around Cheryl's age, thirty nine, skinny where Cheryl was, well, amply covered, and not only having problems striking the right keys but enjoying a seriously bad hair day into the bargain. The ends of her fingers were blotched white with Tippex.

"Mr Dunn?"

Sonia blinked. "No."

"When are you expecting him? '

"Nobody of that name works here.

Cheryl produced the card she had taken from Mary Coles' kitchen. "This says he does."

Sonia eyed Cheryl with suspicion. "Mr Dunn some-times works *for* us. He never works here."

Cheryl was getting fed up with this, royally pissed off. "How does this arrangement work?" she asked. "Fax and mobile phone, or perhaps you're a dab hand with a weegee board?"

The blinking increased, accompanied now by a pronounced tilt of the head. "Mr Dunn telephones here and speaks to Mr McStay." The sign on the door behind her, one of those instant engraving jobs they specialise in at shoe repairers, read *Jason McStay, Manager*.

"And," suggested Cheryl, "Mr McStay tells him to go out and terrify an old woman, half crippled and living on her own, frighten the life out of her for the sake of five fucking pounds."

Sonia pursed her lips. Cheryl half expected her to say, "Language!" and tut-tut. She was the sort, Cheryl thought, for whom the expression 'having relations' didn't mean a visit from your gran or a great aunt.

"Is he here?" Cheryl asked, pointing towards the inner office.

"Not presently."

Jesus, Cheryl thought. "And when will he be here, or is he busy off somewhere threatening old ladies, too?"

"There is no need to cast aspersions," Sonia said, getting older by the minute, "Mr McStay is a perfectly respectable businessman and, besides, you can't see him without an appointment. He never sees anyone without an appointment."

"Oh," said Cheryl, "and how do I get one of those?"

"Write a letter, stating the nature of your business and we will contact you in due course."

"I'll bet," Cheryl said. "I'll bet you will, my arse."

That evening, Cheryl left Vicki watching *EastEnders* with

a friend from school who lived two floors up, and went to Sherwin Road on foot. Mary was bearing up, happy enough to have Cheryl mash tea and butter toast, but worried sick about where she was going to find ten pounds.

"Relax, sweetheart," Cheryl told her. "Don't you worry. I'll look after it, I promise."

And the way Mary had looked at her, squinting up from the one good side of her face, had made Cheryl all the more determined that she would.

There were only two pubs she thought Ted Cole would have walked to for his regular meetings with Reggie Dunn, The Happy Return and the 17th-21st Lancers. Never The Grove, too full of students and student nurses. Cheryl called in both of them and Dunn wasn't in either, but, just as she'd guessed, he was known. "You tell him I'm looking for him," Cheryl said. "Cheryl Wheeler. Just you tell him that." Staring at the barman hard, daring him to make some crack.

Three days passed and nothing happened, nothing out of the usual. Vicki went to school and came home. Cheryl drove her van round the streets of mostly terraced houses, the rent-controlled flats and the back-to-backs. On the Thursday evening, for a treat, she walked with Vicki to the chippie and carried it back, warm through the wrappings of paper, cod and chips twice, two pickled onions, a can of Vimto and a Pepsi. Somebody's birthday, Cheryl thought, when they found the lift still working. It didn't matter, the whole block had been tarted up something righteous, even moved them out for a spell while the work was done, lifts were lifts all the same which meant, more often than not, not working.

Up on the eighth floor, Vicki jumped past the slow sliding door and out onto the balcony and before Cheryl could follow her an arm slammed across in front of her, one foot braced to keep the lift door open. "I hear you been looking for me?" Reggie Dunn's flat, round face glaring in.

"Vicki!" Cheryl shouted, but all the girl could do was stare, mouth wide, at her mother trapped on the far side of the man's spread body. Reggie Dunn, tall, fat, strong.

"Vicki!" Cheryl shouted again.

"Never mind her," Dunn said.

Vicki didn't move; didn't run.

"You been mouthing me in my local, running round my boss, making all these lyin' fuckin' allegations. Sticking your tart's nose where nobody asked it to go. In my affairs. And you got to learn that's not on."

Cheryl ducked her head. "Vicki, run and..."

His hand caught her round the neck, forcing her back. "Never mind fuckin' Vicki. Never mind her. What you want to think about is me. Me. Reggie Dunn." His knuckle was pressing hard against her windpipe, making it difficult for her to breathe. "If I ever, ever, hear of you interfering with me again, the way I do my job, anything, your life won't be worth livin'. Right?"

And faster than he had any right to be, pushing her roughly back, he pressed the bottom button on the lift and sent her down; Vicki's face, shocked and pale, the last thing Cheryl saw before the door slid closed. Vicki and that bastard alone on that eighth floor balcony.

The lift seemed to take hours to descend and when it had, Cheryl wasn't prepared to risk it again. She raced the stairs, lungs rasping, backs of her legs aching by the time she swung around onto the open walkway and there was Vicki, leaning over the railing, staring down, hands clenched fast, her still child's body racked by sobs and tears. Chips and broken pieces of fish, some stamped on, lay strewn across the floor, paper wrapping itself around the metal rails, the backs of Vicki's legs. Of Dunn there was no sign.

Cheryl caught her daughter fast and cursed and cried and kissed her hair.

❒

Resnick had the CID room to himself. The door to his own office, a partitioned-off section of the long, rectangular room, was open, revealing a desk crowded with papers, Home Office bulletins and memoranda, case files and rosters and scraps of paper on which his sergeant, Graham Millington, had scribbled important messages in a hurried and largely indecipherable hand. Around him, typewriters waited silent, VDU screens tilted blankly save for the rhythmic blip of cursors and in ragged tintinnabulation, telephones rang and continued to ring unanswered. Although the windows facing onto the Derby Road were unhealthily closed, the constant drum of traffic underscored everything, accented every now and again by the clash of gears as an articulated lorry approached the Canning Circus roundabout.

Kevin Naylor and Lynn Kellogg were out on the Broxtowe Estate, investigating an attack on the house of a widower who was suspected of having grassed to the police about one of his neighbours. Broken windows, excrement smeared across the front door and pushed in parcels through the letter box, vilification tagged on his walls in fluorescent colours, four feet high. And all the man had done was wave down the local Panda patrol and complain about his bike having been nicked from his backyard, the second in as many weeks.

Millington himself, Carl Vincent in tow, had hurried off in the direction of Angel Row, where a posse of eight or nine youths, the youngest no more than nine years old, had steamed through one of the major clearing banks, waiting for one of the staff to pass through the security doors and barging past him, while others vaulted onto and over the counters. Several hundred pounds missing, one clerk elbowed in the face, a have-a-go customer knifed in the thigh, and all in around three minutes flat.

It was the third such incident in the city centre in the past month; all the kids wore sweatshirt hoods around their heads, scarves across their faces; limber, lithe and fast; black, white and shades between. Caught on the security cameras their exploits would have made an excellent commercial for one of the new alcoholic lemonades or Pepé jeans, but when it came to identification they were next to useless.

Turning, Resnick picked up a telephone at random and identified himself. Forty-five minutes later, Cheryl Wheeler was sitting opposite him in his office, Cheryl dressing down according to the seriousness of the situation, wide black trousers, denim shirt, boots with a three inch heel. Outside, Millington and Vincent had returned and were interviewing the parents of one possible suspect, a youth of fourteen who had already been taken into care twice as being beyond parental control. "What'd you have me do," the father was saying, "tie the little bastard to his bed, burn all his soddin' clothes?" He had tried both and neither had worked.

"I know you, don't I?" Resnick said. "We've met before but I can't think where."

Cheryl's mouth widened into a smile. "It was here in the canteen."

"Right. Carole? Caroline?"

"Cheryl."

"Of course." Resnick's turn to smile. Charlie Parker with Miles Davis and Max Roach. Nineteen forty seven. 'Cheryl'. One of those bouncy little blues themes Bird used to love to play. "Tell me about it," he said. "From the beginning, tell me what happened." Impressed by Cheryl's fire as he listened, the righteousness of the anger brimming inside her, the love.

"Why didn't you come in last night?" Resnick asked when she had finished. "Report it then?"

"I was bloody scared, why d'you think? And I wasn't going to leave her, Vicki, I wasn't going to leave her and no way was she moving out of that flat, not if I'd dragged her kicking and screaming."

"He didn't touch her?" Resnick asked, the second time. Cheryl shook her head.

"You're sure?"

"She wouldn't lie. Not about a thing like that."

"And you?"

Unbuttoning the top buttons, Cheryl pulled back her shirt to show him the bruises, colouring well, to her neck. The most prominent, purple, the perfect size and shape of a large thumb.

"I'd like to have some photographs taken. If you've no objection?"

"Suit yourself. Go ahead. Take as many as you like. Just so long as that bastard ends up inside."

"You would be willing to give evidence? If he were charged."

Her eyes widened. "What d'you mean, if?"

"There was no one else saw what happened, no other witnesses?"

"My Vicki, she was there all the time."

"You might not want her," Resnick said, "giving evidence in court, standing up to cross-examination. Always supposing the CPS would want her on the stand."

Cheryl swept back the chair as she rose to her feet. "You're going to do soddin' nothing, that's what you're saying, isn't it? You're going to let the bastard go scot-free."

"No, Cheryl," Resnick said, "That's not what I'm saying at all."

Sonia thought it would be a good idea if she had one of those signs like the ones on her boss's door, the one that said *Jason McStay, Manager*, right there on her desk. Freestanding. Easy to shift then, when Sonia had a dust and tidy. Not *Receptionist*, though; *Secretary*. No tone. *Personal Assistant to the Manager*. No, that was too long, they'd never fit it all on. But, *Sonia White, Managerial Assistant*, that would be fine. Real class. She would ask Mr McStay when he came back in. At least then, people wouldn't gawp and talk to her like she was part of the furniture; that woman who'd been in the other day, all scarlet nails and scarlet mouth and that ghastly leisure suit… Sonia shuddered. Women like her gave a new meaning to the word cheap.

Five minutes later when the door opened and McStay came in, a bit of a face on him, Sonia hesitated that fatal second too long.

"Get us a coffee, Sonia. Two sugars. It's a bastard of a day."

"Yes, Mr McStay."

What she did was nip across and buy him a cream slice, refresh her lipstick and bring in his coffee and cake with her best professional smile. "Mr McStay, I've been meaning to ask…"

He hardly seemed to listen, uncertain whether to utilise

the plastic knife in his drawer since his last Kentucky Fried Chicken dinner or bring the whole thing to his mouth and hope for the best.

"So, I mean, Mr McStay, what d'you think?"

"I think anyone with half a brain, walking in and seeing you plonked down behind the typewriter can see you're the sodding secretary, so what's the point?"

She'd scarcely got over that when a big man knocked and entered. Quite a nice suit, Sonia thought, a little old-fashioned but she didn't mind that; shame though about the stains on his tie. She wondered if he were the new collector Mr McStay had set on: a nice look about the eyes that might charm a few of the old dears at least.

When Resnick showed her his warrant card, she knew she'd been barking up the wrong tree. "Mr McStay doesn't normally see people without a written appointment," she began, but her heart wasn't in it. "I'm sorry to trouble you, Mr McStay," she said into the receiver, "but there's a policeman here to see you."

Resnick smiled his thanks and went on through.

In the course of McStay's journey from Belfast to Glasgow via Tyneside and Sheffield and a few minor diversions between, there were times when he'd drifted more than close to the wind. Since setting up Sheriff Finance and Loan here in the city, he'd had more than a few warnings – employing personnel with a penchant for violent behaviour, exceeding the duly constituted Codes of Practice, failing to pay National Insurance contributions for all of his staff as well as some little negligence over taxes; the arson attack on a persistent defaulter was little more than a rumour and remained unproved, though not for want of trying.

So McStay sent Sonia in search of more coffee, which Resnick tasted but didn't drink, laying out the case against one Reginald Alexander Dunn, currently in McStay's employ.

McStay was shocked, almost apoplectic with apology. He had no idea of the tactics that Dunn had been using and neither did he condone them in any way, shape or form. And to attack a member of the public, threaten her little girl... "You leave it to me, Inspector. I'll deal with it forthwith. The last thing I want, the name of this firm dragged through the mire. Business like mine, well, you can imagine, trust and confidence of our clients, that's what it depends upon. No, he's in here and I'm telling him straight. He'll not work for me again."

Resnick nodded. "Just one other thing."

McStay's eyebrow twitched.

"Standard loan contracts, the kind your firm uses... You do issue contracts?"

"Yes, yes, of course."

"All the time?"

"Everything above board."

"Each and every case?"

"Yes."

"So the papers concerning Ted Coles' loan, they'll be here on file?"

"Somewhere, yes. Sonia can..."

Resnick leaned forward, just a little. "Isn't there a clause, in the event of the death of the borrower, the remainder of the debt is set aside?"

McStay could smell something distressingly like his own sweat. "Usually, yes."

"And in the Coles' case?"

"I daresay, yes, but, like I say, I can check."

"So you've been collecting on a contract that was legally null and void, in addition to persuading an elderly stroke victim to take out a second loan to cover that non-existent debt?"

"I think... I mean, I can see there's almost certainly been an administrative oversight and..."

"And you'll make restitution immediately? Full financial restitution?"

"Well, naturally, yes."

"Plus, I daresay, a bonus to compensate for your client's deep discomfort?"

"I think we could see our way..."

"A generous bonus?"

"Yes, yes, you have my word."

Resnick rose to his feet. "I think what I'd be happier with, if it's all the same to you, let's have the figures down on paper. Nice and clear. Signed. You know the kind of thing."

"Graham," Resnick said, back at the station. Resnick had nipped into the Gents to relieve himself and found his sergeant doing something decorative to his moustache with a pair of nail scissors. At least it meant he couldn't whistle 'Winchester Cathedral' at the same time.

"Boss?"

"You remember that arson attack, February? Halal butchers on the Ilkeston Road."

Millington wiggled his upper lip, rabbit like, in front of the mirror. "Loan shark we liked for it, if it's the one I'm thinking. McFall?"

"McStay."

"That's him. Sheriff something-or-other. Robin Hood in reverse sort of a thing. Steal from the poor and keep McStay in Alfa Romeos."

"Right. Well, I think we might be able to squeeze out a little insider information."

Millington slipped the nail scissors down into their plastic leather-look case and looked interested.

"Reggie Dunn," Resnick said. "Late in McStay's employ. I thought perhaps you might find the time to have a word."

"Over a friendly pint."

"That sort of thing."

"Happy Return, then. Not been in for a while. Might give Reg Cossall a call, not so far from his place. He might fancy a chat with Dunn himself. Both Reggies, after all."

"Thanks, Graham," Resnick said, rinsing his hands under the tap.

McStay hadn't called round on Mary Coles himself, hadn't had the stomach for it. He sent Sonia instead, even though it had meant giving in to her about having some poncey sign stuck on her desk.

"Yes, Mrs Coles," Sonia had said. "Five hundred pounds, representing a repayment plus a substantial and generous bonus. And your old loan contract cancelled and returned. Now if you'll just sign this form absolving the firm of any further liability, I'll be hurrying along."

And she smiled her prim little purse-string smile and watched Mary fumble with her pen.

"The thing is, Reggie," Millington was saying, Cossall close alongside with a large scotch, Millington himself with a pint of mixed, "it's because we don't want to see you ending up with someone else's shit on your shoes, we're going out of our way to give you a hand."

"Photographs of that woman you nearly strangled in Radford," Cossall said. "Don't look good. And then, of course, there's you up there alone with the little girl."

"Not so little," Millington mused.

"Thirteen."

"Almost."

"I never laid a finger…"

"Course you didn't," Cossall said, "we understand that. But out there in this mistrustful world, who else is going to believe it?"

"Eighteen months inside," Millington said. "Assault. In there with the nonces."

"Look, I fuckin' never…"

"Right, right," Cossall said. "We know. Graham and me, we believe you. Right, Graham."

Millington smiled, a terrifying sight. "Now, Reggie, before you say any more, how about another drink? Bitter was it, or perhaps you fancy something a little stronger?"

Dunn sank what was left of his pint and then a swift Bells, followed by another, and told them about keeping watch with McStay in his new sports job while Mickey Threadgill and Pleasant John Taylor, McStay's money in their pockets, swaggered down to the butchers across the street and torched it.

It was Hannah's half-term and she was off at an English teachers' conference in Harrogate, which meant that instead of spending the evening round at her house on Devonshire Promenade, something he was increasingly likely to do, Resnick was spending a quiet evening at home with the cats.

Of course, he'd put his Charlie Parker on the stereo, the collection with 'Cheryl' as one of the tracks. Not the greatest, perhaps. But honest, genuine. Miles, only young then, sounding a little uncertain in his articulation, hazy; and Bud Powell's piano solo working too hard, perhaps, against the rhythm. But Parker's chorus was fired by the presence of possibility, brilliance waiting for its spark.

◻

Cheryl told the story to her new fella a few weeks later. They were taking a break from dancing, a leaving do for a friend of a friend upstairs at the Irish and the DJ over the top on seventies disco. 'Le Freak' 'Young Hearts Run Free' 'You're the Greatest Dancer'.

New fella. She presumed that's what he was. They'd met at the exhaust centre when she'd taken in her van for some running repairs. Grease on his overalls and a great bum. Twenty seven if he was a day. He confessed to her after, it was the leisure suit he'd noticed. She hadn't told him yet how old she was, though he knew about Vicki so he could likely figure out she wasn't exactly Liv Tyler. Closer, Liz Taylor. Still, pray for a little subdued lighting and hopefully the stretch marks wouldn't show. Vicki was sleeping over with her mate Erica and her two kids, a favour returned.

"And they nicked the lot of them?" Brian asked. A nice name, Brian.

"All three. Pictures in the paper. Arson. Intimidation. Fraud. Enough for half a dozen episodes of *The Bill*."

"Let us know," Brian said, his hand rather high on her thigh, "when you're ready to leave."

It nearly popped out of her mouth. "Right now, sunshine," but there was Gloria Gaynor winding up through the speakers. 'I Will Survive'. She couldn't let that go to waste now, could she?

"Come on, love," she said, dragging Brian back out onto the floor. "Just one more dance, eh?"

WORK

> *"I want you to pay me for my beauty*
> *I think it's only right*
> *because I have been paying for it*
> *all of my life"*
> **Ani Difranco: Letter to a John**

SHE KNEW he loved her: really knew. It wasn't the flowers, though they were frequent and effusive enough; it wasn't the presents, each of them gift wrapped at whatever perfume counter or jewellery store he happened to be passing; it wasn't even the scrupulous care with which he asked about her plans for this evening or that, which party, which friend, never wanting to appear intrusive, over-protective, fatherly. It was none of those things. What it was, Eileen thought, was the way Terry watched her whenever he was sure she wasn't looking, the pain that gathered, waiting, at the backs of his eyes. Terry, waiting to be hurt.

"I don't care," he said, "you know that. Where you go or what you do. You're a grown woman. It's your life."

But it wasn't; not any more.

She felt that pain, his pain, the burden of it: resented it so much there were times it was all she could do to stop herself from leaving, walking out and never coming back. The responsibility of his loving her: loving her that much, the way he did. Terry, this caring, crooked, just-shy-of-fifty, charming, balding man. And Eileen, who had left home at fifteen and was still not twenty-five; who had spent what should have been her childhood fighting off men who wanted to be close to her, greedy for her beauty, the glorious red of her hair, the glow of her skin. When she had stopped fighting it had been for a price.

The first time Terry had seen her she had been booked to do a strip at a pub in Gedling, a private party, fifty quid and all the tips her g-string would hold. Terry had been at a table near the end of the bar, laughing with some mates. And then he hadn't been with them any more; had been on his own, watching her as she turned her body to the music, swirl of her long hair. He was waiting outside for her afterwards in his car, the engine running. Quick to explain why he hadn't poked a twenty between her legs like the others, not wanting to do anything that would make her feel cheap.

At the time, smoke and the residue of sweat stuck fast to her skin, she had thought that was, well, sweet. Now she knew it was foolish: somebody always had to pay.

◘

"So what's she like then?" Jill asked.

"Who?"

"You know who."

Khan looked at her over his shoulder and grinned.

"Bastard!" she said softly and slid her long body beneath the sheet.

He was standing before her dressing table mirror, still faintly damp from the shower; the room lit by candles and his skin a honeyed hue. The way his back tapered in towards his waist, the tight curve of his buttocks – she loved his body. The tautness of it, its colours. Light and dark. She liked to tell herself that didn't matter, the colour part, but she knew it did. So different from her own.

Sometimes when she lay there with him, closed high in the house, safe inside this room, Jill would look at the way they wound around each other and marvel at the picture they made, leg and arm, chest to chest, all those shades from palest white to deepest brown.

"Come here," she said.

"A minute."

"Stop titivating yourself and come here."

He screwed the cap back on the bottle of vanilla lotion he had been rubbing into his hands. "Just thinking of you," he said.

When he walked towards the bed she could see that he had been thinking about somebody. She thought she could read those thoughts. With one leg she lifted back the sheet to let him in. Gasped as his hand pressed firm against her breast.

"Are you sure the kids...?" he started to ask.

"They're my kids," she said. "Let me worry about them, okay?"

There was a faint breeze from the barely opened window, lightly stirring the candle flame, turning the mobile that hung, above her bed.

"Jill..." he said later, breathing the word into her shoulder.

"Hmm?"

"Nothing. Just Jill."

He had met her at the television studio where she worked as a receptionist; there had been a disturbance, a small fracas involving a disgruntled design assistant and the head of production; blows had been exchanged, threats issued, the VDU screen Jill used had been splintered open. Khan, not yet made up to detective, had been the officer nearest to the scene. A month later he had seen her again at a bar in the city and been surprised that she remembered him.

"I didn't know if you would," he'd said, handing her a gin and tonic, "you know, without the uniform."

"I'm good with faces. Have to be."

Khan had grinned. "Even faces like mine?"

Jill had downed three or four already. "It's a lovely face," she said.

She still thought so: she leaned over and kissed it lightly on the mouth, the closed eyes. Khan's breathing caught but he did not wake. The candles had long since burned down and the only light, opaque, was from the window, the partly opened curtains. The digital clock told her it was nearly four. In a couple of hours, less, she would scuttle him into the shower and down to the kitchen, a mug of coffee and then he would be off across the city and changing for work before the first of her children woke.

She had thought that when she told him about the two girls and a boy, the oldest eleven, youngest rising seven, that he would end it. Imagined the calculations inside his head. Lies of omission about her age. She went to the gym four times a week, took care with her clothes, make-up, looked after herself. But she was still the wrong side of thirty and losing ground fast.

Khan had stayed.

"In my community," he'd laughed, "they teach us to

revere our elders. Treat them with the respect their wisdom deserves."

"Bollocks!"

"Exactly."

Somehow they had scarcely mentioned it since. And the children had rarely been a problem. Sometimes Jill's sister slept over and Jill stayed in Khan's flat near the canal; once in a while the kids stayed at her sister's for most of a long weekend and Khan, shifts permitting, moved in. If neither arrangement were possible, like tonight, he came late and left early. It wasn't perfect, but then, she asked herself, what was?

He stirred against her and opened his eyes, smiling.

"Pleasant dreams?"

"Mmm, very."

"Bastard."

"What?"

"Well, I don't suppose it was me you were thinking about. Hardly need to dream about me, do you? Not here in my bed." She could feel his erection against her thigh.

Khan's smile broadened across his face.

She punched at his shoulder with her fist, hard enough to hurt.

"What?"

"I was right, wasn't I? Fantasising about some other bloody woman in my bed."

Khan caught hold of her wrists before she could hit him again. "Nothing I can do about it, right? I mean, out of my control. Sub-conscious and all."

"It was her, wasn't it?" Jill said. "I'll just bet you. That tart you've been watching…"

"Eileen? She's not a tart."

"Stripper, then. Same thing. Bloody fancy her, don't you?"

"No."

"No?" reaching down. "What's this, then?"

Khan grinned. "Didn't notice."

Jill kissed him anyway, feeling for his tongue, and immediately he kissed her back. She kissed his nipples, kissed the dark swirl of hair at the base of his belly, the veins of his cock pulsing against her throat. Who cares if it came from thinking about somebody else? Waste not, want not, wasn't that what her mum had said?

❐

Resnick woke abruptly, pushing back the covers and startling two of his four cats onto the bedroom floor. Seven forty five. What the hell was he doing still in...? He was on his feet and heading for the door before remembering it was Sunday, once in a while his day of rest. By the time he emerged from the bathroom, showered and refreshed, Dizzy, whose hunger knew no days of the week, only the hours of the day, was nibbling at his toes.

He drank his first cup of coffee in the kitchen, opening cans of Whiskas, watching toast beneath the grill, searching for news in Saturday's *Post;* his second he carried out into the garden, musing a little on the disposition of his flower beds and the stubbornness of grass; the third, and positively, he made himself promise, his last this side of lunchtime, he enjoyed in an easy chair, listening to Stan Getz bossa novas and trying not to get worked up about Terry Cooke.

Terry had been a small thorn in Resnick's side for years: a petty thief who had graduated to being a petty fence, mostly working out of the premises he owned at Bobbers Mill, from which he and his nephew Raymond sold everything from second-hand refrigerators to almost complete sets of *The Illustrated History of the Second World War.*

"No need to worry, Mr Resnick," Terry had assured him. "Burma campaign and a fold-out map of the Ardennes, that's all that's missing. Make a good investment. Something to mull over in retirement."

He wished. Resnick was certain Terry Cooke had changed, got nasty, dangerous, and he wasn't going to rest, never mind retire, until he had him nailed.

The nub of it was a job Terry had allowed himself to get involved in, oh, months back. A break-in which had gone badly wrong, shotguns, two police in hospital, and fingers pointed at Terry Cooke and Seamus Coughlan, along with Coughlan's cousin, Norbert Breakshaw, and a couple of real make-weights, young Frankie Farmer and Tommy DiReggio. But mostly it was down to Terry and Coughlan, sometime business partners and long-time friends – friends, that is, until Coughlan discovered Terry had been putting it to his wife, Marjorie, every other Friday afternoon, when Coughlan had thought she was doing yoga at the local community centre.

In the event, the only way Terry had been able to keep himself from a long term inside had been by shopping Coughlan, Breakshaw and the rest. Not that he'd been pleased to do so, Coughlan aside. Grassing up to the law wasn't only against Terry's principles, it was bad for business; quite a lot of choice stuff had failed to come his way since this had happened and Tommy DiReggio's brother had threatened to put a razor to his cheek if he ever passed him in the street. Terry didn't take offence at that; family, it was to be expected. And there was something charmingly old-fashioned about the razor – whoever used razors nowadays except for shaving?

No, what Terry had exercised himself about had been those he rightly assumed had grassed on him. Doris Duke, who had a flower stall in the market, he had let his nephew, Ray-o deal with – something, he thought, that had involved matches and paraffin. But the other – Ronnie, Ronnie Rather – that was different. Ronnie had sat with him at the window table of that café in Gedling Street more mornings than the pair of them had had bacon cobs and mugs of tea; Terry allowing himself to be bored shitless while old Ronnie sucked on one of his vile black cigars and warbled endlessly about his days as a trombone player with Lew Stone and Geraldo. And for that Ronnie had dropped him in it without as much as a second thought.

Well, not any more he wouldn't. Slippery bastard! Terry had bought a pistol in the back room of a pub and gone round to Ronnie Rather's pathetic bed-sitter with the pistol in one pocket, a half-bottle of Bell's in the other. First he had forced the muzzle of the gun so far into the wattles of Ronnie's grizzled neck, the old boy had pissed himself on the spot. Then he had got hold of the trombone that stood, unplayed now and highly polished, in the corner and pro-ceeded to beat Ronnie around the head with it until his anger was spent.

"Drink, Ronnie? Old times sake?"

But Ronnie hadn't wanted a drink.

"Suit yourself." Terry had taken two good pulls from the bottle and then left, calling an ambulance from a pay phone down the street. Never let it be said he wasn't a caring man.

And Ronnie Rather, seventy eight years of age, now spent his days in a wheelchair with severe headaches, slurred speech, and the use of only one eye. Resnick dropped in to see him whenever he could and took a box of

Panatellas, occasionally something to eat; they would sit listening to scratchy old recordings, waiting for the moment when the trombone would take its short, eight or sixteen bar solo and Ronnie Rather's good eye would light up.

Resnick knew the old man would make no kind of witness in court, and besides, Terry Cooke had made sure he was alibied three times over. What Resnick had to do was keep the pressure on, squeeze hard, let him know he was being watched, watch that young woman of his too, Eileen, apply pressure where it hurt. Sooner or later, Resnick was sure, Terry would let it get to him, panic, make a mistake. Resnick intended to be there when he did.

Nine-thirty. The cab was coming for her at a quarter to. Since all of this recent trouble Terry had gone back to asking her if she wouldn't like him to take her himself, drop her off at the job, pick her up once it was over. No call to advertise, just discreet. "You're not my chauffeur, Terry. You know that."

"No?" he had said across the top of the *Mail*, "What am I then?"

Eileen had kissed him, leaving a clear Cupid mark on the bald patch near the back of his head. "You're a sweetheart, that's what you are." But it was a question, she thought, that increasingly had to be faced.

Before the mirror, she applied the final touches to her make-up, turning to see the back of her dress and smooth it over her behind – just a g-string, nothing showing – the rest of her paraphernalia was snug in the white leather case Terry had bought her last Christmas. Tassles, holster, police cap and handcuffs, the plastic banana she sometimes used for an encore. Once she and Terry had actually started living together, Eileen had called a halt to regular stripping, concentrated on Strip-o-Grams instead. Coming in bold as brass and placing some half-pissed bloke under arrest before teasing him down to his y-fronts, that was what went down best. But since the police had been all over Terry money had been tight and when Eileen suggested going back to working a few late-night lock-ins – a hundred quid at least and tips – Terry had turned his head and nodded okay.

"You off then?"

She stood in the doorway, red hair pinned high above her head, light reflecting in the delicate green of her eyes and for a moment Terry's heart seemed to stop. What had he ever done to deserve someone so lovely? What did he have to do to keep her?

"You know you don't have to wait up."

"I know."

They both knew he would.

The cab dropped her at the corner and she went in through the rear entrance: a good crowd already, she could hear it, and Eileen felt the adrenalin start to race within her. All those faces fixed on her in the spotlight, the way she looked, the way she was moving. It was like a drug. As many as a hundred people, hers for as long as she held them.

She was just getting into her stride when she noticed them, the same two plain clothes police, off to one end of the bar, glued to her like the rest. Eileen wondered if they were really working or whether it was more, well, social.

Ever since Mark Divine had been away on extended sick leave, Naylor and Khan had been palling up more and more. The third time this they'd double-dated – Khan and Jill, Naylor and his wife, Debbie. And whereas Debbie would have been happy to go Chinese, Indian even as long as it wasn't one of those really scruffy ones, Jill had insisted, no, it had to be Sonny's, didn't it? And Jill, as was too often the case, Debbie thought, had had her way.

So there they were in a table near the window, surrounded by expensive suits and voices, Jill undecided between the crème brûlée and sticky toffee pudding, while Khan and Kevin, more than a little drunk already, pondered the advisability of a fourth bottle of wine. Debbie sat a little too stiffly in her chair and watched them, the men with their faces flushed and Jill ready to smile across the room at the least opportunity, showing off her boobs in a blue dress that looked like silk and must have cost what it took Debbie to keep both her kids in clothes for a six-month.

"Fancy going on somewhere after?" Kevin asked.

"Clubbing?" said Jill.

"Pubbing?" grinned Khan.

Jill leaned over towards Debbie and touched her sleeve. "You know why he said that, don't you? Fancies getting another look at that fancy redhead doing tricks with her banana."

Kevin laughed while Debbie blushed and Khan, she thought, let his hand rest for the slightest moment close against her knee.

"So long as I come back home to you right after," Khan said with a smile.

"It's true," Jill grinned, her face still close to Debbie's. "Last time he came round after watching her I was in the kitchen fixing a drink for one of the kids, must've been two in the morning. All I could do to stop him having me against the sink. But then, you don't need me to tell you that, your Kev must be just the same."

Jill glanced across at Kevin and winked broadly and

Kevin hid his face behind his glass. It wasn't a hand that Debbie could feel this time, but Khan's leg, rubbing slowly, back and forth, against her thigh.

"Another bottle, then," Khan said, turning his head to look for the waitress. "That's for definite."

Debbie thought about it on the way home in the taxi, the time a few years ago when she and Kevin had just got back together again after breaking up. A night like this it had been, a meal out, plenty of wine; not Sonny's though and on their own. The minute they'd got inside the front door Kevin had grabbed for her, kissing her, hands everywhere, wanting to do it to her right there in the hall.

The cab jolted across a speed bump and Debbie's eyes closed, imagining the two of them stretched somehow across the narrow strip of carpet, her dress hiked up over her hips – Debbie looking down on them the way anybody would who happened to come up to the door and peer through the glass... or suppose they'd forgotten to shut the door properly and someone had walked right in...

Christ! She knew she was wet and she wanted him.

On the way from the cab she tried not to think how long it was since they'd last made love. Thank God the kids were at her mum's. In the hallway she turned fast against him and caught at his hand before he could switch on the light.

"Debbie, what...? Deb... Bloody hell, Debbie, you're treading all over my feet, whatever're you at?"

With a sigh she pitched away from him and slammed her way into the kitchen, the bottle of vodka half-empty in the fridge.

"Should've thought you'd've had enough already."

To spite him she put back the glass and drank from the bottle.

Kevin's face twisted in disgust. "Now I've seen bloody everything."

She listened to him, heavy on the stairs, the pronounced click of the bathroom door. "We all know what you've seen, Kevin. You and your mate going on about it all evening. Well, maybe you should see how much she charges, private? Take it out the fucking housekeeping!"

She seized the jar in which she'd been saving towards the baby's birthday and hurled it at the wall, glass and coins scattering wide across the floor.

Resnick chewed at the last mouthful of his sandwich and brushed crumbs from the front of his jacket and the edges of his desk; a slither of mayonnaise continued its slow journey, unobserved, down the length of his tie. Full twenty minutes the superintendent had given him that morning, boring on and on about resources being wasted on toe rags the likes of Terry Cooke. "Neither here nor there, Charlie, when it comes down to it. Not worth arguing the overtime, not in my book."

But Skelton's book didn't have Ronnie Rather writ large in its pages, beaten half-daft and half-blind.

Resnick eased open his office door and called Naylor and Khan through from the CID room. What they had to tell him gave him little joy: Terry Cooke had been behaving like an altar boy preparing for heaven; his girl friend, Eileen, had clocked them each time they'd showed but carried on regardless, unfazed by their attentions.

"You've spoken to her?" Resnick asked.

Khan glanced at Naylor before answering. "A few words. Not a lot."

"But she knows who you are?"

Naylor nodded: yes. "Take more than us staring at her

to get under her skin," he said. "It's what she's getting paid for all the time."

"And loving it," Khan said.

Resnick stared at him a moment.

"You should see her," Khan continued. "The difference. When she's performing, doing her act. I mean, she's a good looker anyway; beautiful, even. But when she's really getting into it…" He shook his head. "Amazing."

"What about the rest of the time?" Resnick asked. "Day times. What does she do? Help out Cooke and that nephew of his over in Bobbers Mill? What?"

"Got a couple of mates she meets sometimes," Naylor said. "Jallans of a lunchtime, early afternoon. Sometimes she goes there on her own. I don't think she goes near the shop."

Resnick pushed up to his feet. "Okay, leave it be. Let her go. I want Cooke's place turned over. Every day if you have to, twice a day. Get a warrant to go through his house. Stolen goods, whatever. If he thought we were leaning on him hard before, now he'll know better."

"What about the girl?" Khan asked, almost keeping the disappointment out of his voice.

"Don't worry," said Resnick. "I'll talk to the girl."

She had almost the same name as his wife; first wife, the only one he'd so far had. Elaine. Eileen. They could not have been more different.

Resnick sat watching Eileen perched on one of the stools near the end of the bar and smoking a cigarette, toying with a Bacardi and Coke. Resnick listening to the Parker coming through the Jallans stereo. Parker and then – was it? – yes, Monk. One of those Blue Notes trio sessions from the early fifties. Elaine with her red hair loose about her shoulders and wearing a loose silver-grey top, close-fitting black trousers in some material that invited touch. Yes, she was beautiful.

Resnick's club sandwich arrived and then a second bottle of beer. 'Just a Gigolo' had finished and now Monk was playing something Resnick was stretched to recognise. A double bass intro, Latin feel to the rhythm, and Monk himself fleeter over the keys than his usual faltering, fragmentary self; as if, perhaps, to say, listen, you want the fancy, filigree stuff? Well, I can do that. "Work," Resnick smiled, remembering the title before the track had come to an end. "Work," that's what this was.

Eileen stubbed out her cigarette, pushed aside her unfinished drink and swung round from her stool; at first Resnick thought she might be heading for the ladies but she continued up the stairs and out towards the street and, wrapping the untouched half of his club sandwich inside a paper napkin and jamming that down into his coat pocket, he followed her.

At first, Resnick thought, as Eileen headed north across the Old Market Square, that she had a particular destination in mind. But as she hesitated, first outside the Theatre Royal and a second time at the furthest corner of the *Post* building, he realised she was wandering aimlessly. Thinking, perhaps; filling in time. Seeing the downward cast of her shoulders, the dip of her head, he wondered what she might be thinking about.

When she reached the Arboretum, Eileen twice circled the small ponds before setting of along the slight rise that would take her through the rose gardens towards the mounted cannons that had been shipped back from the Crimea. She flapped some dirt from one of the benches with her hand and sat down.

Watching from a little way off, Resnick retrieved the club sandwich from his pocket and ate. Only when he had finished, the last snippet of bacon tasting almost as fine as the first, did he drop the napkin in a wastebasket and continue up the hill.

Eileen scarcely raised her head when Resnick stood a moment near her, then took a seat at the opposite end of the bench. Probably no more than she was used to.

"No," she said after a while, flat and not moving her head to face him.

"No, what?"

"No, anything."

Resnick extended his hand. "Charlie Resnick. Detective Inspector, CID."

She stared at the hand a moment before dismissing it; too dangerous, too large, too real.

"I wanted to talk about Terry," Resnick said.

"It's you then, making his life a misery?"

Resnick shrugged.

"Both our lives. Why can't you bloody leave us alone?"

"Like your Terry, you mean? Like he left that old boy alone?"

She looked at him then, white of her teeth biting gently into her bottom lip. "What old boy?"

"He didn't tell you?"

She shook her head nervously. "What old boy?"

"Nice old bloke, not so far short of eighty."

"What about him?" Her voice was suddenly strident and a few pigeons lifted off from the cannons and flapped through the solid afternoon air before resuming their places.

"I should take you to see him."

"Who?"

"Took his eye out, your Terry. Beat him round the head

with something sharp and metallic until he'd lost an eye and half a brain."

"I don't believe you. You're lying. Winding me up. That's not Terry, I don't believe it."

He could see in her eyes that she almost did. Quickly, she got up but not so quickly that Resnick couldn't catch hold of her hand. "I'll be here, this time, tomorrow. The day after. Most days. Talk to me. We'll talk. Find a way out."

She snatched her hand free and rubbed at it with the other, though his grip had not been strong enough to hurt.

"I think that's what you want to do," Resnick said. "Find a way out."

Without answering, Eileen turned and walked away.

❐

"How come," Debbie asked at breakfast, several days later, "you can get turned on by some slapper who does it for money and not by me?"

Naylor pushed aside his plate and swallowed down a last mouthful of Shredded Wheat. "You're not still on about that, are you?"

"Just answer me."

"Debbie, I don't know." Naylor on his feet now and heading for the door.

"Kevin…" Debbie's voice was shrill and loud.

"What?"

"I am your wife, you know."

"Yeh, well, maybe that's the problem."

He hadn't started the car and slotted it into gear, before Debbie had uncapped the bottle from the fridge and poured a shot of vodka into her tea.

Khan thought Terry Cooke had lost it this time, really lost it. He and Naylor and some carefully chosen back-up had turned up at his house with a warrant, going in nice and early with the milk, except in Terry's street all deliveries had been cancelled and you had to fetch your pinta from the nearest corner shop.

They were on their way upstairs when Terry's mum, startled, came out of her bedroom in curlers and a candlewick dressing gown and proceeded to give them a piece of her mind, lively for a woman of advancing years.

All Khan did was attempt to move her back out of harm's way, when Terry grabbed at his collar, jerked him round against the bannister and threw a punch. "That's my mother, you Paki bastard!"

"Found these, sir," Naylor said, holding up quantities of coloured pills. "In his bathroom cabinet. Thought they might be something, you know, hallucinogenic."

"And?"

"Beta-blockers, stress. Checked it out with his GP. Advised him to go for this massage…"

"Shiatsu," Khan said.

"Yes, that's it. Apparently chose the pills instead."

"Maybe he should double the dose," Resnick said, "doesn't seem as if they're working."

"Living with that girl," Khan said, "got to be a strain. Man of his age."

Resnick looked back at him without saying a word.

She was wearing jeans and a loose leather jacket and her hair had been pulled back tight from her face; she seemed to Resnick to be wearing little or no make-up. He watched as she walked towards the bench, avoiding looking at him directly. She stopped and he waited for her to sit beside him and when she didn't he got to his feet and asked if she would rather walk.

They set off on an uneasy diagonal towards the bandstand, and from there down again to the road and the cemetery that rose gradually from the far side.

"How's it going?" Resnick asked. Overhead the sky was uncluttered Wedgwood blue.

"You could put a stop to it." Eileen said.

Resnick shook his head. "Would it make a difference? To you, now, if I could?"

She stopped in the middle of the path. "No, not now."

A woman carrying a bunch of what might have been chrysanthemums skirted round them, bent-backed.

"Leave him," Resnick said.

Eileen shuddered as if someone had stepped over her grave. "I can't."

"Why not?"

"I'm afraid."

"What of?"

"That he won't let me."

They walked on further, forking left by a headstone blurred with moss – *Ethel Teasdale, departed this mortal toil, December 7th 1894, aged seventy three years: now she rests among the angels.*

"He'd try to stop you?"

"Yes."

"You think he might hurt you?"

Resnick read the answer in her eyes.

"Listen," he said, steering her towards the eastern wall, "if we could find something on him that we could make stick. Something big."

"I'd never give evidence against him, I never would."

"I know."

"I'll not grass. Not on Terry. Not him."

"Of course. But like you said, you could be in danger. Circumstances like that, you've got to look out for yourself. No one would blame you for that."

They walked on almost as far as the top exit before Eileen stopped and said: "Terry, I don't know where he keeps it. Your lot've never found it. But I think he's got a gun."

Debbie had called in sick. She knew that Kevin would be working late, overtime, this other case he'd been working on, hi-jacking. Just Kevin and the sergeant, that was all. Debbie had gone shopping in town. Back home and trying on things, wondering what she'd have to take back, what she'd keep, she knew what she was thinking about, just didn't want to give it a name. Not till the second bottle of vodka had been breached.

She looked Khan's number up in the book out in the hall; after three rings, terrified, sweating, she put down the phone. She was still staring at it, disbelieving, shaking, when it rang.

Picking it up she heard Khan's voice. "Did you just ring?"

"No."

"Shame." Beneath the light ironic tone, she could feel the smile in his eyes.

Fifty minutes later she was in a taxi heading west along Queen's Drive against the tag end of the evening's traffic. The long black dress she'd bought for the reception at her sister's wedding and never worn since. Sleeveless, high at the neck and tight across her narrow hips and bust, it clung to her when she moved. Her shoes had two inch heels. At first she had taken her wedding ring off, then slid it back. When she blinked at her reflection in the taxi window she imagined she could smell the vodka on her breath. She thought about Khan, his voice, the softness of his hands; wondered if he knew that she would come, if he had thought about her while she was drying from the shower, putting on powder, getting dressed. God, she wanted him!

Khan's flat was by the Castle Marina, neat and small with whitewashed walls. Flowers in a narrow vase, she re-membered that; one of them, Kevin or herself, assuming Jill had brought them, but no, he had bought them for himself. Kevin's flat, before they'd got married, all there'd been was the spider plant his mum had given him and that was dead.

"Number, duck?" the driver asked over his shoulder.

Stammering she told him, scarcely able to force out the words.

Khan came to the door in grey T-shirt, pale blue jeans; his feet were bare. From somewhere behind him came the sound of music, that single – what was it? – 'Beautiful Girl'.

He smiled. "I hoped it might be you."

Debbie pushed past him into the bathroom and bolted the door, certain she was about to throw up.

"Are you all right?" Khan called.

Not answering, Debbie leaned up against the mirror, her face against the glass. Her eyes refused to focus. For Christ's sake, Debbie, she told herself, do something for once in your life!

"Debbie?"

She opened the door and he was standing there, amused and concerned. "Are you okay… ?"

"Shut up!"

With one hand she pushed him back against the wall.

Her other hand was reaching for his belt. Then she was kissing him, unbuckling his jeans.

Khan kissed her back; half-pulled, half-led her to the living room at the end of the hall where 'Beautiful Girl' was on repeat. He reached for the catch at the back of her dress and, angry, she told him to stop. Thinking she was teasing he tried again and she pushed him away.

"I said stop. Just stop and watch me. Watch!"

Khan stepped away towards the settee, while Debbie slowly, inexpertly, removed her dress, the wisp of bra, her shoes.

"Well?" she said.

"Beautiful," Khan said. "Lovely. Sexy, too."

"You're not just saying that?"

"Does it look like it?" Khan asked, glancing down. "Now get yourself on over here."

"We don't have to go into the bedroom, do we?" Debbie asked.

Khan grinned. "Not yet."

Eileen did a quick twenty-first for a pimply youth who worked in the despatch department at Raleigh, snapped her fake handcuffs on the wrists of a middle-range executive from Fissons and then called it a night. Her other two bookings she passed on to her friend Gloria, who was getting over a nasty bout of glandular fever and pleased to get the work.

She was home indoors – Terry's home – by something after nine, Terry's mum mumbling something about cocoa and an early night; Terry oddly subdued and scarcely able to look her in the eye. Eileen began to wonder if she shouldn't have carried on as usual after all.

But she poured Terry a large whisky and water, just the

one cube of ice, no sense anaesthetising all the flavour out of it he used to say, and cuddled up alongside him in front of *News at Ten* ; before the first commercial break, he curved his hand around her knee. Maybe it'll be all right after all, she thought, just something we're going through. Couples do. She had been thinking all evening, off and on, about what Resnick had suggested and knew she could never land Terry in it, no matter what he might do. He had taken her in, given her a home, looked after her, right?

News over, Terry switched off the set and put on the Dionne Warwick CD he'd talked her into buying him for Christmas. By the time Dionne had found her way to San José, Terry had swallowed down two more scotches in quick succession.

"Terry? Tel?"

The look he gave her was one she didn't recognise. She shivered a little as she stood. "I'm off to get ready for bed," she said, leaving him alone with the bottle and Trains and Boats and Planes.

Eileen intended to stay awake for him, curl like spoons about him and get him to tell her what was wrong. She only realised she'd fallen asleep when she felt something cold pressing hard against the side of her face, hard and cold enough to hurt.

"Terry, what... ?"

Eileen realised it was the barrel of a gun.

"Terry, you can't..."

"Sshh. Sshh." He rested the middle finger of his free hand across her lips. "Sweetheart, ssh, don't make it any worse."

"What? I swear I don't under—"

His hand clamped across her mouth. "I know you've been seeing him, Resnick. Meeting him. Last week. Today. Talking. About me."

With an effort, Eileen wrenched herself free and turned round in the bed, facing him. "It's not true. It's a lie."

There was something akin to a smile on Terry's face, though it was nothing to do with happiness, nothing to do with joy. "You haven't been seeing him?"

"We weren't talking about you, I swear."

"What then?"

Eileen's mouth was suddenly dry. "I don't know, nothing really, I..."

"Having it off with him, are you? Our Charlie? Bit on the side? An affair?"

"That's stupid; that's ridiculous; you know that's ridiculous; you..."

"Yes?"

"Look, Terry..."

"Mm?"

"It was nothing, I just... I bumped into him, that's all. Honestly, that's all it was."

"Twice?"

"What?"

"You bumped into him twice?" The muzzle of the gun was resting now against the space between her breasts.

Eileen tried to swallow air. "Yes."

"And Jallans?"

"What about Jallans?"

"Lunch in Jallans; little – what-d'you-call-it? – tête-à-tête."

"I never saw him in Jallans."

"He saw you."

Silently, almost silently, Eileen had begun to cry.

"You been a bad girl, Eileen?"

"Yes." Her voice no more than a croak.

"A silly little girl?"

"Yes." The barrel of the gun was pushing lightly now, up beneath her chin.

"You know he's not going to be satisfied, don't you, that fat bastard, till he's done for me once and for all? You know that? Business, family, home, you – he wants all of it. Shut me inside and chuck away the key. Christ, Eileen, I had a life. Mum, Ray-o, a life here with you. And he's going to take it away on account of the stupid old josser, that imbecile toss-pot who grassed me up. Well, he got what was coming to him and nothing less. What the fuck did he expect? Mouthing me off to the law. Anyone who grasses up on me, they know what they're going to get. No matter who. You know that, Eileen, don't you? You know there's nothing else I can do?"

Eileen shook so hard it would have sounded from the next room as if they were making love.

Terry raised her head with the muzzle of the gun and kissed her through her sobs, kissed her eyes, her nose, her mouth. Then he pressed the gun against his left temple and squeezed the trigger once.

Eileen screamed and pushed back in the bed, frantically rubbing at her face and brushing blood and brain and broken bone away.

When Terry's mother came into the room moments later, Eileen lifted one of the pillows and covered Terry's head.

Five minutes past midnight and on the edge of sleep, Resnick was woken by the phone's insistent tone.

❑

Ronnie Rather had his wheelchair wedged between the sideboard and the bed and had exhausted himself trying to get free. Resnick dragged the bed to one side and pushed Ronnie over to the centre of the room, where his record player stood on an old card table, the records themselves in an apple box on the floor.

"Soup, Ronnie? Bread?"

"Not that Polish muck, is it? Rye something or other, can't stomach that, gives me indigestion something awful."

"Wonderloaf, I promise. White and ready-sliced."

"Now you're talking."

While Resnick poured the soup from a thermos and buttered the bread, Ronnie found the Lew Stone recording he'd been looking for earlier.

"Cock an ear to this, Charlie. That section work, the brass. Lew Davis that is, leading the trombones. Nat Gonella, the trumpets. Should've paid Lew to work in that band – and we did work, mind you, two, three in the morning at the Monseigneur, tea dances on top." He laughed. "Not that I'd've told him that at the time."

"How's the soup?"

"Grand. Champion. Tomato, is it?"

"Chicken and vegetable."

"Oh, well."

Resnick tried a spoonful of it himself. "You heard about Terry Cooke?"

"Topped himself, didn't he? Useless bastard."

"Bullet through the head."

"No more than he deserved. Still, like to have seen it, one eye or not."

Resnick reached towards the thermos. "Want to finish this off?"

"Why not?" Ronnie said, holding out his bowl. And then, "That kid he was kipping with – Elaine?"

"Eileen."

"Yes, that's it, Eileen. What's happened to her?"

"London, apparently."

Ronnie folded a piece of bread and carefully wiped it round the inside of the bowl before squashing it into his mouth and starting to chew. "Lovely girl," he said eventually.

"Lovely," Resnick agreed. "Beautiful."

"Well shot of him."

"Absolutely."

When Resnick left, some twenty minutes later, Ronnie Rather was leaning to one side in his wheelchair, eyes closed, lips drawn tight, listening to the only session he played with Jack Hylton's Orchestra, the one where they recorded 'Dancing in the Dark'.

STUPENDOUS

RAYMOND HADN'T recognised her at first. Not till she climbed out of the first car, the one that had been travelling smack behind the coffin. Face all pinched and red from crying. Terry's daughter, Sarah. Black coat, leggings and boots with a three inch clumpy heel. Raymond wondered how long it had been since he'd seen her. Best part of a year, had to be. Eighteen months? Filled out, though, he'd say that for her. If it hadn't been for the cold sore, raw at the side of her lipsticked mouth, she might even have been worth fancying. Not like all those times he'd kept his eyes jammed shut while she was feeling him up, evenings at his Uncle Terry's house when Terry was out down the pub or off for an Indian with his girl friend, Eileen; nights he'd slept over and she'd sneaked her skinny little body into his bed, done the business, some of it anyway, then scarpered bare-arsed back to her room before anyone else woke. His little cousin, Sarah: Raymond had been knobbing her, one way or another, since she was thirteen.

"I shouldn't like to think, Ray-o," Terry had said, the time he nearly caught them at it on the settee, "that you were taking advantage of me."

"No, course not," Raymond stumbled, "nothing like that. Nothing at all. Your Sarah, she's just a kid."

"Got a crush on you, though," Terry had grinned, "Blind not to see that." Raymond had laughed and blushed and nipped out to the kitchen for a couple more beers. Well, he was hardly going to tell his uncle the truth, not the way Terry had looked out for him in the past, stuck up for him even against his own brother, Jackie, Ray-o's old man. Not only that, it was Terry got him a job, working out at the shop he had by Bobber's Mill, managing it more or less, second-hand furniture, stereos, quite a few things that came Terry's way still sealed inside their boxes. Bargain price and no questions asked. Except by the police.

It had been them, Raymond thought, the bastards, Resnick and that lot from Canning Circus, as had made Terry's life a misery, driven him to do what he did. What else? Not money worries, that much seemed certain. And certainly not Eileen, not much more than half Terry's age but with a head on her shoulders, as well as a pair of tits that could earn her several hundred easy at an after-hours lock-in in this pub or that. Eileen up on the bar, eyes half closed, red hair spinning out around her, doing her slow strip to Portishead or Neneh Cherry. Nothing old-fashioned about Eileen.

She was over there now, head bowed, listening to the vicar, no doubt running over what was expected once they'd all gone inside. Eileen, pale faced and serious, her hair died black as a sign of respect. Raymond liked that, admired her for it, that and the way she'd hung around after it had happened, helped the family with the arrangements, sponged off the bedroom walls. Not a lot of women would have had the bottle, Raymond thought, not after watching the bloke you were living with blow his brains out all over the pillow.

Raymond stubbed out his Silk Cut and turned aside as Sarah started to walk towards him, not wanting her to think he'd been watching her, not wanting her to think that he was interested. Sarah leaning a little on her mother's arm, the pair of them back down from Scotland for the funeral. Her mum looking out of it almost before it had begun.

The chapel doors were open now and the mourners starting to edge their way, reluctantly, inside. After you; no, after you. Raymond's dad had been one of the pallbearers along with Norbert Breakshaw and two cousins from Kirkby built like brick shithouses.

"No use asking you, Ray-o, you puny bastard, drop him arse over tip like as not. Ashes, Ray-o, more your mark. Hang about later, youth, see if you can't manage the urn."

Raymond could see his father staring at him now, face sour as last night's piss. Rumour had it his old man had smiled once, summer of ninety-two, but no one had been on hand with a camera to prove it.

"Hope you're not wetting yourself," his father said as Raymond passed, "not on account of Terry's will. Hadn't turned the gun on hisself, most like he'd've come after you with it, once he'd found out what you was up to with his daughter."

Raymond flushed and carried on walking, slow now between the rows of pews. What was his old man on about? Terry, he'd swear, hadn't known a thing, at least not for certain, and who'd have told him different? Sarah herself? Unlikely. Old Ethel? He glanced at the grandmother now, the old woman staring at him from her place at the front of the chapel. Something gouged deep in Raymond's gut and he stumbled, steadying himself against the dark polished wood before sliding along towards the wall.

He hadn't been there two minutes before Sarah left where she was sitting beside her mum, and settled herself down at his side, bold as you like.

"Hello, Ray-o," she said, "how've you been?" And then, whispering. "I've missed you, Ray, you know that, don't you?"

Whatever hymn was being played on the organ wheezed asthmatically to a close and the vicar rose to his feet in the corner pulpit. "We are here to commemorate the life of Terence Albert Cooke…"

Sarah ran the hand not holding the hymnal down along Raymond's thigh and cupped his balls.

Khan and Naylor had stationed themselves some forty yards back from the gates, close enough with a long lens, and a plentiful supply of stone angels to lean on while they went about their business. Several rolls of HP5 aside, they'd armed themselves with flasks of coffee, Naylor's nicely laced; chocolate bars, extra-strong mints and a pair of fine-tuned, police issue binoculars. Naylor, who'd drawn this surveillance often enough before, had pulled on his Marks & Sparks thermals first thing, whereas Khan, cold and virginal in this at least, was fast realising the uselessness of the silk-cotton mix boxers Jill had bought him as anything other than an erotic artifact. Gloves and a tightly wound scarf helped a little, without ever really hitting the spot.

"Why," Khan asked, "couldn't he have had the common decency to top himself in summer?"

"Suicides," Naylor said, shaking his head, "fewer the hours of daylight, more you get." He'd read it somewhere, most likely on the back of a packet of tortilla chips.

There had been four cars at the head of the procession, long and black and hired by the hour, bouquets and wreaths in the first displayed all round the coffin. Then came the grieving relatives, dark suited, sullen, a flotilla of small time crooks and wasters, at least two allowed out on compassionate grounds through the good offices of Her Majesty's prisons.

Trailing in their wake, half a dozen Mercs and BMWs, even an antique Ford Granada with every sign of being Turtle Waxed that very morning. Naylor had phoned in the registrations and they were being checked through the computer. If at least one didn't show up as stolen, he stood to buy Khan a pint of Shippo's and a whisky chaser, large; whoever was it said Asians didn't drink? The same fool, he thought, who put it about Catholics won't eat meat of a Friday.

Once the cars had passed and they were sure there were no stragglers, they shifted position, giving the crematorium a wide berth as they slipped between close rows of gravel and tombstone before setting up with a clear view across a half moon of dodgy lawn and the pruned stems of the memorial rose garden, sighting on the paved area at the rear of the chapel where the flowers would be laid in display.

"That was Cooke's woman," Khan asked, "next to his mum?"

"Eileen. Yes, that was her."

"Nearly didn't recognise her at first."

"With her clothes on, you mean?" Both he and Khan had witnessed more than one of Eileen's performances, strictly in the line of their enquiries.

"No, it's the hair," Khan said. "She's changed the colour of her hair."

"Half-surprised she's here at all," Naylor said. "Now Terry's gone."

"Got her reasons."

Naylor nodded. " I daresay."

They were both thinking about the contents, so far undisclosed, of Terry Cooke's will.

From the building in front of them came the faint, brittle sound of voices raised in praise of the recently departed, while above the roof rose the first wisps of smoke, ash grey against the glowering sky.

Ethel Cooke, mother to Terry and Jackie and several others she'd sooner forget, stood just outside the chapel door, grim faced, straight backed and no more than a handful of days off her seventieth birthday, accepting condolences with a nod of the head while her insides were screaming for a piss. By this stage of her life, Ethel's bladder was as much use as a pint pot in a thunderstorm.

Still inside, Terry's estranged wife, Mary, grabbed Sarah by the sleeve and away from Raymond. She was angry at being upstaged by Ethel but without a quick top up of Temazepam, didn't have the strength to do anything about it. And if that weren't enough, here was her daughter throwing herself at some totally unsuitable bloke like she was a minor royal.

"Hasn't that little prick got you in trouble enough already?" she hissed.

Sarah smarted as if she'd been slapped: trouble was the best thing you could say for it and it pained her to be reminded. She allowed her mother to drag her outside. "You, my girl," Ethel said, stopping Sarah as she made to go past. "You and me, we've got some serious reckoning to do. You know what I mean."

And she stared at Sarah so hard, for an instant the girl swore she could see it, reflected there in the older woman's eyes, her baby, premature, stillborn, cradled inside some old woollens in her bedroom drawer, the buttons she had placed over his eyes before catching the night bus north to Scotland.

"A reckoning, my girl. Once this is over."

Sarah shivered and covered her face with her hands.

A couple of spindly youths, crematorium workers, black suits baggy at the shoulders, short in the legs, shuffled into sight with the flowers.

"What kind of a job is that?" Khan asked.

Naylor took a quick pull at his flask. "Yorkshire Ripper," he said.

"What?"

"Worked in a cemetery. As a kid."

"Where he got his ideas from, you reckon?"

Naylor shrugged. "Who's to say?"

Khan focused the camera and clicked off a couple of shots, just in case. "Hey up," Naylor said, straightening. "Here they come."

A slow coil of mourners appeared from the side of the chapel; the men, unused to sitting so long in cramped surroundings, already reaching for cigarettes in soft-topped packets or slim gold cases, spreading their arms wide, flexing their considerable muscles. Gradually small groups formed and turned inwards with heads bowed; desultory conversations in hushed tones. Only Eileen walked with her head high, moving amongst the others without quite seeming part of them. Naylor, used to Debbie's often sullen stance, the shrewish way she would sometimes screw up her face in imitation of her mother, felt a knot of lust twist inside him like a vice.

"Look," Khan said quietly, pointing, "over to the right, standing with Breakshaw…"

"Frankie Farmer," Naylor said, recognising the man he had twice put an arm lock on, heard the custody sergeant charge with aggravated burglary, seen released by some half-wit judge.

"Right. And isn't that his – I don't know – brother-in-law? Polishing his shoe up the back of his trouser leg."

"Tommy DiReggio."

"Name like that," Khan smiled, "ought to be playing for Chelsea."

"Mansfield," Naylor said, "his kind of form."

They'd never been able to prove it, but the Christmas Eve before last, the occasion of Ethel Cooke's sixty ninth birthday, Tommy had head-butted a man in the face for speaking to the current Mrs DiReggio at the bar, dragged him out back and broken both his arms and one of his legs with a car jack.

Khan paused as the film clicked off and rewound inside the camera, slipping it out into his pocket and sliding the replacement that Naylor handed him neatly into place. The vicar was moving from one group to another, nodding sympathetically and shaking hands, not averse to accepting the odd tenner should anyone feel so moved. Already, one or two were starting to drift off towards their cars. Only when everyone was safely away, would Naylor and Khan move in amongst the lilies and cellophane wrapped roses, examining the black bordered cards with care and copying each of the names down into their notebooks.

At first Ethel had insisted the wake be held at the house, the same one in which she'd raised Terry and Jackie and which Terry had moved back into when that druggie cow of a wife of his fucked off back north of the border where she belonged. It was only a shame, Ethel thought, she hadn't taken that slag of a daughter with her at the time. Instead Sarah had moved into the room along the hall and kept it littered with teddy bears and faceless dolls she'd won at Goose Fair, piles of clothes and tawdry make-up, comics and magazines from which she tore photographs of baby-faced men with hairless chests to stick all over the walls. That wasn't the worst though: that had to wait till Terry convinced Ethel it would be okay for Raymond to have the spare room at the back. Thick as pig shit, Raymond, and still with that smell that lingered on his skin from the time he worked in the abatoir. Family though, mum, Terry had argued, close, you wouldn't want to see him sleeping rough on the street. Besides, a couple of weeks, that's all it'll be. A month at most. Soft sod that she was, Ethel had agreed. And from the first time she saw Sarah, sitting with her skirt hiked up round her waist, licking Raymond all over with her eyes, she knew she'd been wrong.

Wrong about getting everyone back home after the funeral, she'd realised that too and in time. As Jackie had pointed out in no uncertain terms, every time some bastard pops a bottle of champagne, we're all going to be staring up at the ceiling, thinking it's Terry, sticking another one through his brain pan, God bless him.

So they settled for the upstairs room in the local pub instead, lucky to get one so close to Christmas, too. A couple of hundred quid behind the bar to pay for the first few rounds and a nice cold buffet, though she'd put the bar up to cooked meats what with all that e-coli nonsense finishing off pensioners like flies she wasn't about to take any unnecessary chances. Not this close to her seventieth.

Once everyone was nicely oiled, Jackie made a bit of a speech and they all drank a toast to Terry's memory; after which Eileen allowed herself to get more than a little tearful, telling all and sundry how there was nothing Terry liked better when they got to bed of an evening than to take her in his arms and give her a loving cuddle, just like she was a little girl. Well, there were tears at that, you can imagine, and a few raised eyebrows, one or two of the blokes, Norbert Breakshaw especially, voicing what he'd like to do to her instead, given half the chance.

Aside from someone throwing up on the stairs and Sarah's mum locking herself in the ladies, presumably searching for a vein, everything else passed off quietly. Ethel thanked them all for being there to dignify her son's passing; it was only a shame, she said, her Terry hadn't been with them long enough to raise a glass to her on the occasion of her seventieth birthday, that Christmas Eve. And with that she had another brandy and ginger wine and asked Jackie to drive her home. Funeral or no funeral, it was time for her afternoon nap.

Resnick had taken the news of Terry Cooke's death philosophically. Back in those days before he made inspector, there had been evenings when he and Terry had stood shoulder to shoulder at the same bar, trading pints, swapping stories, Resnick filtering truth from lies. It was what you did as a young detective, the company you kept: knowing the enemy. And dangerous. Insidious. Resnick knew of officers who had sunk too far in, drawn by the spurious glamour, the sly offer of a restaurant meal, a case of scotch, front row seats for the fight, a week in Cyprus or the

Algarve, all expenses paid – That girl? The blonde tart over there with the gams? You can have her, no worries. Back to your place, is it, or d'you fancy a hotel?

Compared to other villains Resnick had known, Terry Cooke was affable, a sense of humour, ambitious but not greedy, not vicious either, at least not till near the end. Which was the other side of the coin, the other part of the story. Terry, that last year of his life, with his hands in too many pies, touching stuff he'd have passed on before as too risky, too hot. It was as if, once Eileen had moved in with him, he couldn't make money fast enough. Not that you ever saw the proceeds on her back, around her wrists or neck. No, older man with a woman half his age, Terry felt the need to protect, provide, ensure there was enough there for Eileen if ever anything should happen that meant he couldn't look after her himself.

The result was Terry Cooke's world started to fall apart. The job he set up with his mate, Norbert Breakshaw, went pear shaped, the lads in over their heads, and suddenly there were weapons being waved around and two uniformed police in hospital, touch and go, intensive care. That was just one example. It turned people against Terry, even some of his own kind, and those that might have turned a blind eye were turning it no longer. For a while there were so many dawn raids on Terry's various premises, he stopped bothering to set the alarm. Officers poring all over the house and shop, stripping both places almost down to bare boards, breaking down the doors to the two lock-up garages he used for storing what he optimistically described as surplus stock. Generally making Terry's life a misery.

He felt beleaguered; his mood changed. When he had a tip one of Resnick's regular informers, an old dance band musician named Ronnie Rather, had grassed him up, Terry lost it in a way he never had before, beat Ronnie within an inch of his life and left him in a wheelchair, sightless in one eye.

Resnick and Ronnie had been close – as close as you can allow yourself to get to a snout – and when he heard that Terry had topped himself, Resnick kept what had happened clearly in mind, a corrective to any excessive sympathy he might otherwise have been feeling.

Young Eileen, though – the story was she was in bed alongside Terry when a single .38 shell redistributed Terry Cooke's skull to various parts of the room. Resnick had spoken to Eileen several times in the weeks leading up to Terry's death; nothing ostentatious, out of the way, Resnick encouraging Eileen to talk about how she felt, which was trapped in a situation that was making her increasingly uneasy and wanted to make a break, yet scared to try. Resnick wasn't working for Relate: not pushing it too hard, he encouraged her to leave, suggesting ways in which she might put some space between herself and Terry and assist the police at the same time.

Thinking about it now, Resnick wondered if there was any way Terry might have known what was going on, sensed it at least, felt something changing in Eileen the way you did when you were very close.

Maybe someone had seen them together, Resnick and Eileen, and reported back. It wouldn't have been so hard for Terry to have slotted two and two together; not a stupid man, and not without his sensitive side.

Resnick even wondered if at any point the gun Terry Cooke had stashed beneath his pillow that night had ever been intended for Eileen and not himself.

He would never know. He stood up, stretched, and

poured himself a drink. Not for the first time, he had come up lucky in the Christmas sweep; a bottle of Bushmills and a Melton Mowbray pork and chicken pie. Through the window at the side of his office, he could look out over the tall Victorian mansions of the Park, windows glittering with Christmas trees and coloured lights. In the Old Market Square, revellers would be winding themselves up for the Great Event, singing carols and getting drunk. Like as not, the late night buses home to Bulwell or the Broxtowe Estate would be awash with seasonal good will.

Glass in hand, Resnick looked again at the photographs spread out across the desk, those Naylor and Khan had taken at the funeral. Faces he expected; some he didn't. Coughlan, for instance. Hadn't he and the Cooke clan had a falling out? Resnick knew for a fact, but, of course, had no useful way of proving it beyond reasonable doubt, that Coughlan had three times used a shotgun in the commission of a crime. Resnick wondered who Coughlan's prime source of weapons was now. And there was Tommy DiReggio, another certifiable hard case, shaking hands with one of the Malloy brothers from Kirkby, though whether it was the one who worked as a bouncer or the brother who toured the country as a fairground boxer, Resnick couldn't be sure.

What he did know was Terry Cooke's sudden and unexpected death had left a considerable vacuum waiting to be filled. Left money, too, quite a slice by all accounts. Property, too. But to whom? He glanced again at the photographs – all those back of the hand conversations, deals being struck, incipient betrayals, new liaisons being planned. Time to keep a watchful eye, Resnick thought, stay poised on the perimeter, ready to move in fast when the time was ripe; with any luck they'd be on hand to staunch a few more self-inflicted wounds, mop up whatever blood got spilt.

Ethel dozed a little watching *EastEnders*, woke herself up with a port and lemon, slipped her teeth back into place and shouted Sarah down from her room. The girl stood with eyes downcast, head over to one side, as if expecting to be slapped.

And Ethel, looking at her, a child really, no matter what traps her body had set for her and the foolhardy ways she had tumbled into them, surprised herself by feeling something close to sympathy. After all, in her own youth she had been no stranger to the sins the flesh is heir to, although all that was far behind her now.

Hastily, she willed all such feelings away, much as she had when, searching for some old wool to unpick and reuse, she had come upon the scrap of skin and bones and never breathing flesh Sarah had run off and abandoned. Much like that.

"You listen to me, my girl, and listen good. I want this clear. You and me, no one else needs to know. But you got yourself knocked up, I'd guess by that wastrel Ray-o, though I'd not have reckoned him to have spunk enough to sire a weasel, hid it from the rest of us, from your own family, dropped it early, poor little bastard, stillborn like as not, and left it like it was so much offal on a plate."

Sarah made as if to speak, then curled her fist against her mouth instead.

"I'm not here to judge," Ethel said. "What's done's, done and it's no use pretending anything else. But you have to know, what I did, clearing up for you, protecting you, lying to my poor dead son, that'll live with me the rest of my misbegotten days. You understand?"

Sarah nodded, an almost imperceptible movement of her head.

"I need you to acknowledge that."

"Yes, gran."

"And pay me back."

Sarah started, screwing up her face.

"Whatever else my Terry was," Ethel said, "he was softer than pig shit where the likes of that Eileen were concerned. You, too, though sometimes he might not have shown it. Even that sorry specimen, Ray-o. So come tomorrow, the reading of the will, it won't be the likes of Norbert Breakshaw or those fat bastards from Kirkby as'll be rubbing their hands like they'd won the lottery. And it won't be me, either. You're the one who'll be sitting pretty, you see. You and Eileen, both."

Ethel moved faster than Sarah could anticipate, faster than a woman of her age had any right. The grip she had on Sarah's wrist was like a vice.

"You're going to promise to see me right, anything and everything you can. I want to carry on living here, in this house till they carry me out, and I never want to have to worry about opening that purse of mine and finding it empty. You understand?" Sarah winced. "Yes, gran," she said, little above a whisper.

"Again."

"Yes, gran. I promise."

"Right." And smiling, Ethel released the girl's arm and turned back around; another port and lemon and then she'd be ready for an early night. One thing and another, it had been a tiring few days.

If Ethel had ever hankered after a second career, one more in the line of Original Famous Gipsy Rose Lees who scattered themselves the length and breadth of the land, reading palms, tea leaves and crystal balls and telling fortunes, she would have shot to the top of her profession. Anyone might have thought – and a few did – that she had seen her boy Terry's will before it came to be signed and sealed.

But there in the solicitor's office, a cold December afternoon with the frost still edging the window panes, she sat still and impassive as Cleopatra's needle, listening as Declan Travis intoned the terms of Terence Cooke's testament. Close alongside her, Terry's brother, Jackie, nudged at his moustache with his bottom lip and occasional wriggled his finger back and forth inside a collar one size too tight. Elaine, a new black coat open over what looked suspiciously like a new black dress, sat well to one side, a Kleenex in her hand, anticipating tears. Sarah, the only other clear potential benefactor, was bundled up in a fake fur she had borrowed from her mum, gazing at the polished beech floor and sniffling back what sounded like a dreadful cold.

"No use you wasting your time there," Raymond's dad had said. "Only thing Terry'd leave you'd be a boot up your backside."

So Raymond spent the afternoon in the shop as usual, listening to the Spice Girls on Radio Trent.

"…all of the properties listed above," the solicitor read, "including such of their contents as are mine to dispose of, in addition to the total amounts remaining, after necessary expenses, in my various bank and building society accounts, also listed hitherto, I bequeath in equal amounts to my daughter, Sarah Jane Cooke…"

Sarah squealed and came close to having a little personal accident.

"...and my common law wife, Elaine Patricia Pendleton."

Elaine let slip a controlled sigh and recrossed one slender but athletic leg over the other.

"This on the understanding that the aforementioned Elaine Patricia Pendleton will control and administer that which I have bequeathed to my daughter until her eighteenth birthday."

The solicitor stopped, coughed into the back of his hand, and looked around. "What you tellin' us?" Jackie Cooke demanded. "That's it? That's soddin' it?"

Declan Travis raised a hand. "There is a codicil."

"I should fuckin' hope so," said Jackie, leaning back again in his chair.

"With respect to the lock-up shop in Bobber's Mill, Mr Cooke has requested that his nephew, Raymond, continue to be employed there in the position of manager until such time as he himself wishes to leave."

"That's it?" Jackie said, heaving himself to his feet. "That's fuckin' it?"

"I'll speak with Ray-o," Eileen said. "Find out what he wants to do. You never know, he might want to take the chance to move on elsewhere."

"Bloody dole," Jackie said, standing behind his mother's chair. "That's the only place that poor git's fit for movin' on to."

"Come on, Jackie," Ethel said, rising. "We're through here. You can give me a lift home." And to Eileen, almost without pause for breath, "Seeing as you're babysitting my granddaughter's money, Miss High and Mighty, you'd best find out from her what we already agreed between us. Before you spend it all for her."

❐

Resnick waited around the corner until Raymond had unlocked the metal shutters guarding the shop front and heaved them from sight. Time enough for him to become absorbed in a familiar routine. The youth was midway through rocking a king size fridge-freezer out onto the pavement, when he saw Resnick walking towards him and nearly let go of the appliance, narrowly avoiding blackening several toes.

"Now then, Ray-o," Resnick said, adopting the avuncular approach. "Anything I can do to give you a hand?"

"No way, Mr Resnick. I'm fine. Thanks all the same."

"Just so long as you're sure. Not want to see you causing yourself an injury. Not now you're nicely settled."

"Settled, Mr Resnick?" Sweat was palpable on Raymond's upper lip.

"Uncle Terry. Fond of you he was. You'll have done nicely out of the will, I shouldn't wonder."

Raymond stammered and invited Resnick inside; he didn't fancy talking family business out there, arse to the wind. Within twenty minutes, Resnick knew it all. All there was to know. When Terry Cooke had moved into Ethel's house, he had taken over responsibility for the mortgage and paid it off eighteen months back, but in his own name; the premises they were standing in, shop and flat above, were owned outright, and the two lock-up garages held firm on a ninety nine year lease. At the accountant's final reckoning, the cash value accruing from Terry Cooke's various accounts was close to the seventy five thousand mark after death duties and tax. Pounds, Raymond? Not ECU?"

"Eh?"

"Forget it." Resnick picked up a Black and Decker power drill and surveyed the bit. "Who was it said, Raymond, crime didn't pay?"

"Crime?"

"Just a figure of speech, think nothing of it." Resnick pushed past Raymond on his way towards a wayward pile of old 78s, balanced on top of a Zanussi washing machine, which, unlike the records, had the appearance of being alarmingly new. "How's your dad taken all this, then?" Resnick asked. "Put out a shade, I shouldn't wonder. And then there's all the old crowd him and Terry used to run with. Norbert, of course. Tommy DiReggio. Coughlan, too." Resnick smiled benignly. "Nasty temper, Coughlan. I doubt he's the kind who'd take well to being left out in the cold."

Raymond was shifting his weight from one foot to the other like someone whose Y-fronts have suddenly shrunk several sizes too tight. "Coughlan," he tried, "I don't think him and me Uncle Terry spoke for months."

"At the funeral, though, wasn't he, Ray-o. There to pay his respects. Collect his due."

"I don't know, I..."

"This lot here, Raymond," Resnick said, lifting the uppermost disc towards him and blowing a skein of surface dust carefully away. "Kettelby. 'In a Monastery Garden'. You'll not get much of a price for this kind of thing, I'll wager."

"Take them, Mr Resnick," Raymond exclaimed gratefully. "Take them all. The lot. Yours for free."

Smiling, Resnick reached inside his overcoat and brought out his wallet. "Can't do that, Raymond. Generous as it is. I mean, just imagine how it might look. Senior police officer accepting gifts. Just not on."

Peeling off a pair of fivers, he pushed them into Raymond's unwilling hand. "If there's some kind of a box you could put them in, maybe you'd not mind carrying them out to the car."

Where Raymond was concerned, it was destined to be that kind of a day. No sooner was he back from the local café with a can of Coke and a sausage bap, removing the 'Back in Ten Minutes' sign from the window, than Frankie Farmer and Tommy DiReggio arrived, the pair of them, seeking to establish that as far as Ray-o was concerned, if they should lay their sticky hands on anything movable from lead piping all the way up the line to a score of boxed and unbooted Dell Dimension XPS P133 computers with an extra 16 megabytes of SDRAM memory, then he would be happy to oblige them at the same competitive rates as before.

Raymond assured them that he would. No chance, he asked, of you offloading a couple of those computers this side of Christmas?

One of the Malloy brothers was next – Raymond thought it was the prizefighter, but he wasn't sure and didn't like to ask – stopping by to ask more or less the same question. Raymond guessed he wouldn't be the last. For himself, he couldn't see why they were all getting so wound up, business as usual, surely they could all see the sense in that? But it irked him, the way each and every one of his uncle's old mates were getting in these little digs at one another, expecting him to favour one of them over the rest. Even his dad had been round to slip in his ten pence worth, offering advice where it wasn't wanted. Best thing they could do, Raymond thought, was grow up, the lot of them. Start acting like businessmen instead of extras from some rip-off Tarantino movie – Mr Crap and Mr Shite. Chill out.

It was Sarah last, something bright and agitated about her as if she'd dropped an E before leaving the house. All over Raymond, wanting to know what was he doing after closing. Why didn't he shut up shop now, he was his own boss, wasn't he? No one looking over his shoulder. How about a drink, Ray-o? Let's go up the pub. A curry. Clubbing later. How about it, Ray-o, eh? Eh? Her tongue was quick between his teeth and she had only to reach inside his jeans for him to come in her hand.

They paid court to Eileen, too. Norbert Breakshaw sent flowers, Frankie and Tommy a bottle of pink champagne. Coughlan was waiting for her when she left work, a private party in the conference room of some small hotel on the Mansfield Road, the kind with ideas above its station. A couple of hundred for an hour's work, schoolgirl first and then the nurse; uniforms, they went down a treat. She picked out Coughlan straight off, leaning against a Jag like it was rightfully his.

"Hop in, I'll give you a lift."

Eileen pointed at the waiting taxi. "I'm all right, thanks."

"Hop in."

She opened the cab door. "No, it's fine."

Coughlan reached into the rear of his car and when he straightened there was a sawn-off shotgun in his hands. The taxi driver found first faster than Damon Hill and Elaine was left standing, make-up bag in one hand, week-end case holding her costumes in the other.

He didn't take her straight home; first one drinking club and then another. When she asked for mineral water, he brought her a large gin. When he caught her pouring the bulk of it into a plastic plant pot, he slapped her round the face and no one in the place, crowded as it was, moved to stop him.

"Scared?" he asked, hand high up on her thigh. "Frightened?"

"No."

"You stupid tart, you fucking should be."

Outside the house, Terry's house, as she still thought of it, Eileen waited to see if Coughlan would switch off the engine, follow her in, weighing up in her mind what she would do if he did. But what he did was light a cigarette and sit there, smelling faintly of drink.

"Your Terry," he said finally, "I suppose you think he was pretty big?"

Eileen pushed open the car door and swung one foot onto the pavement.

"I'll tell you this, he was nothing. No ambition. Small time. Terry and all those arsewipes he wasted his time with. You and me, we can do better." He had hold of her arm this time, fingers digging in. "Stuff he would have shat himself silly just thinking about. You know what I'm saying? My connections. Your money. That bundle he left you, eighteen months we'll double it. Treble. You got my word." Still holding her arm with one hand, he reached across with the other and squeezed her breast.

Eileen stared back into his face and gave him nothing, no expression, no word. "Run along," he said.

Eileen closed the car door quietly, made herself walk slowly to the front door, reaching for her keys. Half way up the stairs, she leaned against the bannister and hugged herself till the blood ceased to flow, head resting forward against the smooth paleness of polished wood.

Outside, enclosed in the darkness of his brother-in-law Frankie's Sierra, Tommy DiReggio watched it all unfold. Coughlan and Eileen, he could see the way it was going to be. Unless he and Frankie took steps of their own.

What he didn't see, at the opposite end of the street, binoculars trained through the rear windows of a battered transit van, was Khan and Naylor, watching him.

❐

Resnick took Ronnie Rather half of his family size Melton Mowbray pie, a few bottles of Worthington White Shield, Ronnie's favourite, and the remaining third of the Black Bush. He also took a present, wrapped in bright green paper peppered with crimson Santas and silver stars. It was a little after eight o'clock on Christmas Eve.

The last he'd heard from Kevin Naylor, on obs near the Cooke house, there seemed to be a party going on inside. Late that afternoon, one of the florists from the market had delivered a couple of dozen roses, followed swiftly by a baker's and confectioner's van, from the back of which a ginger-haired youth in a white apron carried a cake thick with pink and white icing. And candles. There was a lull then till early evening, when Sarah and her mother made a run for the corner shop and returned with several six-packs of lager. After that it was Eileen, carrying what might have been wine, Jackie Cooke with a giant card in a pale blue envelope and finally Raymond, hands in pockets, whistling.

Perhaps, Resnick thought, they'd finish up with a family excursion to midnight mass.

He poured Ronnie a beer, careful not to tip in the sediment lurking at the bottom of the bottle, set a generous slice of pie on a plate, adding a pickled onion from the bottle in Ronnie's cupboard and a forkful of Branston pickle. He was glad to see Ronnie wasn't living by meals on wheels alone, although from the light that came into his one good eye whenever he mentioned Cheryl, who delivered his pre-cooked lunches wearing one of a selection of brightly coloured leisure suits, Resnick could tell they were playing an increasingly important part in his life.

After a while, Resnick pointed at the parcel he had placed on the table. "Open it for me, Charlie, will you?"

So Resnick cut the string and folded back the paper, revealing the half a dozen gems he had uncovered amongst the recordings of Joan Hammond and Josef Locke, 'Count Your Blessings' by the Luton Girls Choir and Flanagan and Allen crooning 'Run, Rabbit, Run'.

"By God, Charlie. Where ever d'you turn up these?"

One by one, Resnick settled the prize 78s onto the old gramophone and together they sat back and listened to the music of Benny Goodman, Artie Shaw and Tommy Dorsey, 'Clarinet a la King', 'Begin the Beguine' and 'Getting Sentimental Over You', Ronnie Rather playing along with the trombone parts inside his head. He was sliding through 'Opus One', note by note with Dorsey, when Resnick's mobile sounded. Khan's voice was clear and to the point. Shots had been heard from inside the house, people were injured, the armed response unit was on its way. Not Midnight Mass then, Resnick thought, after all.

❐

The roads were icy and Resnick drove quickly but with care. By the time he arrived, the street was cordoned off at both ends, the Cooke house spotlit and surrounded, armed officers kneeling in front gardens and stretched out along the rooftops opposite. Tommy DiReggio, bleeding heavily from a shotgun wound to the groin and barely conscious, was being stretchered to a waiting ambulance by paramedics. Frankie Farmer was being treated inside a second ambulance, having received a glancing flesh wound to the shoulder. Somehow, in the fracas, Raymond had stabbed himself in the hand with a knife. On the far side of the street, Sarah and her mum were pleading with another of the paramedics for tranquillizers. Jackie Cooke sat on the kerb, numbed, drinking tea.

Khan and Naylor were standing to the rear of one of several police vehicles, hands jammed down into pockets, breath bright and silvery on the air. Close beside them, the officer in charge of the Armed Response team was communicating with his marksmen, a negotiator with a man's uniformed topcoat belted over her ball gown, was talking over a mobile telephone to someone inside the house.

"Who's still inside?" Resnick asked.

"Coughlan," Naylor said. "Locked himself in one of the bedrooms, upstairs, front. Injured, we don't know how bad."

"Anybody else?"

"The old lady and Eileen. That's her we're talking to now."

Resnick looked across at the house and nodded. "Fill me in on what happened. "Ten thirty," Naylor began, "thereabouts, Farmer and DiReggio drove up and went inside. They were carrying what looked like bottles, so we thought, you know, they were there for the party."

"We now have reason to believe," Khan said, "what one of them was carrying was a gun. One, at least."

"Go on."

"How long," came the negotiator's voice from behind them. "since you heard his voice?"

"Just past eleven," Naylor said, "Coughlan arrived. Jackie Cooke came to the door and tried to stop him getting in. After that, it all happened pretty fast. Farmer and DiReggio got in on the act and there were punches left and centre. Eileen comes out and takes Coughlan to one side, reasoning with him. Looks like she's calmed him down, because he's walking back to his car. Elaine ushers the rest back inside. Only Coughlan doesn't drive away. Instead he comes up with a shotgun, fires at the front of house and then he's in through the front door."

"Three more shots after that," Khan said. "Possibly four."

The negotiator took a pace towards Resnick, telephone held against her side. "Eileen's spoken to Coughlan. He wants to give himself up."

Resnick and the Armed Response officer exchanged glances.

"Have your men got him covered?" Resnick asked.

"Three times over."

"Eileen," the negotiator said into the telephone, "tell him to open the window wide, hand the weapon outside, holding it by the barrel, and drop it down into the garden. By the barrel, okay?"

There was silence as the curtain across the street moved a fraction to one side, fell back, then moved again; abruptly, a side window jerked open and a moment later the shotgun appeared, butt end first.

"Chuck it," Khan said, to no one but himself.

Coughlan let the weapon fall and before it had reached the ground the first armed man was through the door.

What extra personnel could be spared from supervising the celebrations in the city centre were helping to take statements, recover physical evidence. Oblivious or exhausted, Ethel Cooke had retired to her bed.

Resnick found Eileen in the back garden, wearing no coat despite the icy cold. "Are you okay?"

"I'll be fine."

"You'll have to make a statement later."

She nodded. "I understand."

"You did well. Kept your head."

An orange glow dulled the night sky that was otherwise bright with stars.

"Why don't you come back inside?" Resnick asked. "You'll catch a chill."

Eileen shook her head. "Sarah told me something, earlier. I didn't know whether to believe it or not. Turning, she looked him in the eye. "I think I do," she said. And then she told him what it was.

Resnick slipped off his coat and put it around her shoulders and she trembled lightly at his touch. Then he called in Khan and Naylor and issued new instructions. Made a call for reinforcements.

After almost two hours of shifting heavy furniture, stripping wallpaper, prising up boards, one of the officers called Resnick's name. The tiny skeleton, less than a foot long, had been buried beneath the back room floor, wrapped in swathe after swathe of newspaper, then tied around with string.

There was a light still shining in Ethel Cooke's room and Resnick knocked and waited, wondering what he might say. Happy birthday? Merry Christmas? The words froze on his lips.

My Little Suede Shoes

"So WHAT do you think about it, Charlie?"

"What?"

"The Millennium."

"Not a lot."

What Resnick thought: I shall be two years older.

They were heading back from lunch at the house of some friends of Hannah's in Southwell, a former art teacher who'd jacked it all in to restore furniture and support his partner who made batik wall hangings. Resnick's stomach was still celebrating the collocation of tofu lasagna and home-made parsnip wine. Hannah was driving. Her friends, Dermot and Belinda, were convinced the Millennium would bring about a positive change in the way people felt about the world's ecology; they could already sense it in the atmosphere.

"I was talking to Trevor Lynton about it," Hannah said. "You know, from Leisure Services."

Resnick didn't think he did.

"Seems there's all kinds of plans – fireworks in the Old Market Square, decorated barges on the Trent, lasers lighting up the sky from a dozen high points all around the county. The one I liked best, though, a giant hologram of Robin Hood across the top of Colwick Wood."

"Lottery funding, all this then?" Resnick asked. "Or straight out the Council Tax?"

Hannah, for whom the idea of celebration, almost any kind of celebration, was a positive thing, accelerated into the centre lane, rounding a maroon Rover towing a caravan and ducking back not so many feet short of a Ford Sierra heading in the opposite direction. Resnick managed not to say a thing.

"I wonder," Hannah said, several miles closer to the city, "what we'll be doing, that New Year, Charlie? I wonder if we'll be seeing it in together."

"Can see Colwick Wood, you know," Resnick said, trying for a smile. "Patch of waste ground at the end of the street."

Hannah switched the wipers on to meet the first fall of rain. "Trevor," she said, "he asked me to see it in with him."

"Sherry party at the Council House, that'll be," Resnick said.

"Condominium in the Virgin Islands."

He turned his head to see if she were serious.

"Those competitions, on the back of frozen food packets, gourmet pickle, something like that. Seems he won first prize. A Millennium holiday for two."

"And he asked you?"

"He's been onto me to go out with him the best part of three years."

"Bit extreme for a first date, isn't it? The Virgin Islands."

"The best he could come up with before was cocktails in the Penthouse Bar at the Royal, followed by a dinner dance at the Commodore. At least this time he's got me giving it some serious thought."

Trevor Lynton, Resnick was thinking, perhaps he did know him after all. Blue braces and spray-on stubble; waved his hands about like he'd just taken a course in semaphore. Not thirty-five if he was a day.

As Freddy McGregor was fond of saying, any performer who doesn't work New Year's Eve might just as well be dead. And, as Freddy would have been the first to admit, there had been some close calls: the year he'd found himself stranded on the Isle of Man without his costume or the price of a ferry ticket to the mainland; the time the Pier Theatre in Hunstanton had burned down, taking his last chance to play Buttons along with it; worst of all, nineteen ninety four, when he had lost his footing clambering over a greasy upper storey window ledge and broken one of his legs – the ward sister had finally agreed to let him sing 'O Solé Mio' from a makeshift stage on top of the linen cupboard, and Freddy had encored with 'Crying in the Chapel' and 'Auld Lang Syne', the nurses blubbing into their blue uniform sleeves.

Already it was late October and he was getting decidedly edgy. Calls to his agent yielded half-formed promises or, increasingly, the blank charm of the answerphone; pubs and clubs which had previously welcomed Freddy with open arms and used tenners, slotting him in amongst their regular array of strippers and comedians, now simply didn't want to know. Plans for a fifty date Solid Silver Sixties revival tour broke down at the last moment, denying Freddy the chance to strut his stuff at the Flower Pot in

Derby, the Regal Centre, Worksop, the Beaufort Theatre, Ebbw Vale. Even the landlord of the Old Vic, where Freddy had long been a regular star of Saturday Night Music Hall, took him to one side and wondered gently whether it wasn't time for him to find another line of work. "Let's face it, Freddy, there's just so many times you can persuade the punters to shell out for a four-foot Elvis in a white satin suit, even if it is an exact replica of the one he wore in Las Vegas. Scaled down, of course." And he slipped a crisp twenty into Freddy's top pocket and patted him on the head.

Patronising bastard, Freddy thought, crossing Fletcher Gate towards the car park. And besides, I've already got another line of work. Why else would I break a leg falling from a second-storey bathroom window?

Most times when Resnick and Hannah had been out together, one or the other, usually Hannah, would pose the traditional question, your place or mine? Once in a while, Hannah, especially if she were driving, would take Resnick's answer as read and head for her place in Lenton without bothering to ask the question. But this particular Sunday, again without asking, she took a left at Mapperley Top towards the Woodborough Road and Resnick's house.

Dizzy, the largest and the fiercest of Resnick's four cats, stared at them from the stone wall, flexing his claws. Hannah sat with one hand resting on the wheel, engine idling.

"You're not coming in?" Resnick said.

"No, I don't think so."

"Quick cup of coffee? Tea?"

"I ought to be getting back."

Clicking open the car door, Resnick suppressed a sigh. "Are you okay?"

"I'm fine."

Her cheek, when he kissed her, was marble against his mouth.

Dizzy wound between Resnick's legs as he walked towards the front door, pushed his head against Resnick's shin as he fidgeted for the key. Behind them, Hannah pulled away a little too fast, shifting through the gears as she turned the narrow corner and accelerated towards the main road.

When he woke it was a little after five, wind rattling the window frames. Bud, as usual, lay with his head close to the edge of Resnick's pillow, one paw folded across his eyes. Miles and Pepper were curled in a black and grey ball near the foot of the bed, impossible to tell at a glance where one began, the other ended. Dizzy, Resnick knew, would be within reach of the rear door, chewing over whatever prey the night had providentially provided.

In the depths of the house, he heard pipes rumble and stir as the central heating came awake. How far from winter, Resnick wondered? Black ice on the roads and mornings that defied the light; storm warnings on the shipping forecast, severe gales force 9, northeasterly winds becoming cyclonic all the way from Cromarty to German Bight.

He massaged lather deep into his hair, stood with head tilted back, letting the water spray across his face and chest. Quickly dressed, he fed the cats, depositing first Dizzy's ritual offering of rodent rump inside the bin. Buttering toast, he toyed with the idea of phoning Hannah before she left for work, but pleasantries aside, had no idea what to say. The first cup of coffee he drank standing up, the second he took into the living room, where the previous evening's *Post* remained unread.

A series of break-ins at late-night chemists in Aspley, Meden Vale and Selston; a children's playground vandalised in Keyworth; two Asian youths attacked on the last bus to Bestwood by a gang of more than twenty; several people injured, two seriously, when a fight broke out during an American Line Dancing evening at Tollerton Methodist Church Hall.

Resnick folded the paper and carried it through to join the ever-growing pile awaiting recycling in the hall. One of these days, he'd throw them in the back of the car, drop them off on his way to work, but not today. The traffic was beginning to build up as he passed the roundabout where Gregory Boulevard met the Mansfield Road and Sherwood Rise.

The station where his CID squad was based sat just east of the city centre, squarely between the affluence of the Park Estate and the down-at-heel terraces either side of the Alfreton Road. The kettle was boiling away in an empty CID room, Resnick's sergeant, Graham Millington, peering into the mirror in the Gents, counting the grey hairs in his moustache.

Resnick flipped open the folder the officer on first call had left on his desk and thumbed through the night's incident reports: sometimes it was easy to believe the houses on Tattershall Drive and around Lincoln Circus were as heavily targeted as Dresden or Hamburg during the last World War.

"Anything on this last batch of break-ins, Graham?" Resnick asked, hearing Millington's cheery rendition of 'Frosty the Snowman'. Millington whistling early for Christmas.

"Nothing as yet," the sergeant said, adding one for the pot, "Kev's down there now. Back entry, though, all accounts. Fire escape, drainpipe, neighbour's balcony, you know the kind of thing."

On his return, an hour later, Kevin Naylor filled them in. Eight burglaries in all, two neat batches of four, nicely professional. Cash, credit cards, cheque books, jewellery – a couple of Rolex watches worth a week of Ravanelli's wages, his and hers. Nothing that wouldn't fit into a set of well-lined pockets.

"Someone flying solo?" Resnick asked.

Naylor shook his head. "Pair of them, sir. One to gain entry – bathroom window, that seems favourite – lets in his oppo, ten minutes later, fifteen tops, they're back out the front door."

"These windows," Resnick said, "ground level?"

Another shake of the head. "Not a one. And small with it. Any of us, not get our head and shoulders through, never mind the rest."

"Kids, then?" Millington said.

"Don't think so, serge. Too clean, no mess. Quiet, too. All but one, occupied. Slept right through."

"What was that father and son team, Graham?" Resnick asked. "Edwalton, Lady Bay – maybe shifted ground."

"Used to boost the lad up on his shoulders, I know who you mean. Regular couple of acrobats. Rydale, some such name."

"Risdale."

"Risdale, that's it. Paul?"

"Peter."

"Peter. Made his boy, Stephen, run five miles every morning, fed him fish and chicken. White meat. Leaner'n a whippet and about as fast."

"Back on remand, is he? Youth detention?"

Millington stroked his moustache. "Easy enough to

check. Won't hurt to give Risdale a pull, any road. Nothing to say he's not been down the job centre, found himself a replacement."

"Good." Resnick was on his feet. "Kevin, best get the details of those credit cards circulated; unlikely, but check if Scene of Crime fetched up anything by way of prints. And it might be worth a word with the home beat officer – might be time for another circular, see if we can't encourage a few more people to keep their windows locked nights."

"Right."

Resnick nodded and looked at his watch. After the meeting with his DS, there was one line of enquiry he'd follow up on his own.

Freddy had been busy since mid-morning, cold-calling bookers and agencies, club and pub managers within a fifty mile radius, anyone with a music licence and half a square metre of stage. Now it was scarcely short of one o'clock and all he'd to show was a kids' party at Snape Wood Road Community Centre and a silver wedding at the Salvation Army Citadel, Main Street, Bulwell. After fifteen minutes haggling, Freddy had promised the proprietor of a new burger bar in Ilkeston that he'd get back to him about performing on the pavement outside to mark the opening, one number every quarter hour, ten a.m. till closing. And he was still waiting for a call back himself from the events organiser at the Rotherham Transport Club, Masborough – we'd love to have you, Freddy, you know we would, but not all that old Elvis, you've got to come with something different, something new. An angle. Find a way to work the Spice Girls in somewhere and then we'd be talking...

Freddy lit the last of his king size and squeezed another half mug of tea from the same bag. It was all very well for someone stuck behind a desk to rattle on about trying something new. Over the years he'd tried them all – Laurie London, Little Jimmy Osmond, Michael Jackson with a full-out Afro and a kiddie voice singing that love song to a rat; once even Little Stevie Wonder, which had been fine until he'd fallen off the front of the stage doing 'Fingertips', unable to see where he was going through the dark glasses.

But no matter what anyone said, none of them worked as well as his Elvis Aaron Presley – the first of Freddy's pre-recorded tapes blaring out into the darkness and then the spotlight catching him from the waist down as his hips began to swivel, his little pelvis to gyrate, black leather trousers, blue suede shoes. A medley of 'Hound Dog', 'Jailhouse Rock' and 'Don't Be Cruel', slow things down with 'Heartbreak Hotel', whip them up again with 'King Creole'. A break then for the strip show or the bingo and Freddy would be back in his shiny white jump suit, perspiration, get some of that chest hair showing, 'Suspicious Minds', 'Burning Love', 'Are You Lonesome Tonight?' and the audience can't help but sing along, then for his encore what else but 'Blue Suede Shoes' itself.

How could it fail? How could he go wrong?

The phone rang and he lifted the receiver on the second ring. "Derek, I knew you'd come round."

"Fuck Derek, you short-arsed little cunt, it's Clayton. I'm in the back bar of the Portland Arms and if you're not here by the time I've downed this pint I'll take those excuses for legs of yours off at the knees."

Clayton Kanellopoulos was the thirty-nine-year-old son of a Scottish mother, a Greek Cypriot father; his family had happily owned a succession of greasy spoons and gentlemen's hairdressers, brother to brother, cousin to cousin, generation to generation: it had taken Clayton to break the mould. He had started out pimping for a string of scrawny girls in North London, got to know each nook and cranny of the Holloway Road, the Cali like the back of his proverbial hand. After that a spell of enforcing for a loan shark in Edmonton, till one razor stripe too many sent him scurrying north for safety. Leicester, Nottingham, Sheffield, Derby. Clayton settled down to an early middle-age of breaking and entering.

"Freddy, what kept you?"

"How d'you mean? I got here just as fast…"

"I know, fast as fat little midgets can go."

"I'm not…"

"What?" One grasp of the hand, and Clayton had Freddy firmly by the balls. "Not what?"

"It don't matter."

"Fat? Not fat?"

"Yeah, that's right." Freddy wincing with the pain.

With a laugh Clayton let go his hold and, tears blinking at the corners of his eyes, Freddy sat himself down.

"Not fancy a half?" Clayton asked, gesturing towards the bar. "Maybe a short?"

Freddy shook his head.

All business now, Clayton leaned in close. "I thought what you and me had was a deal?"

Knees clenched close together, not too close, Freddy's mind was racing into overdrive. "We do, Clayton, so we do."

"Then tell me it weren't you, did all them places up the Park?"

"When?"

"You know all too fuckin' well when."

The bone inside Freddy's left leg began to sing; the last

time he'd gone in for a bit of B&E in the Park, he'd ended up on his back in Queen's. "Not down to me, you got my word."

"Who then?"

All Freddy could do was shrug.

Clayton stared him down a while longer before stretching back and lighting a small cigar with a match that he flicked against the front of Freddy's shirt. "All right, this weekend coming. Sat'day night. I got a job."

Freddy fingered anxiously the ring on the pinkie finger of his right hand. "I can't." The words only just carried across the small space between them.

"Sorry? I could've sworn you said…"

"Clayton, any other time, any other night. Even if you'd asked me – what? – an hour earlier, everything would have been fine. But I've got this booking, Saturday, all agreed. No way I can let them down, you got to see that, no earthly way…" Freddy's voice fading now, words failing him as he watched the broad planes of Clayton's face break into a smile.

Resnick had phoned Hannah mid-morning, knowing full-well that she would be out and leaving a message on her answerphone: hope everything's okay, maybe if you've got a minute when you get in, you'll give me a call.

Immediately after that paperwork claimed him, quarterly crime figures to be checked and okayed before passing on to the Detective Chief Inspector of CID downtown. It was almost two before he crossed Canning Circus to the deli and bought a brace of brie and ham sandwiches and a large black coffee to go. The lunchtime traffic had thinned enough for him to be in the upper reaches of Carlton in time to catch Freddy McGregor just back from the

Portland Arms and still looking a touch anxious around the gills.

"Mr Resnick..." Freddy thinking one shock was enough for one day, one unwelcome interview; though he had no reason to believe Resnick was the sort to use force – not like some of his compatriots – Freddy covered himself instinctively, both hands cupped in front of his crotch as if anticipating a Psycho Pearce free kick.

Without exactly being invited, Resnick found himself inside the living room of Freddy's ground floor flat: posters advertising *Freddy McGregor, the Miniature Elvis* vied for wall space with pictures of the man himself, snarling from the stage of the Mississipi-Alabama Fair in Tupelo in 1956, thoughtfully biting his thumbnail in an off-set still from *Loving You*. Underneath the latter, Freddy had neatly written out one of the lines Presley spoke in the film –

"That's how you're selling me, isn't it? A monkey in a zoo. Isn't that what you want?"

Freddy hovered nervously, watching Resnick's face.

"Working, Freddy?" Resnick eventually said.

"Oh, you know, bits and pieces here and there. Mustn't grumble, Mr. Resnick, you know how it is."

"Tell me."

"Just fixed up a few things this morning, matter of fact. Small stuff, private parties, just while I'm putting a new act together. I..."

But Resnick was already shaking his head. "Not the kind of work I mean."

Freddy could feel himself starting to blush, guilty or innocent, the colour spreading up from his neck to brighten his cheeks.

"I was thinking more," Resnick continued, "the second storey kind."

"Never, Mr Resnick."

"Never?"

"Not any more. Not since, you know…"

Resnick nodded. "Lost the nerve for it, that's what you're saying."

"Absolutely."

"Heights."

"Giddy these days, Mr Resnick, climbing onto that table there, change a bulb in the lamp."

"Vertigo, acrophobia."

"If you say so."

Resnick seemed to think for a while, then moved towards the door. "All this, Freddy," he swept his hand towards the wall, "profession, a career. Show business. Something to be proud of. Shame to see it all fall by the by."

Freddy nodded most emphatically. He knew; he knew.

Resnick hesitated, half in, half out of the room. "Christmas on the way, New Year. Busy time for you, I dare say. Shame to be unavailable for work that festive season, shut away."

For a long time after Resnick had gone, Freddy sat pondering over ways to avoid carrying through on what he'd promised – two twenty minute spots either side of a buffet supper at the silver wedding celebrations; gaining entry through the fourth floor skylight of a large detached house in Church Lane, Watnall Chaworth, its occupants booked into a banquet up in Buxton and due to stay the night.

The first time the phone went that evening, it was a wrong number; the second heralded the membership secretary of the Polish Club, politely wondering if Resnick had received his second reminder. Promising he'd get the cheque in the post first thing, Resnick determined he would give Hannah till nine then try her again. Midway through dialling her number he thought better of it: she would have listened to his message; if she wanted to call him then she would. Just after ten he called Millington instead, television news just audible behind the sergeant's voice; the interview with Peter Risdale had been inconclusive. Lying, Millington thought, almost beyond question, but a man like that would lie to the police on principle, guilty or not. Either way, he'd an alibi that'd be hard to shake. His son, Stephen, was still in youth detention and there was nothing tangible to place Risdale himself at the scene or even close.

Resnick poured vodka over ice cubes in a chilled glass and closed his eyes as he listened to Johnny Griffin guesting with Thelonious Monk. 'Round Midnight', 'Misterioso'. 'In Walked Bud'. Actually, the smallest of Resnick's litter was already making discreet snoring noises in his lap.

When the vodka was finished and the music at an end, he lifted the cat into the cradle of an arm and carried it up the stairs to bed.

Hannah called next morning, not so far after six. "I didn't wake you?"

"No."

"Charlie, I'm sorry I didn't get back to you last night."

"That's fine."

"This meeting after school became one quick drink, and then dinner and then, oh, it must have been nearly twelve."

"Hannah, it's okay. It doesn't matter."

There was a brief pause before she said, "Sunday? Shall I see you Sunday? Maybe we could go for a walk, late breakfast somewhere, brunch, what'd you say?" Somehow she could sense Resnick was already smiling.

"Fine," Resnick said. "I'd like that a lot."

"What d'you mean, you're going?"

Freddy was half in, half out of his Ford van, still wearing his first-half costume, make-up, the whole bit. The anniversary couple's grandson, the one who'd booked him, standing there with both hands on the door. Aside from one slight glitch when the tape had got stuck at the intro to 'King Creole' it had not gone badly – if you glossed over Freddy transposing two of the verses in 'Heartbreak Hotel'. What was he doing? A song he'd sung how many hundred times.

He knew what he was doing. Not flustered he explained to the grandson that in his hurry to get there, he'd left his costume change, his white jump suit behind. Twenty minutes, thirty at most, he'd be back. No worries.

"Forget it," the man said. "You're okay as you are."

But Freddy would have none of it: the whole show was what they were paying for and that's what they were going to get.

Clayton was waiting for him as planned, in a lay-by just past the motorway where they switched vehicles.

"There may be a problem," Clayton said. They were heading east along the Watnall Road, keeping the speed below fifty, not wanting to attract attention.

"What?" In his anxiety, Freddy's voice little more than a squeak.

"Gave it a quick pass-by earlier, checking it out. Just in time to see him getting into a taxi, penguin suit, the whole bit."

"So?"

"So she's standing in the doorway in this quilted dressing gown, all she can do to wave him goodbye."

"She's still there?"

"Sick, my guess. In bed sick."

"Then what the hell are we doing? For Christ's sake let's turn round and get…"

But Clayton's free hand was like a vice right above Freddy's knee. "Easy, easy. Take it easy. What d'you think, she's in there wide awake, maybe doing a spot of housework? Soon as he's gone, she's back to bed. Nurofen, Paracetemol, it'll take more'n you to wake her, eh Freddy? You tip-toeing down the stairs like some fairy in your size four shoes."

In the event, Freddy's shoes were in his hand. Gaining entry through the third floor bathroom window had been straightforward enough, the upper section easing back to admit his child-size body, Freddy pausing just long enough to adjust the way his black silk shirt tucked into his black leather trousers, sit on the side of the bath to slip off his blue suede shoes.

He was down as far as the lower landing when the dog started to bark. Fucking Clayton! Why the fuck hadn't he known about the fucking dog? Freddy jumped so hard his shoes jerked free of his fingers and went spiralling down towards the hall. By which time the aforementioned fucking dog, in addition to barking fit to raise the dead, was hurling itself against the door of the ground floor room it was shut in, a few more times and Freddy could see its nasty vicious snout breaking through the wood. An Alsatian, he imagined, some kind of mastiff, one of those slick and nasty Dobermans.

Added to which, the lady of the house, far from being asleep, was standing somewhere above him, screaming fit to beat the band. Clayton hammering at the front door, wanting to know what the hell was going on, waiting to be let in.

Freddy slipped the bolts, unfastened the chain, turned both handles at once.

"What the fuck's going on?"

Freddy almost head-butted Clayton in the gut as he pushed past him, sprinting now towards the car, Clayton with nothing to do but follow in his wake.

"What... ?"

But Freddy was too angry, too wound-up, too scared to say a thing. It wasn't till Clayton dropped him off back at his van that he realised he was standing there in black nylon socks, a hole beginning to appear round the big toe of his right foot.

"I don't think you're supposed to call them that any more," Hannah said. "Dwarf." They were strolling round the long lake in Clumber Park, nice enough for a walk if you were well wrapped up.

"Not midget, surely?"

"Certainly not that." She paused at the raucous clamour of ducks, a small child lopsidedly hurling them bread.

"Vertically challenged," Resnick suggested, only half in fun. "Something like that."

Doing her best not to smile, Hannah shook her head. "I believe the correct term is person of restricted growth."

"Person of restricted movement, certainly. That'll be Freddy McGregor for the next six months at least."

"There isn't any doubt?"

Resnick laughed. "One pair of little suede shoes, custom made. Better than fingerprints where Freddy's concerned. Even after the dog had got through with them."

"I feel almost sorry for him in a way."

"The good thing," Resnick said, "with Freddy's help there's a really nasty piece of work called Kanellopoulos we can put away for years."

Uncertain about the efficacy of imprisonment, Hannah held her tongue.

They were in a corner of the lakeside café when Resnick showed her the reservations. A hotel in Matlock, five-course dinner and a jazz band ball.

"If you fancy it, that is."

"Of course." Lifting up the tickets, Hannah looked again at the date. "Try-out for the Millennium, Charlie, that what this is?"

Just for a moment, Resnick squeezed her hand. "One New Year at a time, eh? Happen that's best."

COOL BLUES

THE FIRST thing Laughlin noticed about the woman was her purple nails; not long, therefore probably not false, nicely rounded, neat, the purple polish – dark purple – carefully, recently applied. Her hair was fair and fashioned in a long bob, fair but darker at the roots. She was wearing a grey, military-style coat over a paler grey sweater, a black skirt long enough to cover her knees as she sat, the movement of the underground train jolting her occasionally, this way and then that. As they slowed, coming into Camden Town station, she glanced up, and Laughlin thought for a moment she might be alighting, changing perhaps to the other branch, but, no, she settled back into the book she was reading – a romance, Laughlin supposed, one of those paperback books with pink covers, the name of the author embossed; one of those names that always sounded false, made up.

Tufnell Park.

Kentish Town.

At Archway, the woman folded down the corner of a page to keep her place, pushed the book down into a black leather-look shoulder bag, hoisted the bag upwards and headed for the nearest set of doors. Laughlin slid out his foot and as she stumbled, almost falling, he reached up and caught her arm just above the elbow, steadying her.

"I'm sorry. Are you okay?" A concerned smile wrinkled the corners of his eyes.

"Fine. Thanks. Fine."

"My big feet."

She glanced back at him once before pushing her way between the closing doors.

After that it was easy.

❐

Resnick had not seen Jackie Ferris in what – eighteen months? Two years? Some stolen paintings had been whisked away to London for resale overseas and Jackie, a sergeant then in the Yard's Arts and Antiques Squad, had lent him her local knowledge and expertise. Maybe not lent exactly, more traded... and now it was time for the exchange.

The train slowed as it shuffled the tracks on its way into St Pancras station and Resnick folded the newspaper he'd been reading and reached up to pull his topcoat from the rack. All along the compartment mobile phones were switched off, laptops closed down, cases snapped shut. It had been like travelling in a narrow, open-plan office with views of green fields and small woodlands, small towns sleepily shaking themselves awake.

Jackie Ferris was waiting at the end of the platform, her hair darker than Resnick remembered, cut shorter, styled. The suit she was wearing, darkish brown, looked casually expensive. As Resnick approached, she hitched her bag higher on one shoulder and held out a hand. "Charlie... welcome to the big city."

When she smiled her eyes shone blue and he realised the round, steel-framed glasses she usually wore had been exchanged for contacts. "Good journey?"

Resnick shrugged.

"Coffee, then."

"Fine."

"It's a few paces."

He shrugged burly shoulders. "I could use the exercise."

They crossed a road clogged with four lanes of rush hour traffic, away from the station and the new British Library, and in minutes were sitting in a small patisserie with cups of strong espresso, croissants, pain au chocolat – the Left Bank comes to Kings Cross.

"So," Resnick said, "how's the new job?"

Jackie broke off a piece of croissant and held it between finger and thumb. "Interesting," she said after a moment's consideration.

Jackie had transferred from her specialised unit back into everyday police work, and found herself attached, still a detective sergeant, to the CID squad operating out of Kentish Town.

"No regrets?" Resnick asked.

She shook her head. "I could have stayed where I was another five years and not got a sniff at making inspector."

"And now?"

Jackie gave a rueful smile. "Four and a half."

Resnick cut a brioche in half and spread the insides with blackcurrant jam. "This man, the one you wanted to talk about..."

Jackie took a sheet of paper from an envelope in her bag and swivelled it towards him: in the artist's impression the man's hair was dark, quite thick, curling back lightly against his collar; the cheek bones were pronounced, laugh lines etched around a wide, full mouth; his eyes, dark also, seemed to be smiling.

"Handsome," Resnick said. "Attractive."

"If you like that kind of thing."

"Apparently some do."

"Five at the last count; five we know about. All with a similar profile: middle-class, white, single, working; thirty-five to forty-five, living alone."

Resnick studied the picture again, testing it against his memory. "He doesn't hurt them?"

"Hurt?"

"Physically. He doesn't attack them?"

"Not so far."

"There's reason to think he might?"

Jackie fixed him with her eyes before finishing her espresso. "You want another?"

Resnick nodded.

Jackie signalled to the waitress. "What he does," she said when she'd placed their order, "he picks women up on the underground. Sometimes on the actual train, some-times on the platform, by the ticket machines, anywhere around the station. Regular travellers, mostly. He'll make some sort of contact with them one day – a smile, some kind of offhand remark. Then, when he sees them again he starts talking and, maybe because he's not a total stranger, they talk back. Like you said, some women clearly find him attractive." She gave him a look, half-sour. "He suggests meeting for a drink, then dinner, one thing leads to another. After the second or third time they've slept together comes the rude awakening – he's cleaned them out of everything they've got. Cash, valuables, cheque books, credit cards, everything."

"You've not been able to track him down?"

"Not so far. This sketch, that's all we've got."

Resnick glanced down at it again. "Obviously, you've tried watching the underground, having plain clothes officers on the trains?"

She gave a quick shake of the head. "You know how many people use the tube each day? The number of stations, lines? If he restricted himself to one area, we might at least have a chance. But the first two incidents, Ealing and beyond, out towards the airport; after that he's right across the other side of the map, Loughton, Buckhurst Hill, almost in Epping Forest. There was this one isolated incident on the Bakerloo line, Stonebridge Park, and now…" She held up both hands, palms outwards.

"Now it's your patch."

"This last one, yes. But whether he'll stay here, when he'll hit on someone else, who knows?" She leaned forward, elbows resting either side of her cup and plate. "What you said before – had there been any physical attack. If there had – and I'm not saying I wish there was, don't misunderstand me – but if that was what we were dealing with, offences against the person, sexual assault, rape, the whole business would be taken more seriously. More resources, personnel… instead of me chasing phantoms on my own, with a bit of help from whoever I can drag in without it costs overtime." She leaned back in her chair. "No offence meant."

"None taken."

Jackie laughed, sudden and loud. "Once or twice I've been desperate enough to send myself out as a decoy, up and down from Barnet to Balham in the rush hour. As if someone who works women as well as this one does couldn't sniff out a dyke like me at fifty metres."

Resnick smiled along. "Statements from the women, there's nothing there might trip him up?"

Jackie shook her head. "Spun them a different story each time, used a different name. The only one thing that remained consistent, where he comes from. Nottingham. Which is why I thought of you. I thought something, the M.O., the face, might ring a bell."

Heavily, Resnick crossed his legs, shook his head.

"Anyway," Jackie said, "it's part of his spiel. Only recently moved down to London, finding it difficult to make friends."

"And the names he uses? There's not a pattern there?"

"Not that I've been able to find." She took out her notebook and flipped back through the pages, looking for the list. "Usually there'll be a link, similar sound, same initials, something. But these – John Sanders, Edward Preston, Alan Smith, Richard Williams, Leon Cox."

Resnick's expression shifted from the merest of grins to broad delight.

"What? What is it?"

"The Allen – Allen Smith. It's spelt double-L E, not the usual way?"

Jackie shook her head. "I don't know. Not for sure."

"I wouldn't mind betting it is. And Edward, that'll be Eddie, Eddie Preston."

"How do you know all this? Who are they?"

"They're all musicians, the names he's chosen: jazz musicians."

"What? English?"

Resnick shook his head. "American. If my memory's

right they all played with Duke Ellington. Mid-fifties. Sixties, maybe. Brass section, trumpet or trombone. The thing is, though, these aren't the famous ones, not even regulars. They may have only been on one or two sessions, a single recording."

"So to know this, he'd likely be what? A musician himself?"

Resnick shook his head. "Unlikely. Unless he was a keen amateur, semi-pro."

"He'd need to be a fan then, is that what you mean? A real anorak?"

He looked at her quizzically.

"You know, trainspotting type. Ticks them all off in his little book. Snuggles up in bed with – I don't know – lists of some kind. Catalogues."

"Discographies."

"Yes, right. Discographies. When he's not pulling women on the Northern Line."

"You can bet he's loving it," Resnick said. "This little private joke with the names, certain no one's going to find him out."

As they were stepping back out into the street, Jackie touched his arm. "I don't want to make too much of it, Charlie, but the fact you cottoned on so fast... I'd hate to think you were spending all your nights with only a – what was it? – discography for company."

❐

Resnick toured the specialist shops: Mole Jazz at King's Cross was only a short walk away; fifteen minutes in the opposite direction brought him to Ray's Jazz Shop on the edge of Covent Garden. He visited the jazz departments of

Tower on Piccadilly, HMV in Oxford Street, both branches. Showed the artist's impression and asked about a collector, into Ellington, big bands and swing. For one or two, the face was vaguely familiar, but nothing more; one of the assistants at Ray's remembered a telephone enquiry about some Ellington recordings, live sessions from the Travis Air Force Base in California, 1958... whether the man ever came in to collect the CDs, he didn't know.

Strolling back through Soho, jogged by memories of great musicians he'd travelled down to see in the past – Stan Getz, Zoot Sims, Roland Kirk – Resnick stopped off for an espresso at the Bar Italia, wandered across the street to Ronnie Scott's and chatted with the woman at the desk. She didn't think the man was a regular, though she couldn't be sure.

Later that evening and the evening after, Jackie Ferris and whoever's arm she could twist would hit the rest of the clubs: the 100, the Jazz Café, Pizza on the Park; the Vortex, the Bulls Head and the 606.

Nothing clicked.

Back in Nottingham, Resnick trawled round a similar, smaller circuit and get only a series of similar, blank responses. After a few days, he called Jackie Ferris, confessing he had drawn a blank. Maybe, she told him, he's moved on, our mystery man, some other section of the line. Given up, Resnick suggested, while he's still ahead. Neither of them thought it true.

❐

"It's Bill," Laughlin said with a grin. "Just plain old Bill Cooke. William, according to the birth certificate. William John. Not that anyone's ever called me that – William –

except for my mother. And a few of the teachers at school."
He laughed. "The other kids, most of them, they called me
Willie." He laughed again, not afraid to show his teeth.
"You know what kids are like."

She did. Deputy head of a Catholic primary school close
to the Holloway Road, she knew only too well.

"And you?" he asked, smiling now with his eyes, dark
eyes.

"Mary," she said, "Mary Parker."

"Well, cheers, Mary." Reaching for his glass, he brushed
her arm, accidentally of course, with his.

When she had spotted him looking at her on the train,
staring really, she had raised the pages of her *Guardian*
higher and dismissed him from her mind. By Finsbury Park
he was forgotten. But then on the bus that carried her down
to Crouch End he had been there again, rising from his seat
in front of her as she moved towards the exit; apologising
as, for a moment, the pair of them stepping down onto the
pavement, his arm and her bag became entangled. She had
stood too long, a deep flush rising, unbidden, along her
neck.

The bar he had taken her to was new, pale furniture and
green plants, bottled beer from Belgium and Japan. She had
never been there before. She rarely went anywhere, not like
that. Not on her own or with someone she scarcely knew.

She watched him talking, chattering on, a gesture here,
a smile there, not really hearing what he was saying, not
needing to, looking instead at the red of his mouth, the
brightness of his eyes, the way their lashes fanned out in an
almost perfect curve.

When his arm touched hers again, no possible accident
this time, she smiled back.

❐

"Call while you were out," Resnick's sergeant said. "Ferris? Get back to her when you can."

It was almost two months since they had met in London and Resnick had been swept up into the everyday travail of inner city police work, one case of arson especially, a child dead, the mother and two others injured, preying on his mind. Jackie Ferris's con man more or less forgotten.

Her voice was slightly fuzzy on the line, resigned. "He finally did it, Charlie. Our underground jazzman."

"Did what?"

"Lost his cool. A woman named Mary Parker, a teacher; she'd been seeing him, off and on, a couple of weeks. Woke up in the middle of the night, needing to pee. There's our friend, stark naked in the middle of the living room, helping himself to her credit cards."

"What happened?"

"She screamed, threw something at him, threatened to phone the police. He punched her once in the face, broke her nose. Then he punched her again."

"She's okay?"

A pause. "Considering, she's fine."

"What name did he use this time?" Resnick asked.

"Cooke. Bill Cooke."

Willie Cooke, Resnick thought, christened John. Born Louisiana, 1923. Joined Ellington in fifty-one and was in and out of the band until Duke died. He allowed himself a wry smile. Jackie had been right. All that useless knowledge, a sure sign of obsession: too many nights counting jazzmen before he could get to sleep.

It was only three days later, leafing through the pages of *Jazz Journal*, that the advertisement caught his eye. One night only at the Pizza Express Jazz Club in Soho, Joe Temperley.

Resnick had been too young to hear the Lyttelton band of the late fifties, the eight-piece with Tony Coe on alto, the late Jimmy Skidmore on tenor, Temperley on baritone – one of the best reworkings of the Ellington small band sound ever. But he had heard the recordings, knew them well. Knew that Temperley had gone to America to try his luck and stayed; played in a big band led by Ellington's son, Mercer, after the Duke had died. On the soundtrack for the film, *The Cotton Club*, it had been Joe Temperley who recreated the solos of Harry Carney, Ellington's star baritone. And now he was back in England, a flying visit. Resnick wondered who else might have seen the boxed advertisement near the foot of page five.

Resnick had been to the old Pizza Express Jazz Club, not the new; had suffered near heat exhaustion listening to Buddy Tate on a summer night when sweat stuck fast to the walls and finally he'd been forced upstairs and out onto the street where the sound was blurred but at least he wouldn't faint.

This place was larger, still low-ceilinged but air-conditioned; black walls hung with posters, a thick red carpet on the stage. Resnick sat at a small round table smack up against the centre mike, a clear view along the piano keys to his left.

He'd been seated no more than ten minutes when Temperley moved into the spotlight, a wide-shouldered, heavy man wearing a loose, double-breasted suit, a dark shirt, a tie shot through with aquamarine. There was something of Resnick's own father in the broad, almost Slavic face, glasses, dark hair and moustache.

"All the way from America…" said the announcer. "Aye," Temperley scowled, clipping his saxophone onto its sling. "By way of Cowdenbeath." Leaning towards the piano, he called a blues in B flat. After two choruses, bell of the baritone close to the mike, the first notes spilled out, rhythmic, rich; large hands, square thumbed, working the keys with ease.

Tune followed tune, song followed song; the club slowly filled. 'Broadway', 'The Very Thought of You', 'Straight, No Chaser', 'Once in a While'. Waiters and waitresses brought food and beer, bottles of wine. Tempos changed. Between solos, perspiring, Temperley took out a handkerchief and rubbed it back and forth across the back of his head.

"We'd like to finish the first set," he said, "with Duke Ellington's 'In a Sentimental Mood'."

Two tables behind Resnick, and a little to his right, a fortyish man in a gently faded denim shirt, also sitting alone, leaned forward in anticipation and smiled.

As the musicians left the stage, Resnick eased back his chair and drank a little more Peroni; the man in the denim shirt was standing now, talking animatedly to Temperley, jabbing the air with one hand to make a point. After a few minutes, their conversation over, the saxophonist joined the other musicians at their table and denim shirt headed off towards the gents. Resnick wondered which name he was using this evening; whether he ever used his own.

Laughlin was standing at the urinal, whistling, when Resnick entered and took his place alongside him.

"Great stuff!" Laughlin said, fastening his fly. "Great player."

Resnick agreed. When he turned, Laughlin was washing his hands at the sink, still whistling softly between his teeth.

"I thought brass players were more your thing – I mean, rather than saxophones."

The whistle died mid-phrase. In the mirror, eyes stared.

"More obscure the better. Leon Cox, Allen Smith…"

Laughlin spun fast and, ready for him, Resnick stepped to block his path, reaching for his upper arm but failing to evade the knee that jabbed hard into his groin. With a gasp, he stumbled back as Laughlin pushed between two men entering and ran.

There were two exits from the club, one by the iron stairs leading up into the street, the other through the restaurant. Jackie Ferris had positioned officers at both and was sitting near the restaurant door, polishing off the last of an American Hot pizza with extra spinach, when the man she recognised from the artist's sketch, neatly side-stepped a waitress with a heavily laden tray and hurried towards the corner exit.

Waiting until he was almost level, she brought one of her legs up smartly between his, allowing his momentum to send him head first into the glass of the door. All those Saturday afternoons at Highbury, watching the Arsenal defence, had not gone for nothing.

Before Resnick had arrived, slightly breathless, at her side, Jackie had Laughlin's arms cuffed behind his back and was reading him his rights.

❐

It was Saturday morning when the package arrived and Resnick was at home: a square shape, covered in brown paper and bubble-wrapped. The note was on plain card, signed Jackie. *I slipped in a couple of extra questions during the interrogation and the suspect suggested these.* There were ten CDs in all – *Duke Ellington: The Private Collection*. Resnick thought it would look good on the shelf, close by his box set of Billie Holiday on Verve. He thought it would sound pretty good, too.

Ten minutes later, coffee made, he slipped the disc into place. Volume one, track one. Chicago, 1956. The band kicking off with a limber, loose-limbed blues. As he listened, his eyes ran down the personnel: Harry Carney on baritone, John Sanders in amongst the trombones, Willie Cooke on trumpet.

Smiling, Resnick sat back and closed his eyes.

SLOW BURN

SOME NIGHTS, Resnick thought, you knew sleep wasn't destined to come; or that if it did, it would be haunted by dreams pitched just this side of nightmare, broken by the startled cry of the telephone heralding some new disaster, awful and mundane. So there he was, at close to two a.m., ferreting through the sparsely filled refrigerator for the makings of a snack, pouring cold milk – yes, milk – into a glass, opening the back door so that Pepper could join Dizzy in a little night-time prowling, hunting down whatever was slower or slower-witted than themselves. Miles and Bud were upstairs on his bed, missing, perhaps, his bulk and warmth while relishing the extra space.

Carrying his sandwich through into the front room, he pulled an album from the shelf and slipped the record from its tattered sleeve. *The Thelonious Monk Trio* on Prestige. Through the smeared glass of the front bay, he could see the outlines of houses left and right along the curve of street, roofs bulked against a city sky that was never truly dark.

Faint, the hum of occasional cars, one block away on the Woodborough Road. Monk's fingers, flat, percussive, treading their way through 'Bemesha Swing' like an over-grown child lurching along the pavement, crack by crack.

It was no surprise when the phone finally rang, nor that the voice at the other end was his sergeant's, weary and resigned.

That deep into the early hours it was no more than a five minute drive to the old Lace Market, the corner of Stoney Street and King's Place and the Victorian conversion that for years had housed Jimmy Nolan's jazz club and bar. Acrid and pungent, the scent of burning struck Resnick as he climbed out of the car. Smoke eddied on the air. Fire officers, purposeful yet unhurried, damped down smouldering wreckage; making safe. Resnick knew they would already have isolated, as far as possible, the area where the fire began. The building itself was little more than a blackened shell.

Resnick stepped across lengths of fire hose to where, bare-headed, hands in the pockets of a loose, navy blue anorak, Millington waited.

"Graham."

"Sir." When there were other professionals within earshot, it was 'Sir' rather than 'Charlie'.

"Fill me in."

There had been an anonymous call to Emergency Services, logged at three twenty-seven. The first appliances had arrived nine minutes later; by then the fire had taken hold and the immediate concern had been to stop it spreading to the old warehouse buildings on either side.

"And Nolan?" Resnick asked.

Millington shrugged. "Locked up this side of two,

according to his story; home and tucked up by two-thirty. We called him out of course, key-holder. Been here and gone." The sergeant lifted a pack of cigarettes from his pocket then thought better of it. "Know him, don't you? Jimmy Nolan?"

"Over the years, yes. A little."

Millington nodded towards the smouldering ruin. "This place, too, I'll bet."

Resnick nodded. Not so often recently, not as often as he'd have liked, but yes, he had been here, evenings, nights to remember: Nat Adderley, Teddy Edwards, Mose Allison.

"Screeching and wailing till all hours," Millington said, his face taking on a pained expression. "Gives me a headache."

"I daresay, Graham."

"Any road," the sergeant continued, warming to his theme. "Took a sight more'n two of them be-boppers rubbing their trumpets together to get this started."

"We don't know yet what did?"

Millington shook his head.

"And that's not why you called me out," Resnick said. "Me knowing Jimmy Nolan. That could've waited till morning."

Millington blinked. "They found a body. Charred beyond recognition, apparently. Must've been inside when the place went up. Caved in on him."

For a brief moment Resnick closed his eyes, as smuts of soot fell soft against his face, caught in his hair.

Nolan had lived in the same spot in the inner city for close on thirty years; the centre of a Victorian terrace, appropriately facing Victoria Park. While most of his neighbours had sold out to upwardly mobile first-homers with their wooden blinds and self-assembly shelving from IKEA, shrill little loud-mouthed kids named Ben and Sacha, Jimmy Nolan's house had remained stubbornly the same. Plaster flaked off the outer walls and slates skimmed from the roof in a strong wind. The upper floors he rented out, the remainder were his own. Small rooms sparsely furnished, bits and pieces bought at auction, curtains that were faded and mis-matched, wallpaper beginning to peel away. At the front, an upright piano had been wedged between window and door, an uneasy pyramid of manuscript paper and sheet music balancing on top. Rickety shelves opposite held a reel-to-reel tape player, record deck and amplifier; speaker cabinets, solid and cigarette-burned, stood knee-high at either end of the room. White tape boxes, annotated in untidy hand, were scattered in haphazard piles across the floor. Instrument cases and a saxophone stand shared the empty fireplace with an overflowing ashtray and a dying plant.

By the time Resnick rang the bell, morning was already starting to leak into the sky.

Nolan's face was pale save for the shadows pocketed around his eyes; there was a tumbler of scotch in his hand and it wasn't the first. "Fuck, Charlie," he said. "Why you?"

"You'd rather somebody else?"

For an answer, Nolan stood aside and ushered Resnick through. He was no more than medium-height, with hunched shoulders and a stooped back; greying hair fuzzed around his ears, the bristle on his cheeks was white. He was wearing a collarless striped shirt under a sleeveless pullover, baggy trousers that needed a belt. Far from the man Resnick remembered, sharp-witted and smartly-dressed, up on stage at the club.

"You'll not be wanting one of these, duty and all that."
Nolan swayed a little as he raised his glass.

"A small one, Jimmy. Thanks."

"I've no ice."

"Water's fine."

They sat facing one another across the small room, the
silence broken by the short scratch of a match as Nolan lit
a cigarette.

"Remember the first night at the club?" Nolan asked.

Resnick nodded, not raising his head.

"You were just an ordinary copper, wet behind the ears."

Resnick looked at him then. "You were still playing saxophone."

"Al Cohn and Zoot Sims. Up from the smoke in a black
Daimler, half a mile long, looked like a fucking hearse."

"You sat in with them."

Nolan laughed, a dry crackle. "My club, Charlie. They
weren't exactly going to throw me off the stand."

"'Four Brothers', I remember."

"Just the three of us."

Resnick sipped at his scotch. "You were good."

"I was bollocks!"

"Jimmy…"

Nolan got up and walked to the window: it was light
enough to see across the slope of grass to the old Victoria
Baths. "It doesn't matter now, Charlie, none of it. Not a flying fuck." He laughed again, brittle and short. "I could've
sold it, Charlie, that place. Down the years. A dozen times
over. But no, stupid bastard that I am, I wouldn't listen,
turned 'em down. And now…"

"The insurance…"

"Not half what I could've got before; not a quarter."

"But you'll be all right? Financially, I mean."

Nolan shook his head and swallowed down more scotch. "What are you, Charlie? My fuckin' social worker?"

Resnick shook his head and leaned back in his chair.

Nolan stubbed out his cigarette. "Let's say, when I've paid off all the debts, any luck I'll be okay. Least, not be knocking at the poor house door."

Resnick let the silence settle round them once more. "When you locked up tonight," he asked, "there wasn't anybody in the building?"

Nolan's glass was empty. "Of course not. Who would there be?"

"You checked?"

"There was no need. I knew."

Resnick was staring at him, waiting.

"What? What the hell you saying?"

"Someone was in there when it went up. They found a body. Somebody died."

"Oh, fuck!" Nolan said, lowering his face into his hands. "Oh, fuck! Oh, sweet, sweet fuck!"

Resnick got to his feet and lifted the almost empty bottle of Bells from the floor; the majority he poured into Nolan's glass, the remainder into his own. Nolan's eyes were bright with tears. "Why, Charlie, why?"

"I don't know," Resnick said. "But we'll find out." He squeezed Nolan's shoulder hard. "We'll find out for sure." Even as he was speaking, he knew it was less than the truth.

Back home, Resnick fed the cats then showered the soot from his hair, lathered, as best he could, the stench of burning from his skin. Forty minutes later he was backing through the door into the CID room, an espresso from the Canning Circus deli in one hand, an almond croissant in the other.

Lynn Kellogg and Kevin Naylor were both busy on the phones, Graham Millington, tie at half-mast, top button of his shirt undone, was artlessly two-fingering his way along the computer keyboard.

As soon as he saw Resnick, Millington pressed *Save* and got to his feet. "Pathologist, got through half-hour back. Deceased was male, young, likely between fifteen and twenty-four, cause of death carbon monoxide inhalation. At this stage not a lot more she can say. Ceiling collapsing on top of him the way it did. Badly burned. Identification's going to be a bugger. Dental records, of course, but outside of that..." He shrugged. "Possible to build up some kind of reconstruction of the face if all else fails, but it'll not come quick. Or cheap."

"Missing persons?"

Millington nodded across the room. "I'll get Lynn or Kevin off down there soon as one of 'em's free."

Resnick lifted the lid from his espresso. "Nothing from the Fire Investigation Team yet, I suppose?"

Millington shook his head. "Early days."

Resnick checked his watch. "I'll give it a couple of hours, call the Station Officer. See if I can't hurry things along."

Resnick's own office was a deep corner, partitioned off from the main room. He was almost through the door when Millington spoke again. "Jimmy Nolan, make a lot of money out of that place, did he? Jazz being the fashion item that it is."

Resnick wasn't certain how sarcastic he was being. "Last couple of times I was there, the band just about outnumbered the audience."

A leery smile creased Millington's face. "This business last night then, might've done Nolan a bit of good?"

Resnick was thoughtful. "Yes. Yes, one way or another, it might."

The sun was breaking through the clouds as Resnick crossed Bath Street and re-entered Victoria Park. Mothers sat in small clusters, watchful of their children; red-faced men with wiry hair and veined hands sat nursing cans of cider, cursing their fate; a shaven-haired youth, elongated swastika tattooed on one cheek, sat with two mongrel dogs curled asleep at his feet. From Nolan's house the sound of a saxophone rose, rough and uncertain, above the shuttle and hum of traffic. Scales, broken phrases, runs that began and never finished: music without flow or melody.

"I didn't know you still played," Resnick said when Nolan answered the door.

Nolan's face was flat and unsmiling. "I don't."

"I thought I heard…"

"You heard nothing." Nolan had shaved and combed his hair, changed into a faded green shirt and dark corduroys.

Resnick followed him into the cramped front room, the saxophone, Resnick noticed, no longer in its case but resting on its stand, its sling draped across the back of a chair. The cassette boxes which had been piled haphazardly, were stacked now along the piano lid, some freshly labelled: Pharoah Saunders, Art Pepper, Art Themen, Pete King.

"Just about everyone ever played at the club," Nolan said. "I've got 'em on there. Good quality too." He chuckled, low in his throat. "Marvellous stuff."

"Worth something, I shouldn't be surprised."

The room was heavy with the scent of tobacco and last night's scotch. Or maybe it was today's. "There's been one or two, sniffing around. Record companies, you know.

Nothing major, not your Blue Note or one of those, but straight up, legit. Course, there'd be permissions to be worked out, rights; even so, end of the day, might fetch in a quid or two."

"Those debts."

"Eh?"

"The insurance, for the fire. You said that's where it would mostly go, paying off debts."

Nolan lit a fresh cigarette. "Tea, Charlie? Not take more'n a few minutes to mash."

Resnick shook his head.

"Coffee, then. Instant, that's all it is. Or a drink, maybe. A beer. There's a decent lager in the fridge, I…"

"Answers, Jimmy. That's what I want. That's what I'm here for."

Nolan stopped short of the door and turned his head. "Christ, Charlie, I thought…"

"You thought what?"

"We was mates. History together. History."

Resnick touched him lightly on the arm. "A fire, Jimmy. Somebody dead. So far, we don't know how or why."

"And you think that I… ?"

"I don't know." Resnick's voice was even, almost reassuring. "Jimmy, I don't know. But a business that's not faring well, debts needing to be paid, sometimes all you want to do is throw in the towel, walk away. Find some other way out."

"You think I torched it." Pain edged its way round Nolan's eyes.

Resnick lowered the saxophone sling to the floor and sat down; after a moment Nolan sat opposite him, tipping ash into an empty mug.

"Ten or twelve years back" Nolan said, "this brewery

came to me, all over 'emselves wanting to buy the place, rip the guts out, turn it into one of them state-of-the-fuckin'-art café bars with all the personality of dog turd on the underside of your shoe." Nolan snorted. "Daft bastard that I was, I wouldn't listen. Course, the club was losing money even then, leaking it, but I thought, no, I've got out of worse holes before, I can bring things round." He glanced over at Resnick and shook his head. "Like bloody buggery I could!"

"I tried everything, Charlie, everything I could think of. Fly-posting, ads on local radio, prices cut back to the bone. Nothing seemed to make a scrap of difference. Oh, you'd pick up a few new faces here, lose 'em a week or so later." He took a long drag on his cigarette. "I thought, right, it's the music, that's what's got to change. Too old-fashioned, maybe, too straight ahead. So I tried it all: jazz funk, jazz fusion, Afro-Caribbean, Afro-Cuban, Hip-Hop even. Got in a DJ – what they call acid jazz." Nolan shook his head. "By the time the accountants had finished going over the books I need scarcely've bothered."

"You couldn't sell up then?" Resnick asked.

"Too late. Too fuckin' late."

"So you borrowed?"

Nolan watched a smoke ring drift, widening, towards the ceiling. "The bank reckoned I was over-extended already. Well, they're not stupid." He shrugged. "I had to go elsewhere, cap in hand."

Music was seeping through the wall from the house next door, the theme from some television programme, Resnick thought. He looked at Nolan and waited.

"Russell Venner," Nolan said eventually. "You know him, I daresay?"

By reputation, Resnick did. Local businessman made

good. At one time or another, Venner had been a member of the City Council, a Justice of the Peace, on the board of County or Forest or both. He guessed he was still director of more firms than you could shake a stick at.

"He bailed you out?"

Nolan lit a fresh cigarette from the butt of the last. "Someone at the club knew I was in trouble; he was on some board with Venner, volunteered to put in a word. I told him there was no need. Knew him, you see, Venner, could've gone to him myself, we had connections. Anyway, this bloke, he wouldn't listen. Upshot of it was, Venner came round, called me a fool for not going to him sooner. Offered to lend me ten grand there and then, interest free. Cheque book in his bloody hand."

"Philanthropist, is he?"

"So he'd like you to think. And I didn't want the money, not from him; reasons of my own, personal, but in the end I agreed." Ash fell along Nolan's trousers and, absent-mindedly, he smudged it away. "Of course, it wasn't enough. It never is. Next thing you know he's offering to buy a share in the club. Nothing threatening, ten per cent; then twenty, twenty-five. A few more shares for his pals, eager to help out. His wife, Nicola, fifteen per cent in her name."

"But the controlling interest, that's still your's?"

Nolan held his gaze. "On a good day, Charlie, I can just about control where I piss, inside the bowl or out."

"And Venner didn't try and force you to sell out altogether? Stop throwing good money after bad?"

Nolan sighed. "He talked about it once or twice; knew I'd never agree."

"Surely he could've forced the issue, all those shares?"

"His wife, he couldn't do it without her, her say-so, her shares."

"And she sided with you against her own husband?"

Nolan's face twisted into a rueful smile. "Not that straightforward, Charlie. Nicola, she's not only Venner's wife, she's my god-daughter too."

Parker's café nestled in the shadow of the flyover which carried the ring road west from hospital and university towards the airport and motorway. A single-storey building close alongside the fire station, it was a regular mecca for personnel coming on and off duty, a comfortable haven, cholesterol rich and welcoming of tobacco.

"Eight sharp, Charlie," Tom McLean, officer in charge of the Fire Investigation Team, had said on the phone. "And if you're there first, mine's a mug of tea, two sugars, and the full works."

As it was, when Resnick entered, more or less to time, McLean was already settled in a window seat, sleeves rolled back, a heart-defying fry-up overlapping the edges of his plate.

Eating habits regardless, the Fire Safety Officer was a fit-looking mid-forties, bright-eyed, brown hair that he had worn cropped short long before it became fashionable. Resnick had worked with him before and had learned to trust his judgment, enjoy his somewhat brittle company.

The two men shook hands before Resnick went to the counter and ordered a sausage sandwich with brown sauce. "Nothing on the body, Charlie?" McLean asked as Resnick pulled in his chair. "No idea who the poor sod might've been?" Though he'd been living south of the border for most of his adult life, there was still a recognisable Scottish tang in his voice.

Resnick shook his head. "List from missing persons longer than your arm. Not a lot of help as yet." Lynn

Kellogg had a meeting scheduled that morning with the manager of the City's Homelessness Support Centre, to see if she could get any leads from there.

McLean sliced through a length of sausage, speared an inch with his fork and dabbed it into a pool of yellow mustard. "Far as we've been able to establish, the fire started in the basement. Place'd been used for dumping rubbish: old papers, boxes, broken bits of furniture – not been cleared out for years. Lad we found, could've sneaked in there, not difficult apparently; looking for shelter, place to doss down, skin up maybe, enjoy a quiet smoke." McLean took a swig of tea. "Wouldn't've taken much to get it started. Stray match would have done the trick. Once it took hold nothing to stop it reaching the storage cupboard on the ground floor – turpentine, several litres of paint, white spirit. That and a good draught…" McLean brought his hands together with a sharp clap, causing conversations to break off, heads to turn.

Resnick chewed at his sandwich thoughtfully. "All this gubbins in the store cupboard, enough to make you suspicious?"

"Of its own accord, no. Little bit of DIY, place that size, pretty much what you'd expect."

"Not arson, then? That's what you're saying?"

McLean broke the yolk of his second egg. "If it's something in black and white you're after, something I might stick my signature to, it's too early. Too many questions still to be answered. I'll need a few more days. But gut feeling, no, likely not." He pointed his knife towards Resnick's chest. "Unless there's something you know and I don't."

Resnick laid out the bare bones of Nolan's financial situation, as far as the club owner himself had explained them.

McLean pushed his plate aside and reached for a cigarette. "Like I say, Charlie, we'll keep looking. A little patience, we'll have it sewn up, one way or another."

Back at the station, Resnick had scarcely time to check through the overnight reports before Lynn Kellogg was back from her meeting and knocking at his office door. Brown hair cut short and shaped close to her face, a faint suggestion of make-up, Lynn was wearing a pale T-shirt, tan chinos and a jeans jacket, Reeboks on her feet. A leather bag, satchel-shaped, hung from one shoulder and she was balancing two polystyrene cups in her opposite hand.

"I called in at the deli on the way back."

Resnick grinned his thanks as Lynn set a double espresso on his desk. Lifting the lid from her cappuccino, she sat down.

"How'd it go?" Resnick asked.

Lynn pushed her fingers into the edges of her hair. "Interesting. Depressing. Probably not a lot of help."

Resnick sampled his coffee and waited for her to explain.

"Single people recognised as being homeless, by the City that is, numbers've stayed pretty constant the past few years. Two, two and a half thousand. Close to a thousand of those in the age range we're interested in, eighteen to twenty four." She freed her note book from her bag and flipped it open. "A thousand youngsters, right? A hundred or so'll be found permanent accommodation, another hundred and fifty some kind of shelter."

"And the rest?" Resnick asked.

Lynn shook her head. "I suppose they get by as best they can. And remember, that number, all it includes is those who apply to the Housing Department for help. There could be twice as many who've never even bothered. The youth that died in the fire, he could be any one of those; any one from a couple of thousand."

Resnick nodded. "Have a word with Kevin, farm it out. Check the hostels, trawl back through missing persons, you know the routine."

A resigned look souring her face, Lynn got to her feet; she knew the routine only too well.

Alone in his office, Resnick sat at his desk, scarcely moving, thinking about the youths he was now so used to seeing, palms outstretched, around the edges of the bus station or along the newly pedestrianised shopping streets, sitting cross-legged on the grassed areas close by the fountains in the Old Market Square, the man with his dogs in the park; people he mostly walked past, hands tight in his pockets, staring straight ahead. His espresso, when he picked it up, was bitter and growing cold.

South from the city, Resnick drove between fields studded with cattle, patches of arable land that rose towards a calm horizon. When he turned off, it was along a narrow, tree-lined road that opened gradually onto a small enclave of houses sitting back, detached, deep into their own grounds. Venner's house was the last on the left, three storeys of mock-Tudor with a modern extension to one side, a two-car garage to the other. A broad drive curved between neatly landscaped lawns towards an arched portico and a front door that looked to be made from Sherwood oak. Resnick was surprised they'd missed out on the drawbridge and the moat. When he pressed his finger to the bell he was treated to an abbreviated version of 'Greensleeves'.

The woman who answered the door was younger than Resnick had anticipated, fair hair tied back from her head, blue eyes that didn't seem immediately to focus. A white silk shirt hung loose outside black trousers, black flip-flops on bare feet. Resnick noticed that her toenails and her lipstick matched.

"Yes?"

"Mrs Venner?"

"Nicola Venner, yes."

Warrant card in hand, Resnick identified himself.

"This isn't something to do with Neighbourhood Watch?" The slur in her voice was only barely noticeable; Resnick wondered how many drinks she was into the day.

"I'm afraid not," he said. "I was hoping I might have a word with your husband."

"Which one?"

"I'm sorry?"

"Which word?" Amusement brightened her eyes. "I've always wanted to ask that. When they say, on tele, you know, all those sad little policemen, Frost and Morse and the rest – I just want to have a word."

"I rang your husband's office," Resnick persevered, "the woman I spoke to, she didn't seem too certain of his movements. She knew he was due at a meeting, but after that she wasn't at all sure."

"And you thought he might be here?" Nicola Venner leaned sideways against the doorway and stared.

"A possibility, yes." He tried for a smile. "It seemed worth a try."

"Chance to get out of the city."

"Yes."

"Grime and dirt, carbon monoxide."

"Exactly."

She shifted her balance, standing away from the door. "Well, he isn't here. Not since this morning, early."

"I see, I…"

"These days you'd have to move pretty fast to catch him here at all. Always working, Russell. One deal after another. Whatever it takes to keep us in this place. Safe and secure." She looked beyond him towards the road. "Glimpsed through the shrubbery, driving by."

"Mrs Venner?"

"Mm?"

"What I wanted to talk to your husband about, it was Jimmy Nolan."

"Jimmy?"

"Yes."

For a moment she seemed to hold her breath. "What do they say, all those women, when people like you turn up on their doorsteps unannounced? I think, perhaps, inspector, we should go inside."

He followed her across a tiled hallway and into the kitchen. Pans, copper-bottomed, hung down from a square iron frame; a stainless steel industrial oven dominated the end of the room. Glass bowls of varying sizes, some in use, clustered on the surface near the sink; a cookery book stood open behind a perspex shield. On a movable butcher's block, where Nicola Venner had been chopping spears of asparagus into one inch lengths, there was a vodka bottle, two-thirds empty, and a lipsticked glass.

She gestured theatrically round the room and laughed. "See? All the evidence you need. Another poor neurotic wife, drinking her way through the afternoons."

"Really?" Resnick said.

Nicola shook her head. "Not really. Well, certainly not

poor and scarcely neurotic; just once in a while when the hormones kick in and everything goes a tiny bit crazy." She lifted up the vodka bottle and squinted at it, as if marking off some notional measurement inside her head. "Only today I thought I'd knock up something fancy for dinner, not even fancy, really, more fiddly. So I poured myself a glass of wine to help the concentration, which was fine, except after slicing those shallots over there the wine ran out, which was when I started on the vodka, and then there you were at the door, looking more than a little dishevelled, but otherwise awfully serious and wanting to talk to Russell about Jimmy. And I was – am – just a little drunk."

"Maybe some coffee," Resnick suggested.

She made a face. "Can't stand it. Gives me a headache. Mineral water, that's the thing." Taking a bottle of Evian from the fridge she offered it to Resnick, who shook his head.

"Tell me about Jimmy," he said.

"What about him?" She drank a tumbler of water almost straight down, then refilled the glass.

"You must know him pretty well."

"Must I?"

"I understood he was your godfather."

She laughed; almost a giggle. "So he is. But, you know, spiritual welfare, well, nobody bothers with that much nowadays, do they?" She looked across at him, one hip leaning against the sink. "A custom – what does Shakespeare say?"

Resnick didn't know.

"More honoured in the breach than the observance. I think that's it. Though he was at my first communion, I remember that. There's a picture somewhere, Jimmy looking fearfully proud, me in this ghastly white dress, more bows and tassels than a prize Pekinese."

"Jimmy's club," Resnick said, "you had shares."

"I did?"

"You and your husband, you both had shares."

Turning away to the sink, Nicola rinsed her glass under the tap. "Then it was a tax thing. Russell does that when it suits him, puts shares in my name."

The water was still running, overflowing the glass, the pressure high. Resnick leaned in past her and turned the tap off. Her arm grazed his. "According to Jimmy, you owned the controlling shares."

Her eyes were focussed now; there was no faltering in her voice. "Do you really think Russell would be so stupid as to allow that to happen?"

He could feel the warmth of her breath. "Then Jimmy was wrong?"

"Jimmy's a romantic. He always has been." She smiled ruefully. "If I'm no longer that poor pale creature in a communion dress, I doubt I've grown in his eyes since he introduced me to his pal Russell Venner when I was scarcely out of my teens. 'Tell me if I wasn't right', he said. 'Isn't she the most beautiful thing you've ever seen?'" Still holding Resnick's gaze, she took a step away. "Oh, yes, he had my spiritual welfare uppermost that day did Jimmy, no mistake about it."

It was quiet, save for the ticking of the clock.

"You've no idea, then," Resnick said, "where your husband might be?"

Nicola shook her head.

"Nor when he might be back?"

"I'm afraid not."

With a slight nod, Resnick turned away. "You'll tell him I was here?"

"Of course."

At the front door, he held out his hand. "Thanks for your time."

Her fingers were warm, only the slightest tremble. "It was a pleasure," she said.

Back in the car, Resnick was trying to figure out the difference in ages between them, Russell and Nicola Venner. Twenty, twenty-five years? More? In all probability Venner was in his early sixties. Nicola was what? Thirty-five? That at most, Resnick thought.

He was past Ruddington and joining the ring road when his mobile broke through his thoughts. Kevin Naylor's voice was faint, the line unclear. "Reports coming in, sir. Been a body found. Colwick Wood."

Tight-lipped, Resnick acknowledged the message and accelerated into the outside lane.

The woods were close by the Trent, no more than a mile or so from the city centre. A favoured spot for dog walkers, errant kids and fair-weather picnickers, they were a well-used urban amenity. The car was in a clearing near the northern edge, a few hundred metres from the road. A BMW, maroon, its nose was close against the trunk of what Resnick thought to be an oak. The body was slumped sideways across the front seat, the face, what was left of it, pressed fast against the glass.

Uniformed officers were cordoning off the scene.

Millington came across to where Resnick was standing. "Shotgun, down by his feet."

"Self-inflicted?"

"Looks that way. For now, any road."

Resnick glanced at the blurred flesh, the rose of blood across the windscreen. "Any identification?"

Millington scuffed the toe of his shoe in the dirt. "Likely a wallet or some such, inside pocket. Didn't want to move him while the pathologist got here. Vehicle registration, though. Just got through checking as you arrived." He paused and looked at Resnick, eyebrow cocked. "Russell Venner."

Soft and involuntarily, Resnick swore and swore again.

"That in itself," Millington was saying. "not conclusive. But if that is Venner, local paper'll have a field day. Not just local either."

Resnick was thinking of Nicola Venner's face at the door, blue eyes, slightly amused, fair hair pulled back.

"The body," he said, "who found it?"

"Couple of youths, off fishing. Heard something they reckoned might've been a shot." He pointed off beyond the cordon. "Lynn's talking to 'em now."

Resnick nodded. He was glad she was there. Once identification had been established, he would need her to drive back out with him, help him break the news.

Somehow, Resnick hadn't expected there to be children, he didn't know why. Perhaps because there had been so little sign. But when Nicola Venner came to the door, there they were, crowding round her, fair-haired and clean-faced, the oldest still wearing his braided prep school blazer, two boys close in age – six, Resnick guessed, and eight.

"Mrs Venner…"

"You again…"

She looked enquiringly at his face, glanced at Lynn Kellogg, serious at his side. A nerve darted, sharp, behind her eyes.

"The boys," Resnick said, "is there somewhere… ?"

Over faint protests and with promises of future treats,

she sent them scurrying off to some distant part of the house until they were called. Resnick and Lynn she led into a living room that was long and cool with facing settees and pale green walls.

"Tell me," she said. "Just tell me." Her hands fluttered close to her face, nervous for something to hold on to, a cigarette, a glass.

When Resnick told her, her fingers gripped the honeyed upholstery and her mouth opened wide.

"I'm sorry," Resnick said finally. "I'm really sorry."

Nicola pushed a fist against her face and bit down into the skin.

"Is there something I can get you?" Lynn asked, leaning forward.

Nicola stared at her as if seeing her for the first time.

"A cup of tea? A…"

"Another husband?" Rocking back against the cushions, Nicola laughed. She continued to rock, then, forward and back, arms clasped tight across her chest.

Resnick and Lynn exchanged glances and Resnick gave a quick, almost imperceptible shake of the head. Somewhere, a neighbour's dog was barking, the same sound, short and harsh, over and over again. Nicola slowed and was still.

"Your husband," Resnick began, "did he own a gun?"

Ham off the bone, cucumber, lettuce, mustard of course, a strong, slightly smoky Dijon, slices of fat tomato, pepper, salt; Resnick pressed the sandwich down with one hand before cutting it across. The potato salad he enlivened with a dollop more mayonnaise, a scattering of chopped spring onion, a shake or two of Tabasco. The fat piece of tomato that had squeezed free, he popped into his mouth; mayonnaise he licked from his fingers. A small brewery had obtained a licence to make Worthington White Shield, rather than letting it disappear altogether, and, miraculously, they had started stocking it at his nearest Tesco. Opening a bottle, cold from the fridge, he poured it gently into a tall glass, wary of the sediment lingering at the bottom, and carried glass and plate across to the kitchen table. Art Pepper's *So In Love* was playing through the auxiliary speakers, recordings made in seventy nine, just a year before Resnick had seen him at Jimmy's club, only three before he died. The front page of the *Post*, close alongside Resnick's elbow, was dominated by a photograph of Russell Venner, hooded eyes, greying hair, mouth no more than a razor line across his face. Praise for his achievements vied for space with speculation about his death: rumours of financial problems and fears about his health, both of which were contradicted by associates and friends on an inside page. The other picture was of Nicola, recently snatched, a hand half-raised to ward off the camera's flash. *Young Widow Mourns, see page two*, where you find, also, photos of the children in their school uniform, smart and self-assured and shining.

The shotgun had belonged to Venner, properly licensed; the angle of the wounds consistent with a self-inflicted injury. There was no note, of course, and a note would have helped. Venner's secretary had confirmed the bare details entered in his diary, he had been to a meeting that morning with his accountant, eleven thirty in offices near the Playhouse; Venner had left the meeting after less than an hour, earlier than expected, items of business unfinished. When the accountant had talked to Kevin Naylor he described Venner as being preoccupied, his mind not wholly on matters at hand; his departure had been abrupt and unexplained, he had no idea where Venner had been going nor who, if anyone, he might have been going to meet.

But two hours later he had been parked in his car in Colwick Wood and so far there was no indication of what had happened in that intervening time. Had Venner spent them alone or with someone else, and if the latter, who? And why? Curiosity stalked Resnick like an itch.

The post mortem was scheduled for the middle of the following day and Graham Millington, who was developing a taste for such things, would most likely attend. The final notes of 'Stardust' faded, a soft fall of saxophone spiralling to silence. Resnick thought tomorrow he would talk to Nicola Venner again.

He woke to the faint hiss of rain: dark earth and shiny roofs. Dizzy's paw prints damp and well-defined across the kitchen floor. The quiet ritual of making coffee, feeding the cats, listening to the local news. One by one, Russell Venner's contemporaries testified to his business acumen, his concern for the community, the common good. Resnick found a clean shirt that barely needed pressing, a striped tie he scarcely recognised. He took more than a little trouble over cleaning his shoes.

Venner's accountant was long-limbed and lean faced; squash, or whatever it was, had kept his body trim, encouraged the firmness of his grip. Farquarson, James Edward Farquarson – if not accountancy, Resnick thought, it would have to have been the law; failing that, possibly, dentistry.

"Inspector, please, have a seat."

They were in a sort of anteroom, a suite of offices converted from an imposing double-fronted Victorian house.

Austere furniture, cut flowers, high ceilings, all of the original archetraves and cornicing intact. Through the window you could see the Catholic cathedral, the green square and broad pavement outside the Playhouse theatre.

A pleasant-looking woman, middle-aged and smiling, popped her head round the corner of the door.

"Tea, inspector?" Farquarson asked. "Coffee?"

Resnick declined, Farquarson shook his head, the woman disappeared. Resnick asked about Venner's mood the previous morning, the morning he had died.

Farquarson leaned forward, hands on his knees. "Ours was merely a routine meeting; there was nothing for Russell to latch his teeth into, no decisions of great moment to be made. I expect he was bored." Farquarson smiled. "For someone whose life largely revolved around the acquisition of money, he was signally bored by figures."

"So there was nothing unusual about his behaviour?"

Farquarson steepled his fingers and considered. "I've been thinking about it of course. On reflection, he might have been a shade more distracted than usual. Preoccupied."

"You've no idea what by?"

"I'm sorry, no. I only wish I had."

"And when he left?"

"As I said to your subordinate, it was sudden, without apparent reason."

"He must have said something, Venner?"

"Not really. 'James, we can finish this another time. I've got to go.' That was all."

"And you've no idea... ?"

"None."

Resnick readjusted his weight. "If you thought by staying quiet, you were in some way protecting him or his family..."

Farquarson shook his head. "Inspector, please believe me, I'd help you if I could."

"There was nothing in his financial affairs that might explain his death?"

"Absolutely not."

"No rivalries; plans for expansion, take-overs; nothing that might have given somebody else cause to feel unduly threatened?"

Farquarson pressed his finger tips together and, more emphatically than before, gave a slow shake of the head.

"Jimmy Nolan?"

Farquarson smiled. "Let me explain, Inspector, Nolan and that club of his; it was never a good investment as it stood. Russell was acting against my advice when he became involved. All that was of real value was the site, but with Nolan feeling the way he did..." The smile had gone from the accountant's face. "There had been several approaches, sound propositions, a consortium, for instance, wanting to open a casino. If Nolan had been willing to step aside, he could have been comfortable for the rest of his life."

"And Venner?"

"My client would have realised a not unreasonable profit on his investment."

"Instead of which..."

"Instead of which the opportunity passed."

"Surely Venner could have forced his hand? Tried to, at least."

Farquarson smiled with his eyes. "They were friends, Inspector. It went back a long time."

"I thought there'd been a falling-out?"

"A good many, I daresay, over the years. I don't know the ins and outs. But argue as they might, when it came down to it, Russell would never have pushed Nolan out of that club and I think Nolan knew that for a fact."

Resnick got to his feet. "I've taken enough of your time."

"Not at all, Inspector."

As if by some sign, Farquarson's secretary, still smiling, was waiting to see him out. Rain was falling from an opaque sky, slanting into Resnick's face as he turned and began to climb the hill towards the station.

Nicola Venner said, yes, she would meet him, but not at the house. They met by the boating lake in the University Park, her suggestion; twelve o'clock. The rain had stopped and the air was fresh, leaves and grass a lustrous green. Nicola was wearing jeans, nicely faded, a thin cotton sweater with a high, wide neck. Her eyes were dark from lack of sleep.

"How're the boys?" Resnick asked.

"My mother, she's taken them off with her for a few days. Northumberland."

They walked without talking, a slow circuit of the lake. Above them, the university buildings, gift of Jesse Boot, clean cut in Portland Stone.

"I did my degree here," Nicola said. "Modern languages. Translation, that was what I really liked. Got off on. Novels, poetry, you know, literary stuff." She laughed wryly. "When we went abroad Russell let me order the food, argue about the bill."

"And nothing else?"

She walked on a little further, Resnick alongside. "You're a grown woman, he'd say, independent. Act like it. Make your own decisions, your own life. And he meant it.

Every time." They were at the mid-point, crossing the bridge towards the second loop of a figure eight. "I'd arrange for some work, freelance, once or twice here at the university, and Russell, he'd say good, fine, and then start raising these objections, obstacles, the children, the house, reasons why it was going to be difficult." She shook her head. "It got so that some days, after he'd left, I'd feel winded. Paralysed."

"You talked to him about it, though? I mean, he knew?"

She laughed again, freer this time. "Oh, he knew. We talked and he promised and the next month or the next week or the very next day we'd be having the same conversation again. So I stopped saying anything. Put up with it. I stopped caring."

"For him?"

"For everything."

"You thought about leaving him."

She stopped. "Did I?"

"If things were as bad as you said."

They stood back, allowing a woman with a push chair and a sleeping child to walk between them.

"Sometimes," Nicola said, "I'd wear myself out thinking about it. It seemed so huge, impossible. Much easier to drink my way through the day."

Resnick smiled. "Make asparagus something-or-other."

"Yes. Lots of it." Her eyes were brighter now, taking in the blue of the lake. "I should have taken a lover. That would have slapped me back to life at least."

"Maybe brought," Resnick said, "problems of its own."

"I dare say. And now we'll never know. A little difficult to commit adultery without a husband, I suppose." When she stopped again, she rested a hand on Resnick's arm. "I'm sorry, that sounds callous, horrible."

"It's all right."

She looked away. "There were times, he'd drive away in the morning, and I wanted... I wished..." Her fingers bit sharp into Resnick's arm. "I wanted him dead. Not hurt. No pain. Just absent. Not there. So I wouldn't have to deal with him again. Dead."

Releasing him, she turned her back and bowed her head.

"I was married once," Resnick said. "Whatever it was that was wrong between us, it went on for a long time." He hesitated. "When we talked about it, not then, but later, years later, she said pretty much the same. 'You know, Charlie, I wished you dead.'"

Nicola turned towards him, sniffing back tears. "You must have been so hurt."

He shook his head. "I think by then most of the hurt had gone."

"And now?"

Resnick smiled. "Just a few bits I've kept around on purpose. For when I want to feel sorry for myself."

They sat in Resnick's car, windows wound down, and he took her through the previous morning: there was nothing she'd noticed out of the ordinary, nothing her husband had said or done, nothing in his mood or manner. She was due to see Farquarson herself later that day, but, no, as far as she knew, everything was financially stable. A row? No, of course they hadn't had a row. As she'd already told him, all that had been behind them. Her husband had left a meeting, driven to Colwick Wood in his lunch hour and pressed a double-barrelled shotgun against the underside of his chin. She didn't know why.

Resnick drove into the city along Castle Boulevard and

dropped Nicola Venner at the corner of Victoria Street and Bridlesmith Gate. By the time he'd got back to the office, some fifteen minutes later, Graham Millington was waiting.

A sense of glee, almost childlike, illuminated the sergeant's face. "Pathologist had himself a field day. Found this bruising, side of Venner's head, round the temple. Didn't reckon too much to it at first. No obvious cuts, you see, abrasions; allowed as how it'd happened when he'd smacked against the windscreen, after the shot'd been fired."

Millington paused and grinned. "Not on your life. Venners' neither. He'd been struck twice, hard. Something cushioned, covered in cloth maybe, so as not to leave an obvious mark. But, like I say, hard, whatever it was, the weapon, swung with force." He hesitated again, adjusting his tone. "Severe subdural haemorrhaging of the brain. Chances of him firing that shotgun hisself close to nil. Some other kind bastard took a whack at him then did it for him."

Resnick took a pace back, weighing up the implications. "Okay, Graham. The car, Venner's BMW, we want the interior checked for prints, marks, fine tooth comb."

"In hand."

"Have a word with the Support Group, see if they can't spare a few bodies, go back over that area where he was found."

"Right."

"Canvass local residents too, anyone who uses that section of woods regular, dog walking, whatever – somebody must've seen something."

Millington nodded. "Even with a bit of help, be spreading ourselves a bit thin. But, yes, we'll do what we can."

Resnick walked across to the window and stared out at

the traffic backing up both ways along the Derby Road. "Why does Venner suddenly up and leave that meeting? No excuse, no explanation."

"Someone he had to see," Millington suggested. "an ultimatum maybe. And not public, out in the middle of the Old Market Square for all and sundry to be gawpin' at."

"Then why not simply cancel the original meeting, reschedule?"

"Perhaps he doesn't take too well to the idea of being ordered around. Except when push comes to shove, he can't do it, can't stay away."

"From what? Who?"

Millington shrugged. "Business? Some shady deal gone sour."

"Something his accountant didn't know about – it's possible." Resnick sighed. "Let's get Lynn out to talk to Venner's secretary. See if she doesn't know more than she's letting on."

"Hanky-panky, you mean?"

"Always possible, Graham."

Finger and thumb, Millington smoothed his moustache along his upper lip. "Force with which he'd been hammered, Venner, I doubt it was some woman. 'Less he went in for your Russian shot putter type of thing."

Resnick shook his head. "Someone young enough, Graham. Fit enough. Angry enough." He half-smiled. "Maybe they don't build shot putters the way they used to."

"Maybe not. But who we're looking for here, a bloke, mark my words. Jealous husband, something of the sort."

Resnick nodded and turned towards his office. There were one or two calls he wanted to make before he headed back out again. And the super would have to be informed of fresh developments, brought up to speed.

"One thing to keep in mind," he said from the door. "The shotgun – if he wasn't intending to turn it on himself, what was Venner doing with it in the car?"

As soon as Nicola Venner saw Lynn and Resnick side by side, she knew something was wrong. Something new. Like a trapped butterfly, a nerve pulsed beneath the pale skin high alongside her face.

Without speaking, they followed her through into the house. Cut flowers stood fresh in vases in the living room; a book Nicola had been reading, a novel, lay open on the arm of one of the settees.

"There've been some developments," Resnick said when they were all sitting down, "concerning your husband's death." Hating the way he sounded, pompous and heavy. "It now seems unlikely that he... that he took his own life."

"What d'you mean? I don't understand, I..."

"The evidence suggests somebody else was involved."

"What evidence?"

"The post mortem."

"What happened? What do you... ?"

"Mrs Venner," Lynn Kellogg said, leaning towards her. "We think your husband was murdered."

For a moment, Nicola stared at her, wide-eyed, before folding back into one corner of the settee, arms clasped tight across her body.

"I'm very sorry," Resnick said, conscious of the futility of the words.

Without waiting to be asked, Lynn went in search of the kitchen, the kettle, a pot of tea.

Resnick crossed and uncrossed his legs, watching Nicola rock herself slowly back and forth.

"How?" she asked finally.

Resnick told her.

Lynn reappeared with cups of tea on a tray.

"How did it happen?" Nicola asked again.

Patient, Resnick told her a second time. What little they knew.

"Have you any idea," she asked, "who?"

"No," he replied. "Have you?"

Nicola's hand jerked and Lynn reached across and took the cup and saucer from her grasp. "The question of who your husband might have been meeting, Mrs Venner. It's all that more important now. Any suspicions you might have."

"I don't have any bloody suspicions."

"Just some idea. Someone... something he wanted kept secret."

The nerve was ticking again at the side of Nicola's face; fast, wayward.

"Mrs Venner," Lynn's face close to hers now, her voice quiet. "Is it possible your husband was seeing somebody?"

"Somebody?"

"Somebody else."

Nicola sprang to her feet, with a quick fling of the arm knocking cup and saucer spinning from Lynn's out-stretched hand. "Jesus! You... the pair of you. So bloody clever." She jutted her head towards Resnick. "You especially, sitting there as if butter wouldn't melt in your hypo-critical bloody mouth." She laughed, bitter and raw. "I thought you were a bit pompous, maybe, a bit old-fash-ioned, but basically okay. A decent bloke. The way you talked to me. Listened. So bloody understanding. And all the time you were just waiting, biding your time, playing me along."

"Nicola..."

"Don't. Don't. Don't fucking Nicola me. Look at you, you're pathetic, the pair of you, sticking your noses in the trough and snouting round."

"Mrs Venner…"

"So bloody simple minded, all of you. Russell's got some assignation, something he wants to keep to himself. A bit on the side, that's what it's got to be. Stands to reason. Your reason." She was midway between Resnick and Lynn and the curtains, bending forward, arms still locked across her chest. "Something going on, something wrong with our relationship, our marriage; not enough sex, too much sex; husband can't get it up, can't get it up enough. Sticking it to somebody else. Is that what you think? Is it? Is it?"

"Nicola…" Resnick on his feet now, a pace or two towards her.

"Well, is it?"

"A possibility, yes, we have to consider it."

She moved to meet him, colour charging her cheeks. "I bet you do. I bet you love it. The possibility. Oh, yes… rubbing my face in it. Hmm? Pushing me down and rubbing my face in it." She lifted her head towards his. "Is that what she did, that precious bloody wife of yours? The one you told me about when you were trying to wheedle round me, convince me of how loving and sincere you were. Is that what she did? Screw around and taunt you with it? Flaunt it? Rub your face in the fucking sheets?"

"Yes," Resnick said, his voice so low it was almost as if he hadn't spoken at all. "Yes, she did."

Nicola looked at him frankly. "Good. Good, I'm glad. Now go. And if you're thinking of coming back and telling me who it was he was having – how many – just don't bother because I don't want to know." She turned from them and walked, brisk, towards the door. "Go on, what are you waiting for? Get out of here the pair of you and leave me alone."

"I'm sorry," Lynn said. They were passing alongside the county cricket ground, a scattering of dingy pigeons perched at intervals along the Radcliffe Road stand. "What she said about you and your ex."

"It's okay," Resnick said. "But thanks."

"Venner, he was carrying on with someone, behind her back?"

"It looks like."

"And you think she knew?"

"One way or another, probably." There were knowing and admitting and often a vast space between them, as well he knew.

A few pale shafts of light reflected off the waters of the Trent. Past the City Ground, lone fishermen sat or stood at intervals, hopeful into the evening's slow fall. However careful they had been, Venner and whoever, someone would have noticed, someone would have seen. Hotels in the general area would be checked, the airport, restaurants and bars.

Back at the station, Tom McLean's report was on his desk, delivered by hand. All the evidence suggested the fire at Nolan's club had started accidentally, a cigarette, a careless match thrown down by the still unidentified youth who had broken in looking for a place to sleep. The insurance company would probably carry out its own investigation, but in the end it would pay.

Kevin Naylor was following up on an approach from a couple whose oldest son had gone missing from home two nights before the fire; a family friend had spotted him in the area earlier the same evening. There was also an incident report from a patrol officer who had questioned a young man with a local accent, loitering in the vicinity of the multi-storey car park close by the club.

Resnick finished reading through Naylor's file and slid its contents back into place. Jack Skelton's extension yielded no answer; the superintendent returned early to the acid bosom of his family. Street lights burned a faint orange outside and cast no shadow. He knew there would be others in the pub across the street, winding down, colleagues, and often he would join them, a quick half and away, but this particular evening he chose to drink alone. Did it matter, what Nicola Venner had said about Elaine? *Screw around and taunt you with it? Flaunt it?* And why now, after all this time?

In the back bar of a pub he seldom if ever used, he ordered a large scotch and then another. *Just a few bits I've kept around on purpose. For when I want to feel sorry for myself.* Or angry, Resnick thought. Venner had married her, Nicola, when she'd been little more than a girl, swept her off her feet. Tied her down with kids and promises: a fine house behind a high hedge: money. Allowing him the freedom to do what? Fool around? What if this were more? Suppose it serious. What if he'd been leaving her? *Someone young enough, Graham. Fit enough. Angry enough.* Easy then to explain another car, the gun.

He shook his head and drained the whisky from the glass. He himself was Nicola's alibi; no way she could have been chopping asparagus at home and meeting her husband in Colwick Wood. It wasn't possible.

And yet it continued to nag at him as he nodded a goodnight to the man behind the bar and shouldered his way out onto the street. It or something like.

The homeless man was stretched out inside a stained sleeping bag near the edge of the park, dogs curled at his head and feet. Resnick hefted a handful of change from his pocket and, approaching, he bent forwards, hand outstretched. Low in their throats, the dogs growled and one bared its teeth. "Fuck off," the man breathed. "Fuck off and leave us alone."

Resnick let the coins fall across the bag and hurried on.

A light showed faintly through sagging curtains. The sound of a saxophone. Not Nolan himself this time. Someone playing a ballad. Breathy and melodic, smooth-toned. Stan Getz but not Stan Getz. More than a hint of Lester Young. Variations that curled like smoke around the song. Zoot Sims?

Cigarette in hand, Nolan drew back the door. "Charlie. Don't suppose this is a social call."

Without waiting for an answer, he wandered down the narrow corridor towards the kitchen and returned, unasked, with a bottle of Budvar, which he pushed into Resnick's hand.

There was one small light burning in the front room, turned close towards the wall. The tape was still playing and Resnick stood in the half dark, listening, as the improvisation wound its way, logical and surprising, through the closing chorus; cadence following cadence to the final chords, the last lingering note, so delicate as to be almost unheard. 'Someone to Watch Over Me'.

"At first," Resnick said, sitting, "I thought it was Zoot."

"No." A shake of Nolan's head.

"But now I'm certain."

"Yeah?"

"Spike. Spike Robinson." Resnick nodded towards the

tape player. "I was there, the club, the night this was recorded."

"Ninety-four."

"I daresay."

Nolan drew on his cigarette, tapped ash into the palm of his open hand. "What else d'you know, Charlie?"

"Venner, it wasn't suicide. Someone hit him, barrel of the gun most likely. Fired the shot on his behalf."

"No more'n he deserved."

Resnick tilted the neck of the bottle to his mouth.

"She was lovely," Nolan said, "Nicola, when she was a kid. A young woman. Bright. Russell, he'd seen her, asked me to introduce him. You're her godfather, he said, least you can do, put in a word. Not twenty she was then." More ash fell from his cigarette, unheeded to the floor. "Married soon after. Kids, lovely boys. That was when he started, Russell, fooling around. Didn't matter he was no oil painting, knocking on. For him it was easy, always easy. Position. Money. When Nicola couldn't look the other way no longer she came to me. I talked to him, argued, he said it was nothing, didn't matter, just a bit of fun. Then he met this girl, Katie, nineteen."

In the background Robinson's tenor was still playing – 'Who Cares?' – 'How Long Has This Been Going On?' – languid, knowing.

"For him it was like meeting Nicola all over again. And nothing else mattered. He was going to leave Nicola for her, get divorced, remarry. When I found out I went to him and told him, you can't, you can't do that, not to her. And there's the kids, what about them? 'Don't worry, Jimmy', he said, 'I'll look after them. Your Nicola, make sure she's properly taken care of.'"

The tape spooled free mid-phrase, spun a few more times

and was still. Nolan's broken breathing aside, it was quiet.

"I gave him one last chance," Nolan said. "Pleaded with him, threatened; it didn't make a scrap of difference. He wasn't going to change his mind." He cast Resnick a quick glance. "I'd already taken the shotgun from the house a couple of days before. Snuck it out when I'd called round to see Nicola." He looked Resnick in the eye. "It was my responsibility, you see. There didn't seem to be anything else I could do."

The beer had grown warm in Resnick's hand. "You'll have to tell it again, Jimmy, down at the station. You know that?"

Nolan nodded. "You don't reckon it could wait till morning?"

"Best not." Resnick got to his feet and Nolan followed suit.

"You got to believe it, Charlie," Nolan said, "Nicola, what was going on, she never knew."

Uncertain whether he did or not, Resnick nodded just the same.

At the doorway, Nolan hesitated, glanced back into the room. "All these tapes, Charlie. This music…"

Resnick touched him on the shoulder. "Don't you worry, Jimmy. I'll see it comes to no harm."

Next morning he threw back the covers before dawn, fully awake and broken from a dream. Nicola Venner had been leaning over him and he had felt the warmth of her breath on his face, of her bare skin on his arm. There had been tiredness and want in her eyes and he had been going to help her, heard the words forming in his mind. Slowly, he swung his legs round and rose to his feet. He could call her later, drive down.

In the bathroom, he splashed cold water into his face, not once but several times. The last thing she wanted, he thought then, offers of help from him. Hadn't she had help enough from men such as himself already?

He splashed more water, cleaned his teeth, shaved, stepped into the shower. Outside, night was gradually becoming another day.

CoDA

Some of you will have recognised the provenance of the titles of these stories: they are all culled from the Charlie Parker Songbook; titles of tunes he composed and recorded. It began with 'Now's The Time' and, thereafter, seemed a good idea. Sometimes the story came before the title, as with, say, 'Cheryl' or 'Work'; in other instances – 'My Little Suede Shoes' or 'Bird of Paradise' – it was the title that suggested the content. Either way, the Parker references helped to stake out the territory and underlined Charlie Resnick's – and this writer's – musical predilections.

But Charlie, it must be remembered, was not always a jazzman, a jazz fan, pure and simple; in the novel, *Wasted Years*, we learn how, a young man, he first met his wife, Elaine, at the Boat Club on the banks of the River Trent, drawn there by the hot soul and blues approximations of whichever local bands were squeezing out their versions of Sam Cooke and Otis Redding, Booker T and the MGs.

Music has always been important for Charlie, you fancy – as background and as entertainment, as a way of easing a stressful life, papering over emptiness, and more positively, helping him to measure and assess emotion, helping him to understand. And where had it begun for him, this musical affiliation, this need? A tailoring uncle, returned from the States with a pile of chipped and scratched 78s and Charlie, in his early teens, open-minded and keen-eared, set loose amongst them. Bing Crosby. The Ink Spots. Sinatra. Dick Haymes. The Mills Brothers. Ella Fitzgerald's 'A-Tisket, A-Tasket' and 'Stone Cold Dead in the Market'. Teddy Wilson and his Orchestra with Billie Holiday (vocal refrain).

This, as it had been for me, a couple of decades earlier, except he was the uncle of a friend and we would spend hours foraging through his collection, slipping roundels of shellac off and on the gramophone, assessing and reassessing the worth of this jazzier stuff against our more poppy favourites of the time – Johnny Ray, probably, or Frankie Laine; Guy Mitchell and Doris Day.

And whereas my personal tastes have always ranged pretty wide – last night, for instance, as well as the Stan Getz bossa novas and some Mozart, I was listening to Dave Alvin, Dusty Springfield, Big Bill Broonzy and Charlie Feathers (some might call that eclectic taste, others would say no taste at all) – Charlie is pretty much locked into jazz whose roots and style are found in the '40s and '50s, the years of classic bop and swing. Lester Young. Ben Webster. Milt Jackson. Parker, of course. Thelonious Monk.

Certain artists have been important for certain novels; in *Lonely Hearts* it was Billie Holiday with Lester Young; Milt Jackson began *Still Water* with flow and swing. Overall, however, it's Monk whose music I've returned to again and again when writing both the books and the stories; Monk whose broken rhythms have underscored the emotional landscape of Resnick's journey and helped to suggest their form.

John Harvey, London, 1999.

RESNICK
A partial soundtrack

MILES DAVIS
Bag's Groove
featuring Milt Jackson
Prestige / Original Jazz Classics

Kind of Blue
CBS

DUKE ELLINGTON
The Blanton-Webster Years
RCA Bluebird

The Great Ellington Units
RCA Bluebird

The Private Collection Vols 1-10
Kaz

STAN GETZ
East of the Sun
The West Coast Sessions
Verve

Getz/Gilberto
Verve

BILLIE HOLIDAY
Lady Day & Prez 1937-1941
Giants of Jazz

The Quintessential Billie Holiday Vols 1 - 9
1933 - 1942
CBS

The Complete Billie Holiday on Verve 1945-1959
Verve

Lady in Satin
with Ray Ellis and his Orchestra
CBS

MILT JACKSON
Milt Jackson
with Horace Silver
Prestige

Bags & Trane
with John Coltrane
Rhino / Atlantic

Django
with the Modern Jazz Quartet
Prestige / Original Jazz Classics

THELONIOUS MONK
Genius of Modern Music, Vols 1 & 2
Blue Note

Thelonious Monk Trio / Blue Monk Vol 2
Prestige

Thelonious Monk Plays Duke Ellington
Riverside / Original Jazz Classics

Straight No Chaser
Music from the Motion Picture
CBS

Monk Alone
The Complete Columbia Solo Studio Recordings
1962-1968
CBS

CHARLIE PARKER
In a Soulful Mood
The Dial Sessions
Music Club

The Charlie Parker Story
The Savoy Sessions – includes 3 takes of 'Now's the Time'
Savoy

SPIKE ROBINSON
The Gershwin Collection
Hep

JOE TEMPERLEY
Nightingale
Hep

With Every Breath ...
Hep

BEN WEBSTER
The Tatum Group Masterpieces Vol 8
Pablo

The Ultimate
selected by James Carter
Verve

LESTER YOUNG
A Lester Young Story
featuring Count Basie, Teddy Wilson & Billie Holiday
Jazz Archives

Lester Young 1943-1947
Giants of Jazz

The Complete Aladdin Recordings
Blue Note

Pres & Teddy
with the Teddy Wilson Quartet
Verve

The President Plays with the Oscar Peterson Trio
Verve

For further information about Slow Dancer Press
visit our web site
www.mellotone.co.uk
or join our free mailing list.

Slow Dancer Press
91 Yerbury Road London N19 4RW
slowdancer@mellotone.co.uk